THE SERPENT'S COIL

THE
SERPENT'S
COIL

PROPHECY OF DAYS: BOOK II

CHRISTY RAEDEKE

flux™
Woodbury, Minnesota

First Edition
First Printing, 2011

Cover design by Kevin R. Brown
Cover illustration by Chris Down
Ouroboros illustration by Chris Down
Interior art by Llewellyn Art Department

Flux, an imprint of Llewellyn Worldwide Ltd.

Library of Congress Cataloging-in-Publication Data
Raedeke, Christy, 1966–
   The serpent's coil / Christy Raedeke.—1st ed.
      p. cm.—(Prophecy of days bk. 2)
   Summary: While attending a boarding school that allows her to travel around the globe, Caity continues her mission to fulfill a Mayan prophecy and mobilize the world's young people to stop the devastating global reign of the Fraternitas.
   ISBN 978-0-7387-1577-3
[1. Prophecies—Fiction. 2. Conspiracies—Fiction.
3. Mayas—Antiquities—Fiction. 4. Indians of Central
America—Antiquities—Fiction. 5. Travel—Fiction.] I. Title.
   PZ7.R1233Se 2011
   [Fic]—dc22

                                                    2011004573

Flux
A Division of Llewellyn Worldwide Ltd.
2143 Wooddale Drive
Woodbury, MN 55125-2989
www.fluxnow.com

Printed in the United States of America

For Hank

Just as they had wished the death of Seven Macaw, so they brought it about.
They had seen evil in his self-magnification.

—Popul Vuh, Mayan Book of Creation

AN ASSESSMENT

ere's what I've got: a monkey who communicates with origami, a prophetic poem with my name in it, and a mission. I've got a boy, I think. Alex and I haven't actually spoken since our first kiss but we've traveled more together than some people who are actually married. I've got a best friend who has proved she'd do anything for me. I've also got Bolon, my ... Well, I'm not sure what he is. Guide? Mentor? Friend who consistently puts me in harm's way? And of course I've also got the *Fraternitas Regni Occulti,* the worldwide Shadow Government wanting to stop me and what I represent: freedom from their control.

What I don't have: Uncle Li, my long-time family friend and main confidant, because he betrayed me and took off with some ancient books that were apparently important to my success. And I don't have a lot of time to carry out this prophecy to unite the youth and overthrow this Shadow Government so that we can be free—the *Fraternitas* is working hard to keep us so repressed that the shift in evolution and freedom cannot happen. And I don't have a home since an "unknown arsonist" (a.k.a. the *Fraternitas*) set fire to it while

I was being chased by dogs through lava caves and flying in a Vimāna. But that, as you know, is another story.

When I assess my life this way, it looks like things are not weighted in my favor. But I can't give up. Not yet. Because when Uncle Li betrayed me, essentially leaving me to fail at my mission, I realized nothing can stop me. I have to fulfill this prophecy. I have to take the world from the elite few and give it to the kids.

The Maya call it the fall of Seven Macaw, the vain and false ruler. I call it the fall of the *Fraternitas*, the Shadow Government. Either way, if something doesn't happen soon, we're doomed.

ONE

Sometimes it takes being away from a place to make it seem like home. Before I went to Easter Island, I only considered San Francisco home. Now, having arrived safely back in Scotland, I can also look at Breidablik Castle as home. This fact is really comforting considering our old house is now gone. *Burned to the ground.*

I'm purposely keeping this information distant. I don't want to see pictures of the damage; I don't want to sift through old photos with charred edges or try to salvage damp and ashy stuffed animals or inhale the smell of burned and melted things. I realize that losing something material like a house shouldn't matter in the bigger scheme of what's happening, but I know if I saw it I'd be devastated. So I keep it abstract—like something that may have happened to a distant relative or to me in another dimension of some kind of weird String Theory.

This is why I am not going back to San Francisco with

my parents to deal with the disaster. Once it becomes real to me, then I have to take full responsibility, which I just can't do right now. Not if I'm supposed to continue down the path of helping fulfill this prophecy.

My parents understand. I think if they didn't *have* to deal with it they'd rather keep it abstract as well. But for insurance purposes they have to go. They have to sift through the wet charcoal remains of What Was Our Life. Their plans to leave were made just hours after I'd returned back to Breidablik Castle.

Waking up in my own enormous bed on the Isle of Huracan after so many nights in weird places—a warehouse floor, planes, trains, even a Vimāna—is divine. Last night I bolted the door and shuttered the windows, then closed my purple velvet bed curtains and used four pillows around me to make the perfect nest. I must have gone deep; the clock shows I slept for eleven hours but when I wake, I am in the exact same position I fell asleep in.

I'm not certain of anything when I first open my eyes. My life comes into focus like Google Earth—the big picture is fuzzy and colorless but with each second that I zoom in, more things become clear. Except in my case it's not the leaves on trees and street signs that come into focus, it's the aches in my body and the realization that nothing will ever be the same again.

My parents are packed and ready to go by the time I get to the kitchen for breakfast, which at that time should really be lunch.

"I was just coming to wake you, Caity," Mom says, handing me a toast-and-bacon sandwich. "We've got to run to catch the ferry. Will you keep us company on the drive?"

"Wouldn't miss it," I lie. I would rather stay home. It's not that I don't want to see them off, it's just that there's something infinitely sadder about seeing your parents sail away than seeing them drive away.

The three of us sit together in the back of the Land Rover, with Thomas up front like a proper chauffer. Dad's arm is over my shoulders and Mom's hand is on my leg. I've barely been home, and having to say goodbye again is making my throat feel swollen and dry.

I try to remember every sensation of the moment: Being bookended by my parent's warm bodies. Their voices. Mom's Cristalle perfume, Dad's tea-tree shampoo. The comfort of being together.

My future is starting to look like a series of farewells that I'm not ready for.

I hold it together until they get aboard, but watching the ferry head out into the sea, with the water black and cold even at mid-morning, I can't keep my emotions in any longer.

I put my sunglasses on and drop my head, hoping to conceal my breakdown from Thomas, but it's no use.

"Ah, Caity, I know 'tis hard to say goodbye, but they'll be fine," Thomas says, arm around my shoulders like a parenthesis at the end of a sentence.

Thomas may be the only one I can be completely honest with. The only one I can freak out in front of. The only one who knows the whole story.

"It's just—"

"I know, lass. I know," Thomas says. "You haven't had an easy time of it this go 'round, have you?"

"Until this summer, life was great. Well, boring, but great," I sniffle. "It's this place that changed everything."

"What's happening now has been in the works for centuries, for millennia." Thomas turns me so I have to look at him. "I reckon you're just going to have to endure, press on, make do."

"I know," I answer. "I'll pull it together."

And I do. Driving silently to Breidablik Castle, I remind myself of what's at stake for our future as well as what atrocious things the *Fraternitas* has done in the past, and my problems start to look miniscule.

Once back, I go to the kitchen to get Mr. Papers. He puts both arms around my neck and holds tightly. When I was on my trip I missed him so much it literally hurt inside my chest; I vow that from now on I will take him everywhere.

As I turn to leave, Mrs. Findlay walks toward me with a basket of large manila envelopes. "These came whilst you were traveling, dear."

I see fancy crests above the return addresses that can only mean one thing: boarding schools. Mom must have sent away for them even though I thought that conversation was over. I roll my eyes and take them from her.

"So is Alex around?" I ask as casually as I can. Since I left Easter Island earlier than he did and took a much faster ride back to Scotland, I doubt he'll be back until later today or tomorrow.

"He's off the coast fishing with a friend. Should be back soon, I reckon. But his mother has hired him out to old Cormag, the butcher. He's redoing the shop and needs help, what with all those dead beasts dangling about."

I try not to look disappointed. "Oh, okay. So will that take all summer?"

"Nae, just a fortnight or so. With your folks heading back to deal with the … situation, and not wanting to take any guests for a few weeks, Alex was available for other jobs."

"Makes sense," I say, though it makes me profoundly sad.

"I can have him over for dinner when he gets back if you'd like," she offers.

I decide *not* to play this one cool. "Definitely," I say, without any hesitation. "That would be great."

Two

Back in my room, I set the basket of boarding school packets on my desk and sit down to check email. Mr. P grabs the fancy Mac Fireland silver letter opener and like a knight with a giant sword, he starts neatly opening the tops of the envelopes and pulling out the folders and brochures.

They all look pretty much the same. Sturdy gloss paper, solid old fonts, high-quality photos. All the photos fit neatly into five categories: Academics (students looking at a teacher with the kind of intensity that's only really seen on the faces of kids playing the last level of a first-person-shooter video game); Inclusiveness (attractive students wearing uniforms and walking together in very large groups as if there were no such thing as cliques or dorks); Long History (beauty shots of buildings that look like they were built in the Middle Ages); Fresh Air and Exercise (snaps of students playing obscure, expensive sports not offered at public school); and Lifelong Power Networking (beautiful white boys in ties with their arms around each other).

School mottos? Select three words and translate to Latin: Conquer, Honor, Knowledge, Excellence, Character, Faith.

School colors? Pick two and combine: burgundy, gray, navy blue, forest green.

They all just seem like fancy storage units for kids.

All of the brochures are so similar that only one stands out from the rest. Mr. Papers hands it to me as carefully as if it were the Shroud of Turin. There are no photos of intense students, no classroom shots, no old stone buildings gracing the cover—there is only a gold twelve-pointed star and some writing in the bottom right corner.

¡Siga la Chispa!

La Escuela Bohemia

On the first page there is the gold embossed star and this small block of text:

> *The motto of La Escuela Bohemia, Siga la Chispa (Spanish for Follow the Spark), is resonant in everything we do. Students drive curriculum with their personal interests or sparks. Teams of research and curriculum professionals work to build courses of study around these sparks. Finally, our world-class Pedagogues then teach and guide the students as they follow their sparks*

of interest around the globe. With a ratio of one Peda-
gogue for every two students, the learning is intense and
tailored specifically to each student's learning style. Our
methods are not for every student; our classroom is the
world at large.

I immediately pull up their website to see if this could really be true, and it is. It's a school based on travel—exactly the kind of place I need. Suddenly Mom's cruel alternative to the local school seems like the perfect way to do what I need to do. But the only way I would possibly go is if Justine went, too.

I do the time-zone math and realize she may still be awake.

I dial and she picks up immediately.

"So, I drove past it today," she says even before a hello. "It's grim, Caity. I cried like a baby."

"Is it, like, *gone*?" I ask.

"Do you really want to hear about it?"

"Do I?" I ask.

"No," she replies quietly. "Sorry, I shouldn't have said anything at all. Your parents are taking care of it, right? Anyway, what's up? Everything okay?"

"Pretty much, yeah. I just need to ask you a question."

"Of course," she says. "Anything."

"If it were possible for you to help me more, would you?" I ask. "I mean, would you ever take on more of a ... like a partner role with me?"

"Hello? I tried to get into the *Fraternitas* offices in the

Transamerica Pyramid, I helped you steal a briefcase and almost got killed on the streets of San Francisco, I slept in a warehouse and then went to Machu-freaking-Picchu for you! I'd say I was pretty committed to helping you already."

"Okay, you're right. You're totally committed. But this next step I'm talking about? It's big."

"What do you mean by big?" she asks.

"I mean monumental big."

"Well, if Machu Picchu isn't monumental big, I don't know what is," she replies. "Lay it on me."

"Well, it's about school—next year. Would you ever, uh, move schools?"

"Like move to your island? You said they had a crappy little school."

"No, I'm talking about a boarding school."

"You know I love you, Caity, and I'd do most anything for you, but boarding school—um, *no*. Academy of Cruelties may live up to its name, but at least I have a lot of freedom. I don't want to be locked up in some brick dorm and live with snobby kids who will more than likely torment us."

"What if it wasn't that kind of school? What if the whole goal of your education was to learn through travel?"

"Ha! My parents would never let me go to some offbeat school that didn't count toward college, you know that. If I don't get into Brown, they'll freak."

"The school is totally legit, and would for sure get you into the Ivy League, Justine. It's a school in Buenos Aires called La Escuela Bohemia and the whole point—"

"Buenos Aires? As in *Argentina*? No way would my parents

let me go to school in South America—you know how image conscious they are."

I knew this would be a factor. Justine's parents are all about image. "According to the school's website, Buenos Aires is *the Paris of South America*. Seriously, you have to check it out; it really looks like a European city."

"But do you really want to *live* there, Caity?"

"No, but you don't have to live there. The whole point is that you travel all the time. You're paired with another student and one teacher, and you plan your own curriculum."

"That's kind of cool."

"I know! Seriously, imagine how fun it would be. No pressure, but I can't really see doing this with anyone else."

"Right! 'I can't save the world unless you go to this weird school with me, but you know, no pressure at all.'"

She's right, of course. I've put her in a bad spot.

"Look, I'm kind of open to the idea, but I can tell already that my parents would not be that crazy about it."

"So let me arm you with statistics: In every senior class, 99 percent go on to college. The average SAT score is 2100. But the real kicker—which will make your parents sign you up immediately—is that it's one of the three most expensive boarding schools in the world! Seriously, no one loves paying too much for something more than your dad. Isn't that the whole reason you're supposed to go to Brown?"

"Actually that *would* be the thing that tips them to the pro side, for sure. Dad could easily work that fact into conversation daily."

"It would be so fun, Justine. Just think about it—we

would be able to go anywhere, do anything, as long as we can justify it with some 'lesson' from school."

"Wow. I've never really thought about moving from San Francisco. But it's not like I see my parents much anyway; I think I've had more dinners with Esmeralda than with my parents."

"Yeah, why sit around and be raised by your crabby housekeeper when you can go to Buenos Aires with me?"

"Send me links and I'll print out my arsenal for the 'rents," she says.

"Done."

"Wait, how can you be sure I'll get in?" she asks.

"Our GPAs easily qualify us. It just comes down to the cash; if you have the GPA and can afford it, you're in."

"Being one of the most expensive schools in the world must narrow down the possible pool of students. But again, that will totally appeal to Dad."

"I'll email you all the info about the school," I tell her. "I'll even send links to some of its alumni—Middle Eastern and Russian royalty, world leaders, and heads of international corporations. Your parents will eat that up."

"And then some."

Now that's she's interested, I have to deliver the not-so-good news. "The only downside is that they're on a different schedule than we're used to—they do four quarters, with much longer breaks in between."

"Meaning we start really soon or a long time from now?"

"Um, soon. Like mid-July."

"Caity, we just got out! June hasn't even ended and we have to go back to school in a few weeks?"

"Yeah, but it's not like we'll be sitting at desks or anything. Plus, we have to go to the Dunhuang Caves in China like, stat, anyway."

"So Uncle Li is our first stop?"

"Yep."

"It's still hard to believe—"

"I know," I say, interrupting her. I really, really don't want to talk about Uncle Li right now. It's still like squeezing a lemon with a cut on your finger.

"Is it weird that we're casually talking about going to school in Argentina?" she asks.

"After having the weirdest few weeks of my life, this seems totally normal."

"Roger that, my friend."

"So will it be hard to leave David von Kellerman?" I ask.

"Over it," she replies flatly.

"Why? What did he do?"

"I found him in the equipment locker in the gym with Amanda Moore. It makes me throw up a little to think about it."

"Not Demanda More! She's so high maintenance!"

"No joke," she says. "Get this: Curran Williams told me she's been to her house and Demanda has a tanning bed in the workout room."

"No! That's *so* last millennium."

"Whatevs. They deserve each other."

"Well, you'll always have Peru … " I say, unable to stifle a laugh.

"Oh my God!" Justine yells.

"What? What happened?"

"I just pulled up the La Escuela Bohemia website—it's like the most beautiful place I've ever seen!"

"Isn't it amazing?" I squeal, relieved that she's interested.

"Done," she says. "We're *so* going."

THREE

I spend the next day getting what I can of my application for La Escuela Bohemia in order and waiting to hear from Alex. By the afternoon I realize that if he doesn't arrive on the 4:00 ferry, it will be another day. I decide to see if Mrs. Findlay knows anything and before I even reach the first floor, I get a good indication that someone will be here for dinner: the smell of roasted lamb and fresh bread.

What I'm not prepared for is Alex. He's already in the kitchen, leaning against the tiled wall eating a carrot.

I know I should play it down, but because I'm so happy to see that he's alive and well, I give him a full-body-press hug, despite the fact that I did not put defrizzer on my hair this morning. Mrs. Findlay looks startled at our reaction to each other, so I pull back, give him a brotherly punch on the shoulder and say, "Hey, good to see you."

"You too," he says, sparring back with a soft punch on

my shoulder. "Did you have a nice trip to see your friend in San Francisco?"

"Oh, yeah, great trip." I answer, fully aware that Mrs. Findlay is still watching us closely.

Motioning to the door with his head, he asks, "Want to go have a chat?"

"First floor only, son," Mrs. Findlay says sternly.

I turn bright red—does she really think I'd take him up to my room to make out?

Okay, I see her point.

"Go on into the library; I'll bring your dinner in there," Mrs. Findlay adds. Her strategy is clear: keep us in the room nearest the kitchen so she can check on us by constantly bringing in food and drinks.

We close the glass doors and settle into chairs by the fireplace. I draw in the utterly unique smell of Breidablik's library, which will stay with me forever. The scent of old books bound in leather and rugs from faraway lands mingles with the static, electric smell of technology coming off Dad's wall of computers and servers. It's the smell of old and new, of ideas captured on the written page and flying through the Internet.

Mr. Papers hops onto the ottoman between us, sits with his tail curled around himself, and begins peeling a banana. Cuteness overload.

"So, you're alive," I say, looking at Alex. "That's a very good thing."

"I'd have to agree," he says, leaning over in the chair to scratch Mr. Papers' neck.

"Seriously, though, I have to thank you. There's no way I could have done it without you."

"It was … an experience," he says, looking at me through hair that has fallen forward.

"So sorry to leave you with Donald."

Alex shakes his head. "How could we have known that Thomas had a twin that was a bad seed?"

"An evil twin—it's so cliché! So what happened to Donald after I left?" I ask. "Did he ever come to and freak out on you?"

"Nae. The doc from the hotel knocked on our door really early in the morn' while Donald was still groggy from the pills. He checked his eyes and his pulse, cleaned up his hand and put a new dressing on it, and then gave him a shot of antibiotics with a painkiller."

"Nice. So that kept him groggy."

"Meanwhile I found your note—I was so worried about you, mate."

"Well, I felt terrible having to leave you there."

"I didn't stay for long—after giving Donald the shot, the doc told me to get my things and then he took me to the airport. I got on the morning plane out and made my way back, sure that I'd see you on one of the flights…"

"I'm sorry; I had no choice. Did you hear the helicopters and dogs late that night?"

Alex's sky-blue eyes widen. "Those weren't—"

"They were," I say, sliding up the sleeves of my shirt to show him the cuts and bruises still on my hands and wrists. "They chased me through the lava tube caves that run under the island."

"Bloody hell, Caity! How did you get out? How did you get home?"

"Bolon came to get me," I say, stopping myself before I added anything about the Vimāna; I wasn't quite ready to explain that. "Anyway, at least we're both safely back."

I like being able to say the word *safe*. For the first time in my life that word really means something, and I'm unsure of how long this feeling of safety will last.

Thinking the same thing, Alex asks, "But for how long?"

"Thomas is on high-security alert. He's keeping the gates locked and the alarms on, so as long as we're in here, we're good."

I see Mrs. Findlay outside the doors with a tray in her hands, so I run over to open them for her. She seems happy to see us talking in the library like eighty-year-olds. Scooting Mr. P. off the ottoman with her foot, she sets the tray down and asks if we need anything else. We thank her and say we're fine, but she says she'll be back in a jiff to bring some water. Clearly she thinks she has to babysit us.

Once she's gone I say, "There's one thing I haven't told you … and it really complicates everything."

"What?" he asks, brows furrowed as he hands me a plate. "Something wrong?"

I hate saying this out loud. I look down and whisper, "Uncle Li is with the *Fraternitas*."

"What? You're joking!"

"I wish," I say. "I'm dead serious. If it wasn't Donald who tipped them off that I was on Easter Island, then it was Uncle Li."

"But I thought you'd known him since you were just a

wee girl?" Alex digs into his plate of lamb and potatoes, but I seem to have lost my appetite.

"I have. I don't know if he's always been with the *Fraternitas* or if this was a recent thing. I don't know much other than that he took the two Sanskrit books that are super important. They're the books Donald came back for. Uncle Li left a note, saying he had to 'follow his path,' whatever *that* means."

Alex leans back, plate balanced on his lap. "Oh, Caity, I'm sorry. That is such a betrayal. Do you think he went back to the States?"

"I don't think so. When Mr. P. saw me freak out about the note, he immediately made an origami cave and put the rabbit ears key inside it."

"Which means?"

"This rabbit ears symbol traces back to the Dunhuang Caves in China, where the prophecy started."

"And that's where you think he went?"

"Yep. And it's where I've got to go next."

"You're a mad rocket! Easter Island is one thing, but some cave in China? How are you going to pull *that* off?" he asks with a laugh before popping a small roasted potato in his mouth.

"Well, now that our house in San Francisco has burned down, my parents have no choice but to stay here for a couple of years and they're encouraging me to find a good boarding school."

I look at Alex's face and see what I had hoped for: a hint of sadness.

"Honestly, I would much rather stay here and hang out

with you and be with my parents," I say, "but there are bigger things at stake."

He just nods.

"Before all ... this, I was totally opposed to going away to school. But now, with what I have to do, I don't really have a choice. And I found a school that will allow me to travel."

"In Scotland?" he asks. I love that I hear a trace of hopefulness in his voice.

"No, actually, it's in ... uh ... Buenos Aires."

"As in Argentina? Is that the farthest point on Earth from the Isle of Huracan?"

"I know, I know. It's a million miles away in a country I know *nothing* about."

"Well, it's the Paris of South America," Alex says.

"They totally said that on the school's website! How did you know that?"

"Mum's travel magazines," he says. "So why this school in Buenos Aires?"

"It's called La Escuela Bohemia, and the whole curriculum is based on travel that is designed by the students."

"Sounds pricey," he says.

"It is. But my parents said I could choose *any* school. The thing is, this all hinges on one person: Justine. I need her to enroll with me because there's no way I could make some random girl go to places like the Dunhuang Caves and other far corners of the world that I may need to travel to."

"Will she go?"

"I don't know. She seems up for it but it's really up to her parents."

We sit quietly for a moment, Alex eating his lamb, me pushing the same little potato around the edge of my plate.

When he's done he sets his plate on the ottoman. "So is there anything I can help with before you go?"

"There's so much to do I don't even know where to start! We need to get that phone widget into use, set up a network connecting kids, translate the Mayan dates into the daily Mosquito Tone so that adults can't hear it—"

Alex laughs and puts up his hands to stop me.

"I know. I'm freaked out." I take a deep breath through my nose to try to calm myself down. I look at him and say, "I don't know how I'll do it all."

"You don't have to—I'll help," he says, slipping his hand over mine. Just as we lock eyes, Mrs. Findlay knocks on the door with a tray of water. I pull my hand away and put it on my lap as she walks in.

"Time to leave, son. Your mother has just called for you."

Way to ruin the moment, Mrs. Findlay.

FOUR

We have exactly two days before Alex has to start demolition on the butcher shop, so we have to get a lot done in a short amount of time. We decide to set up shop in the library because Mrs. Findlay would probably freak out if we were in my room all day, and she doesn't know enough about computers to even question what we're doing.

We meet Thomas outside to strategize, and he commits to keeping Mrs. Findlay occupied as much as he can. We already have the website up, we've started the viral use of the *Tzolk'in* numbers and day signs through an email with links to the site, and now we have to get down to translating the *Tzolk'in* calendar into Mosquito Tone sound waves that only kids can hear. Thomas says he's been in contact with Tenzo, who is still using the lab to check global patters of unification or coherence based on things that are happening. We seem to be on track, so we go inside to make all this happen.

We sit side-by-side in the library, each at our own computer. I can't seem to get started; I pretend to read my screen but instead I watch Alex's hands fly over the keys. I look at his profile out of the corner of my eye until I get a headache and have to scrunch my eyes together to make them work again. When he makes sudden moves, I secretly breathe deeper to catch his scent—that pine smell that wafts from his pores as if amber tree sap runs through his veins.

I want to say, *Do you remember that we kissed? What was that? Is whatever it was gone now?* I think that maybe because it happened so far away, in such bizarre circumstances, it sits out there like a dream so real you have trouble figuring out if it happened or not.

I'm not sure how long I'm lost in Alexness before I'm pulled back to reality by his sudden outburst.

"Done!" he says. "I just wrote a little piece of code that takes each day, translates it from the Mayan calendar number to a hertz tone, and then translates that into a super-high frequency Mosquito Tone so no one over twentyish can hear it."

"Amazing," I say, trying not to gush. I think I may be the only girl in the world to swoon over talk of algorithms and hertz tones. "Did you bundle it with a picture of the Daylord and number for each day?"

"Of course, take a look." He clicks on the day, and four dots—the Mayan symbol for four—and the Daylord symbol of *Lamat* pop up, along with a super-high-frequency tone.

"Nice! Now it's a multimedia experience! No coincidence that today is Four Lamat, huh?" I say. "Lamat is opposition, risk, and daring mixed with Four, which is challenge and change. Perfect for creating a subversive app."

"After reading about how the Russians are making changes to DNA with sound, I really think there might be something to this."

"Speaking of sound, do you think the website should be sound-driven?" I wonder out loud.

"What do you mean?"

"Like when you get to the home page, maybe we should record the instructions in Mosquito Tone to keep it all subversive."

"Aye!" Alex says, slapping me heartily on the back. "You can have the home page show a 404 Error but then have a Mosquito Tone message play that's saying the address of the hidden site."

"It's perfect."

So we work together on each of our freaky little projects. But it seems like I'm the only one stealing glances from the corner of my eye.

I'm astounded when I look at the number of people who have given addresses for email alerts. "We made it over the one million mark," I tell Alex. "Adults have absolutely no clue about the power we hold."

"My guess is they will soon … " Alex replies.

"Yes!" I reply, holding a fist in the air. "I shall unleash the power of the *Tzolk'in* upon the world!"

"I shan't miss that, mate!"

"Wow, I've never actually heard someone use the word 'shan't' in real life," I say.

Alex does not look amused. "Okay, then I'll um, like, try to talk, like, a lot more like you, then. Like, seriously," he says in a perfect imitation of my tone.

It's a weird moment. I try to laugh but it feels awkward. Like we've just insulted each other for no good reason.

Thankfully, Mr. Papers hops up onto the long wooden table that Alex and I are working on. He has a sheet of blue paper and a pair of small scissors, like the kind you use for sewing.

"What's up, friend?" I say as he starts to fold and cut and fold and cut the paper.

"Can you tell what he's making?" Alex asks.

"Not a clue. I didn't even know he could use scissors."

"S'pose that's where the opposable thumb comes in handy."

Mr. Papers puts down the scissors and turns his back to us. We can hear him unfold and refold the paper but we can't see what he's doing.

Finally he turns around and holds in his hand a perfectly made blue paper harp.

"A harp?" Alex says.

Papers pretends to pull a string of the harp and then mimes an expanding wave.

"Oh!" I say, getting the pun. "He means HAARP!"

Papers puts a finger to his nose, sets the harp down on the table, and then crushes the tiny paper instrument.

"What am I missing?" Alex asks. "I said harp then you said harp and then he destroyed it!"

"Open a browser and do an image search on the letters H-A-A-R-P," I tell him as I lean over to look at his screen.

The first image that pops up looks like something out of a sci-fi film—acres and acres of land in the middle of Alaska.

Forests have been cleared and in the place of trees lies a massive tangle of antennas and wires.

"What the bloody hell is that?" Alex asks.

"This was one of the things those guys from the *Fraternitas* were talking about, and it showed up in that binder Justine and I stole from Tremblay! There's this antenna farm in Alaska where they send out frequency waves into the upper atmosphere and magnetosphere."

"Why?" he asks.

"They say it's about defense, like for blocking weapon pulses or something, but what if it's really about blocking this incoming energy from the galaxy?"

"Keeping us sealed off as another form of control?"

"Exactly!"

"So they're jamming the frequencies that would otherwise cause this leap in evolution."

Papers nods and taps Alex on the nose.

"The question is, can what we're doing with the *Tzolk'in* tones rebalance that?" I ask, and Mr. Papers comes over and taps me on the nose. Then he goes back to the crushed harp and ferociously wads it up.

"But we must also do something about HAARP?"

Papers nods and then hops down into my lap, curls up like a spiral, and falls fast asleep.

Alex looks at me. "You do realize we just had a very sophisticated conversation with a monkey, don't you?"

FIVE

Alex and I work together and by the end of the second day we manage to get everything accomplished, even stuff we didn't originally think of, like a live stream of data from the PEAR center that shows this slow, steady climb in coherence, or unity.

In the late afternoon, Mrs. Findlay comes in to tell us she needs to go to town, emphasizing the fact that she will be back in no more than forty minutes. We pretend to be so engrossed in our computer screens that we barely say goodbye, but the minute I hear Thomas start up the Land Rover, I say, "Do you want to see inside the tower?"

"Aye," Alex says, jumping up so fast it startles me.

"Come on, then!"

We run as quickly as we can upstairs. From the rabbit ears key to the ladder in the hole, he is completely fascinated. It isn't until I show him everything, even the *vesica pisces* that drops below ground, that he even looks at me. But it's worth the wait.

Right after I show him how to make the rocks glow with the lanterns, he pulls me close to him, takes my chin and tips it up so I can look into his blue eyes. Then he bends down and gives me the longest, sweetest kiss. Saving the best for last, I gently push him from the edge of the rock to the center. Slowly, because we're entwined as one, we start to rise. He pulls away and starts flailing his arms at first, not knowing what is happening. Then I grab him tightly and we rise together. When we're about two feet off the ground, we lose our balance; he starts tipping backwards and I tip on top of him.

And there we stay, locked in a magnetic kiss, for the best few minutes of my life. Even the feeling of floating seems mundane compared to the swirling I feel in my heart.

The faint beep of a horn startles us both. Thomas must be alerting us that he and Mrs. Findlay are home. We scurry back up to my room and then take separate staircases down—Alex runs straight out to help Mrs. Findlay with the groceries and I run back to the library.

When I sit back down at the computer, it feels like my heart is four times its size, pumping blood and love and fear and excitement all at once.

A few minutes later Alex is in the doorway with Mrs. Findlay. "I've got to go, Caity," he says.

"Oh, bummer. Hey, thanks so much for your help on the project." When Mrs. Findlay turns to leave, Alex stands for a moment and gives me a crooked smile.

After he's gone I move to his chair and close my eyes. If

everything in this world leaves an energetic imprint, I want to bask in his for as long as I can.

———

That night, my parents call. They sound far away in every sense; preoccupied, distracted, sad. They tell me they spent the day going through a storage unit where the insurance company put all the stuff that could be salvaged from the house. Mom said she'll have the nauseating smell of wet, burnt things in her nose for weeks.

"Is there really anything that's okay to keep?" I ask.

"Some silver, some porcelain, things like that," Mom answers. "I'm afraid not much from your room survived."

"That's totally the least of my worries," I tell her. It's true. I picture my room with its lavender walls and corkboards full of magazine cutouts and the white furniture that seems doll-like after the enormous furniture in the castle. It was all so innocent.

That naïve Caity is gone, up in flames with the furniture and stuffed animals and childhood toys.

"Do they have any idea how it started?" I ask.

"They're still investigating," Dad says. "Most likely an electrical thing. These old houses are just a rat's nest of wires."

We chat a bit more about the weather and what we've eaten, all of us wanting to stay connected but not wanting to go back to heavy subjects. Finally, when there is nothing left to say, we hang up.

My bedroom windows and doors are shuttered and bolted and a large club-like weapon that I got from the wall of the Salon sits beside my bed, but I still shiver as I try to fall asleep.

I can't seem to get the image of Barend Schlacter's nasty face out of my mind; it was probably he who started the fire.

When I close my eyes all I see is his fat hand striking a match, burning down my childhood.

———

I spend a lonely week by myself trying to tie up loose ends with the website and the tones that Alex created. Mrs. Findlay, Thomas, and I eat every meal together in the kitchen and I live for little updates about Alex and what he's doing. Apparently the butcher shop is a complete nightmare of rotting wood and the demolition has been tough.

Mrs. Findlay is staying in the room off the kitchen and Thomas is sleeping on site in one of the East Wing rooms, yet I still bolt my door every night.

The day before my parents are scheduled to come home, I get great news from Justine: her parents are letting her try La Escuela Bohemia. It was the exclusivity of the place that tipped it over the edge with her parents. Anything with "world's most expensive" in front of it attracts Mr. Middleford like ants to a Popsicle stick.

Meanwhile, I have everything submitted except the parental agreement and wire transfer, the only things I could not do by myself.

Seeing the bit about the transfer of money made me think about Dad's covert operating style and the fact that we should not enroll with our real last names. So I used the fake email address I'd made for Mom to email the school about a couple of key things, like can we enroll with covert names (for security reasons) and could two students who enroll together be paired with the same teacher—or Pedagogue, as they call them. The answer was "yes" to both. Students can use whatever name they choose at school as long as one person in the travel department has the student's real passport name on file. Best of all, students can pair up prior to coming if both parties consent and both parties keep up their grades.

I think this might actually happen.

———

Mom and Dad arrive home looking older than I've ever seen them look. Without question, sadness can change a person's appearance.

They're worn out, so we spend the day together playing Scrabble and reading in the parlor while being fattened by Mrs. Findlay, who is happy to have lots of people to cook for again. It feels good to just do nothing.

In the evening, after they've relaxed a bit and the sadness has lifted, I spring the school thing on them, being sure to include the fact that this was one of the brochures *they* sent away for. I fill them with info about La Escuela Bohemia's unique concept, the notable alumni, the teacher-to-student ratio. I save the money bit for last. They both gulp and look at each other. It's a *lot* of money.

"If you want me to stay here, I'm totally cool with that," I say. "That little island school should be fine."

"Um, no," Mom says.

"Well, any boarding school will be expensive," Dad says, "so I guess it's matter of scale."

Mom adds, "And it is just two years..."

"Small price to see the world, I suppose," Dad replies.

Mom shrugs. "The whole reason we work so hard is to give Caity a good future."

They are trying to convince themselves, and are getting pretty close.

I trot out the part about SAT scores, college acceptance, and royal alumni. As they're chewing on these tasty facts, I play my last card. "I haven't even told you the best part yet—*Justine* wants to go with me!"

They both look shocked.

"Her parents agreed to this?" Dad says.

"When did this all happen?" Mom asks.

"We talked about it while you guys were in San Francisco," I say. "So what do you think?"

No one answers. Wanting to fill up the dead air, I say, "Honestly Mom, you know how much I did *not* want to go away to school. Now I've found one that actually has me excited to go and has all the academic requirements you guys want."

"I know, Caity," Mom says.

Dad runs his hand through his hair and says, "I'm sorry we're not more excited, Caity. I think we're still getting over the shock of the house."

"Let me call there tomorrow," Mom says. "I have some questions, but I suppose if the Middlefords approve, it must be top notch."

I squeeze her hand. "I just think you're right about me

needing a much more challenging school. I'm really glad you're supportive of this. It would just be a tragedy if I ended up being the dumb one in our family."

Without it ever having being said, I know their greatest fear is having a dumb child.

I'm as good as in.

SIX

Once my parents find out I'm accepted—and how soon I have to go away to school—they don't let me out of their sight. Suddenly they want to spend every waking moment with me. It's difficult to even find a sliver of time to say goodbye to Thomas and to Alex, who has been totally monopolized by the old butcher's remodel. I honestly think we'll be able to get more face time over Skype sessions from school than in real life, because of my parents stealing all of my time and Cormag stealing all of his.

By mid-July, just when I'd usually start getting into the swing of summer, I have to pack up and leave. Mom was definitely regretting her decision when they watched me walk through security at the Edinburgh airport; Dad had to hold her up because she was sobbing so hard. I think if she could go back and change things, she would have chosen home-schooling for sure.

I'm only holding up because I know what's at stake. But

secretly I'm so sad to leave the island and my parents and Alex. I tell myself it won't even be a year, to keep me going. If Justine and I can do what we need to do, maybe in a few months I can be back at Breidablik with my parents and Alex.

———

Justine and I meet up at the Miami airport for our last leg to Buenos Aires. As soon as I see her I get nervous—because I'm reminded that it's really happening. She's cut her long black hair a few inches so now it's just to the top of her chest, which makes her seem older. A couple of weeks at her family's place in Santa Cruz has given her olive skin a deep tan that makes her eyes look as vibrant as green glass marbles in sunlight.

We jump up and down and hug, both nervous and excited and scared. It's one thing to imagine going to school across the world, it's another to be doing it.

I hold up the travel carrier—more like a puppy purse—that Mr. Papers is in. "Justine, meet Mr. Papers. Mr. Papers, Justine." Justine holds a finger to the mesh window and Mr. P touches his palm to her finger.

"Seriously, I have to hold him right this second!" she says.

"We need to go somewhere private." I look around and see a sign for a family bathroom and motion to it. "We're a family of sorts, aren't we?" Locking the door to the little room, I set the dog tote on the small settee and zip open the top.

Mr. Papers looks up at Justine and holds up an origami peony with what seems like hundreds of intricate petals.

"Unbelievable!" she says as she pets him on the head. "Okay, having a monkey makes up for everything."

"I know, right? Can you believe we ever lived without one?" I ask, showing her how to scratch him right below the ears so that his leg twitches.

We let Mr. Papers run around since he's been cramped up for so long until a knock on the door forces us to pack up and go. A woman travelling alone with two kids and a baby is standing impatiently outside and does not look amused when two teen girls open the door.

Knowing we have a nine-hour flight ahead of us, we eat a big meal and stock up on snacks for our bags. I slip a banana and some dried mango into the carrier for Mr. Papers.

We have a little time, so I fill Justine in on all that Alex and I have done—and why. She didn't know that the daily *Tzolk'in* picture and tone was key to unifying the youth in a unique and subversive way, just as the gathering had. It's all a part of literally getting us on the same wavelength, I tell her.

The flight takes all day, but it's night to me so I sleep the whole way. I don't wake up until Justine nudges me and opens the window shade to show me the pink sun setting over miles and miles of lush greenery.

After we weave our way through customs at the massive and modern Buenos Aires airport, we see a man holding a board with "Caitrina and Justine" professionally printed on it like we're diplomats.

We walk over and smile at the man. "I am Ramón," he says, as he offers his hand. "On behalf of La Escuela Bohemia, I welcome you to Buenos Aires."

Justine and I giggle at the formality of it all and he gives us a little smile and a wink.

"Please, your bags," he says as he takes our two large rolling suitcases from us and leads us out to the town car he has waiting.

Once in the car, I let Mr. Papers out. He sits on my shoulder with his nose through the cracked car window like a dog. He seems younger, more alert. I think he's been cooped up in the castle for far too long; this experience will be good for him.

Justine and I both call our parents to let them know we've landed safely, and I'm surprised to hear that they have already been notified. Ramón was one step ahead; he'd texted the school to let them know that he'd picked us up, and the school had called to let our parents know we were en route. I guess that's what super steep tuition gets you.

One of the rules of the school is that first-year students only get to talk to their parents when they arrive, and then not again until fall break around Thanksgiving. You can email all you want, you just can't call or Skype. I guess psychologically there's a difference between hearing your parents' voices and reading their words. Apparently a lot of boarding schools do this to fend off the homesickness that happens with first-year kids. This fact makes me stay on the phone longer that I normally would even though there's not much to report. It's just weird that once I hang up I won't talk to them for a couple of months.

Even though the sun is going down, it's hot and sticky in Buenos Aires. The city is beautiful in the golden glow of evening as lights flick on and candles are lit on sidewalk cafés. The smell of meat and garlic cooking is driving me mad. People are laughing, walking arm and arm, and stopping for drinks and dinner. I like Buenos Aires already.

The city seems to go on forever. When I think about how many massive cities there are like this around the world, my head hurts. There are so many people doing so many things, and trusting the people in power to have their best interests at heart.

Can we really change any of this?

From the isolated view of the Isle of Huracan it seemed reasonable, but in this city teeming with people—just one of hundreds of thousands of cities like this around the world—it seems absurd.

I hear Bolon's voice in my head saying, *Focus on the quality of the frequency.* I say it again in my head, in my own voice, so I'll remember it.

We finally get to the outskirts of the city and turn up a driveway, under an arch that bears a golden star and the school's motto: *Siga la Chispa.* Follow the Spark. I love that their motto isn't something stupid and boring like *Commitment to Excellence.*

I wonder where the spark will lead us.

When Ramón stops, rolls down his window, and puts his thumb to a fingerprint reader, two massive iron gates open up. The number of thick trees on either side of the winding drive block out the fading light completely. When we round the final corner, we both take a breath. It's stunning—a fairy tale of lights and limestone and wrought iron that no brochure or website can come close to capturing.

Justine grabs my hand and Mr. Papers wraps his arms around my neck.

We are here.

SEVEN

The car pulls through a roundabout and stops right in front of a building of pale pink limestone with a black roof; it looks like a gorgeous drawing of a French estate that you might find in a *Madeline* picture book. I put Mr. Papers back in his carrier, and Ramón leads us to a two-story-high wooden door that bears the La Escuela Bohemia crest and the words *Siga la Chispa* emblazoned at the bottom. Beside the door there is a brass sign that reads *La Administración.*

It's dimly lit inside, and set up like a hotel lobby—a large reception area, cushy seating around low tables, and soft classical guitar music playing. I can hear what sounds like a party in some distant part of the building, but the foyer is quiet except for the sound of our shoes on the creamy polished-stone floor.

As we approach the check-in desk, a door opens to the side of it and out walks a tall man with gray hair and the posture of a model. His dark suit fits him so perfectly that it looks as if it were part of his body.

"Welcome, *mademoiselles*," he says as he holds out his hand. "I am Monsieur Didier, the Dean of Students here at La Escuela Bohemia."

We shake his large, tan hand and introduce ourselves. I have to consciously remind myself to use my new name, "Caitrina Luxton," and once I say it Justine remembers to say hers. She picked "Devereux" because she's in love with all things French and thinks it sounds good with "Justine."

After introductions, Monsieur Didier pulls out two business cards from the inside of his suit jacket. "It is my responsibility that you receive the finest education in the world," he says, while handing us each a card. "To that end, there is absolutely no time or day that I am not available. Should you need me, all of my contact information is on this card."

We thank him and slip the cards into our pockets.

"You'll find a schedule printed on your desks in your dorm room. Most notable is orientation for new students, which starts at ten tomorrow morning, and the Spark Ball, which will begin after formal dinner at seven."

I give Justine a quick worried glance. A *ball*? I don't have anything even close to appropriate for a ball.

Monsieur Didier must have caught my look, because he says, "Should you need gowns, the school has an exquisite collection of vintage *couture*, donated by alumnae."

Of course.

Justine's eyes are gleaming and we share a giddy smile.

"Your housemother, Señora Garza, can help you to the archives where they're kept."

The word "archives" reminded me of the Dunhuang Caves. Because I'm distracted by the elegance and promise of the new school, this works like smelling salts to snap me back to the reason we are there in the first place: to leave.

"It has been a pleasure, Mademoiselles Luxton and Devereux," he says with a bow of the head. "Ramón will take you to your dorm. Now, if you'll excuse me, I have to get back to the Senior Mixer."

"Of course," Justine says.

"Lovely to meet you," I add.

As soon as Monsieur Didier is through the door, Justine and I grab each other's arms and start squealing.

"Vintage *couture*?" she squeals.

"I *know*!" I say, "We've hit the jackpot of schools!"

Mr. Papers squawks from inside the carrier. "Sorry pal," I say, looking in through the mesh front. "Didn't mean to scramble you when I jumped."

"I'm dying to see our room," Justine says. "Let's go!"

Ramón leads us back to the car. As we drive around the administration building, I look in through the floor-to-ceiling windows at what looks like a foreign film: gorgeous boys in suits and ties milling around girls with sparkly jewelry and light-as-air chiffon dresses you only see in magazines. Tuxedoed waiters glide through with silver trays of hors d'oeuvres and champagne glasses—it's feast of fabulousness for the eyes.

One boy gazes out the window and seems to look right at me. He stands with that indefinable posture, sort of a relaxed elegance, that Europeans have. His long, straight nose might look out of place on a smaller, less masculine face, but his strong square jaw balances it and also works like a display shelf to feature the most unbelievable mouth I've ever seen. He's more Italian marble than human.

Justine elbows me. "Check it!" she says as we drive slowly by.

"Is that a guy or a statue?" I ask.

"Either way, it's art," she replies. "I love it here already."

———

Ramón parks in a roundabout in front of another building similar to the administration building but bigger. Standing in the door is a short, round woman wearing a skirt and suit jacket she can barely close.

"*¡Hola amigas!*" she says, as if she has been waiting all day just for us. "I am Señora Garza." After we introduce ourselves, she leads us into the residence hall. The first floor has a dark wood study room, a kitchenette with a small eating area, and a student lounge complete with leather sofas and oversized armchairs you could get lost in.

"Eat only in the dining area and no boy past ten at night in this building," she says, leading us to an elevator. "And no boys anywhere but first floor!" she adds as she pushes the "Door close" button. We get off on the second floor and walk to the end of the hall before Señora Garza stops at room 260.

That's the number of days in the *Tzolk'in* and a key number in all Mayan calendars. I take this as a good sign.

"Your room," she says, with a sweeping gesture as she opens the door. It's small but beautiful, like a boutique hotel room. There are two large desks with bookcases attached, two beds with beautifully carved headboards and white linens, and two large armchairs with ottomans. The furniture all looks expensive, not like standard institutional furniture you see in college dorms. The walls are painted a creamy yellow.

Señora Garza pulls back the curtains to reveal a tall glass door that opens to a small balcony. Enclosed by a wrought-iron railing with all kinds of scrolls, the balcony is just big enough for two chairs and a table.

"Perfect," I say, setting Mr. Papers' bag down on the bed close to the window and unzipping the top.

Jumping out of the bag, Mr. Papers hops onto the railing in one leap. Señora Garza screams and tumbles backwards.

"Oh, no! I'm so sorry! It's just my pet, Mr. Papers. He's totally tame!"

"*¡Un mono!*" she says, clutching her chest.

"He's fine. They said I could bring him. He'll be no trouble," I promise her. "Just look at him!"

Mr. Papers is sitting on the railing taking deep breaths of the warm, moist Argentine air with a tiny smile on his face.

Señora Garza scrunches up her nose and hisses, "*Bestia asquerosa.*"

Justine puts her hand on Señora Garza's arm and says, "Mr. Papers is *not* revolting, and he's *not* a beast." Then she takes Monsieur Didier's card from her pocket and adds, "Shall we talk to someone in administration?"

Señora Garza shakes her arm away from Justine and says, "No. It is not a problem. No need for Didier."

Then she looks at us both as if we've just pulled something over on her, turns on her toes, and heads for the door, tossing two keys on the bed as she leaves.

"Wow. Señora Crabby is going to be a lot of fun," I say.

"You mind if I take the bed by the window? That way I can make a little space for Mr. Papers over here."

"Don't mind at all," Justine replies, opening the door for Ramón, who has our suitcases on a rolling cart.

When he's finished bringing them in, Ramón asks us if we need anything else. Then he gives us his card and says to call whenever we need to go anywhere. We thank him and I reach in my wallet for a tip, but when I try to give him a ten, he puts up his hand in protest.

"Gracias, but no tips. Against school policy and I am paid well."

Just as the door is closing behind him, Ramón slips his head back in the door. "Amigas, one last thing. Monsieur Didier sees all. Careful with him."

"Thanks?" Justine says, closing the door and looking over at me. "Uh, that was weird."

"Good to know, I guess," I say, not wanting Justine to get too freaked out her first day here—I need her to stay. But it was odd.

In order to give Mr. Papers his own space, I pull the side table that was by the reading chair over to the corner next to my bed. The pillow from the puppy carrier fits perfectly underneath the table, and he scurries in and gives me a happy squawk. The walls cover two sides of the table but it still doesn't seem like quite enough privacy, so I grab a scarf and put it over the whole table.

I peek under and see Mr. P. reclining on his back, hands clasped behind his head. It makes me happy to see him comfortable; I'd been feeling guilty about taking him from his home, but he seems to be really digging the change of scenery.

There's only one last thing to do.

"So, should we light this candle?" I ask Justine.

She looks at me sideways. "What now?"

"I'm thinking of emailing the *Tzolk'in* to the whole Escuela Bohemia, like I did at the Academy of Cruelties."

"Do you have the email list?"

"Remember that welcome email we got? It was to the group 'All Students,' so I can try to reply all and change the body of the mail."

"Perfect overachiever move. Let's get this thing rolling the first day here!"

I use Bolon's secret PayPal account to get an email name with a shady company that guarantees absolute privacy, even when authorities are involved. I need this account name to be ultra mysterioso and untraceable. Then I type up a message.

"Should I go short and sweet?" I ask Justine. "I'm thinking of just saying, 'Have you ever wondered about the Mayan calendar? Here is your chance to explore it. Click here to start.'"

"Perfect," she says. "That gives them just enough to want to click through."

So tired I'm barely able to write the email, I send it off and hit the pillow.

But I have a bad feeling in my chest. Maybe it was too early to send that email.

EIGHT

The first thing I see when I wake up is Mr. Papers sitting next to me with an origami banana in his hand. How can you not laugh? "Sorry pal," I whisper as I fish around for the bag with food in it.

The sound of me opening the dried mango package wakes Justine, who grabs the clock and yells, "Holy crap!"

Mr. Papers and I both jump.

"It's 9:40, Caity! We have to be at orientation at ten!"

We scurry around, splashing water on our faces and trying to find our least wrinkled clothes, then both take a handful of dried mango. I crack the balcony door for Mr. Papers so he can get some fresh air if he wants, and then we run out. We're late and everyone else has already gone so the halls are empty, which is kind of creepy. As we run through the lobby, we see Señora Garza by the door holding two cups.

"Café con leche," she says as she hands them to us. Stunned by the service, we thank her, then take the cups and walk as quickly as we can while sipping. Last night we looked at the campus map and worked out where the orientation would be, but the trees and bushes are so lush it's hard to see the buildings. We finally make it to the right place almost five minutes late, and when we open the heavy, carved doors to the auditorium, all eyes turn to us.

"Please mademoiselles, take a seat," says Monsieur Didier from the stage. His voice is sweet, but calling us out in front of a packed auditorium is clearly a lesson.

We sit in the far back. I try to take in as much as I can but I'm distracted by the sheer beauty in the room. Seriously, each and every one of these kids could be a model. Are there any nerds here? Any dorks? Where are the zit-faced World of Warcraft types or the bookish girls with bad glasses and thin hair? Who are these people? This is clearly not the public at large.

Justine can totally pass as one of these beautiful, aloof creatures but I cannot. I glance at her and wonder if she's ever embarrassed to be with me and my tall awkwardness and curly hair.

Monsieur Didier blathers on about the philosophy of the school, the character it builds, the global citizens it creates— all standard brochure propaganda. I pull out my notebook as if to take notes, but instead sketch Señora Garza with two big crab claws. Just as I'm shading the bigger fighting claw, something sticks in the back of my hair.

I reach back and feel a small paper airplane. It's a crude folding job that Mr. Papers would be ashamed of. I look back, but no one is behind us; I look up at the balcony, but see no one there. Inside the poorly folded plane is written:

You are not like the others. This may or may not be a good thing.

I show it to Justine, who looks around. She can't see anyone above us either.

The plane's creator has vanished, but the weird feeling in my stomach stays. Who is watching me?

After the general orientation, where I learn nothing new, Didier brings up a matter of great importance. He looks at the audience, scanning every face, and says, "I was made aware of an all-school email this morning about the Mayan calendar. We pride ourselves on shaping students who look carefully and scientifically at things, students who do not get caught up in pseudoscience or chicanery. I ask you now, whoever sent the email with the link to the Mayan calendar, please reveal yourself."

The crowd falls dead silent, and everyone is looking around to see who will stand up. My face feels like it's being stung by a hive of bees. I start looking around too, so I don't look suspicious. I quickly run through all the steps I took in sending the mail, and am still confident he can't trace it to me.

"If no one comes forward to claim ownership of this email—and I assure you the authorities will eventually track you down—the entire student body will have one more day of school than originally scheduled."

A groan makes its way through the audience like a wave at a football game. And then something incredible happens: I start hearing the *Tzolk'in* tone of the day in the super-high

Mosquito Tone—kids are playing the *Tzolk'in* app on their phones! First just a few, and then enough to make me wonder if Didier might sense it. Justine and I share a tenth-of-a-second smirk before looking down.

"You will have twenty-four hours to accept culpability," he goes on, clearly not hearing a thing. "If you do not accept responsibility we will prosecute you for illegal use of school property; every email name issued belongs to La Escuela Bohemia."

Didier is on fire, but if he'd just clicked through he would have seen the 404 Error page. At his age, there's no way he could have heard the Mosquito Tone directions to the hidden site and he wouldn't be making a federal case out of this.

"We will not tolerate this kind of proselytization here. Unfounded ideas perpetuated as truth are dangerous and are exactly what we do not represent."

I nudge Justine—everyone knows that bad PR is the best kind of PR. After hearing the word "dangerous," every kid in the room who has not yet looked is going to go back to that email and open it up out of sheer curiosity. You'd think after working with students for so long, Didier would get clued in to stuff like that.

When he's done unsuccessfully trying to shame the student body into admitting who did it, Didier finally excuses us to go meet with our Pedagogues. Our paperwork says that our Pedagogue is Dr. Clath, who will be waiting for us in room 312.

"What do you think she's like?" I ask Justine as we make our way up the grand central staircase, with its marble floor and scrolled wrought-iron handrail.

"Well, if she's really a doctor, that means she could teach college—why would anyone want to teach younger kids when they can teach at college?"

"Maybe she's into travel," I say. "Or maybe she's running from something … "

"Like the law … " Justine replies as we make our way to the cracked door of room 312. "Hello," she says, peeking her head through the doorway.

"Oh, hello. Hi. Yes, come on in," replies a nervous voice.

As we push open the door, a tall woman with fuzzy brown hair and the kind of face that could be forty or sixty or anywhere in between stands to greet us. She's wearing oversized, out-of-style glasses and a baggy La Escuela Bohemia T-shirt tucked into elastic-waist jeans that are just short enough to feature the kind of Velcro-adjusting black shoes they sell in the drugstore for diabetics. I may be unglamorous compared to the other students, but next to this woman I feel positively breathtaking.

It's almost as if she is trying to look like a "before" shot in a makeover story—to have made all the choices she did that day in her appearance would have taken a massive dose of personal disregard. I'm kind of intrigued by her, but I can tell Justine is let down. I mean, we have to spend the whole year with this person and she could, just by the look of her, be mildly insane.

NINE

As we say hello and walk toward her, she holds out her long arm stiffly. I know this is to shake hands, but it also feels like she's putting up a barrier wall, as if to say, *Don't even think of entering my personal space.* Part of me wants to give her a big bear hug to see if she'd freak out from human contact, but instead I shake her hand, keeping my distance. Then she motions to the two chairs set up on the other side of the table.

"So. I'm Dr. Clath." She smoothes out a perfectly flat piece of white paper in front of her, obviously nervous. "Tell me, girls, what exactly do you want to learn? Whatever you're interested in, we'll build a curriculum around it and make sure we hit all the subjects."

Justine and I glance at each other. She gives me the *you go* look, so I say, "Well, we're very interested in symbols." We already discussed the fact that we have to keep the Mayan stuff and the precession stuff on the down low, and work that into the curriculum on the side.

"Alright. What kind of symbols?" Dr. Clath asks.

"Mostly symbols that are found across different cultures but have mysterious origins," Justine says.

"Good, good," Dr. Clath replies. "Like the Flower of Life, I assume?"

"Exactly! Do you know a lot about it?" I ask.

"Only from a math perspective. It's the blueprint for all geometry."

As she gets less nervous she seems less odd, and I get less worried about having to spend 24/7 with her this year.

"What others, specifically, are you interested in?" she asks.

Justine says, "The snake eating its tail—"

"Good old ouroboros," she interrupts. "Always a classic. Others?"

"Well, the one we're most interested in is the Three Hares," I say.

"Three hares? I'm not sure I've heard of it," Dr. Clath says in a way that makes me think she doesn't like not knowing stuff. "Can you refresh my memory?"

I fish out my sketchbook from my bag and thumb through, looking for the drawing I'd done of the carved panel doors in my room at the castle. I don't dare pull out the key ring that fits in the center of the Three Hares; I don't want her to know that I have any personal investment in this study.

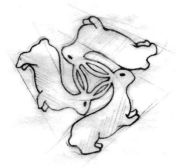

"This is just a sketch, but you get the idea," I say, pointing to the center of the drawing where the three rabbits all share the same ears.

Justine adds, "It's a symbol that's been found all over the world, but no one knows exactly what it means."

"Interesting," Dr. Clath replies, examining my sketch as if it were evidence of something. She takes the sheet of white paper before her, sets it over my drawing, and begins to trace the ears. "See the center part here? This is the beginning of the Flower of Life symbol."

Uncle Li had shown me that already, but I pretend to be as surprised as Justine is by it.

"Yes, I could see this turning into a very interesting primary curriculum," Dr. Clath says. She looks back at her tracings and then jots down some notes that I can't read because her left-handed writing looks more like jagged lie-detector results than actual words.

She looks back up at us and says, "Any ideas for a secondary subject? We must be studying two tracts at once, but they can overlap."

"We're also very interested in old myths," I say. "Like, *really* old ones."

Dr. Clath shakes her head. "You know, all really old mythology is based on astronomy, Precession of the Equinoxes and such, which might take this more into the realm of science than humanities."

"Oh, we know that," Justine says.

"That's what we want." I agree.

"Glad to have some girls who aren't afraid of science!" Dr. Clath says, leaning back and pulling up on the already impossibly high waistband of her jeans.

"Is that your background?" I ask, wondering if it's okay to get personal information from her. "Science?"

"I'm a right-brain, left-brain hybrid," she says, waiting an awkward beat for a laugh that we don't deliver. "I taught Philosophy of Math."

"Really?" I say, "I've never heard of that."

"Well, that must change post-haste!" she replies, mustering a little fire for the first time. Then she goes into a long lecture about what philosophy of math entails, which honestly might be interesting if I understood a word she was saying.

After a long-winded, one-way conversation, Dr. Clath asks where we would like to go first and both of us say, "The Dunhuang Caves" at the same time, as if we'd practiced it.

I'm not sure she's ever heard of the place and I don't want her to feel uncomfortable about it, so I say, "The caves in

China where they've traced the oldest known example of the Three Hares symbol. But I'm sure you already knew that."

Just saying the words "Dunhuang Caves" gives me a chill. I try not to think of how I'll ever be able to find Uncle Li on the other side of the world. I just have to go for it—it's my only chance to get answers.

"Right, right. Yes. Dunhuang," Dr. Clath says, jotting more words down in her crazy handwriting. When she's finished writing she gathers her things together, looks at her watch, and says, "I have an appointment with Monsieur Didier and the travel coordinator to plan our first quarter. Be prepared to pack tomorrow and leave the day after."

"Already?" Based on how long it took us to get here, I assumed we'd have a week or two to settle in.

"Already," she replies, zipping up a backpack that looks older than I am. "I know there's some kind of ball tonight, but remember, you are here for an education. An education for which your parents are paying dearly."

Clearly this is a woman who had no fun in high school.

Justine and I walk out of the meeting room. Once we're out of earshot, we discuss the problem of Dr. Clath. We both agree the only solution is a makeover.

We vow that sometime, somewhere, we will turn that middle-aged duckling into a swan.

———

With nothing left to do for the day, we walk around the grounds. There's something wild and untamed about the lush greenery here. While everything is trimmed and tidy, you get the sense that if the gardener took a few weeks off, nature might start to reclaim this land.

"So, what do you think, Justine?" I ask as we lazily weave our way back to our dorm. "Any regrets so far?"

"Not yet," she says. "You?"

I shake my head. "I just have to keep reminding myself why we're here, what it is we have to do. And what the *Fraternitas* might do if we don't stop them."

I take out my phone and click on the app that gives me the daily *Tzolk'in* tone, along with a picture of the day's number and glyph.

"Isn't it weird that no one over twenty can hear that?" I ask as we reach our dorm.

"Yeah, like why would your high-tone hearing start going out at twenty? Is that so you can block out the screams of your obnoxious children?"

"Seems the perfect evolutionary answer," I reply.

———

At the dorm kitchen we find the South American version of ramen and eat a quick lunch. Neither one of us wants to brave the cafeteria, and the throngs of beautiful people, quite yet.

On the way back to our room we can hear other students in their rooms, talking all sorts of different languages, but no one is out and about. Just as we approach our room, a door opens. In the doorway, a very tall girl with cat-eye makeup like a French movie star stands looking at us and smoking.

She actually does the judgmental full-body scan of both of us, totally without emotion, and then closes her door.

"Friendly neighbors," I say.

"Oui," Justine replies.

Suddenly, something becomes very clear. "Wait a minute—do you think we're like the poor white trash around here?"

Justine laughs, "That's it! We are so low-rent compared to these people!"

"That would totally explain why we got Clath. I'll bet the beautiful people all have Pedagogues that look like Didier."

We open the door to our room to find Mr. Papers sitting on the floor next to an envelope that must have been slid under the door. We open it to find a cream-colored stationary card with *Siga la Chispa* embossed in gold letters at the top. In loopy writing it reads:

> Gown fitting:
> Justine – 1:30
> Caitrina – 2:30
> Check in at the front desk of La Administración

"I am going to pick the most amazing gown ever!" Justine says, then adds, "Unless it would be perfect for you. Then I'll leave it alone."

"Do you think they have shoes?" I say, looking in the closet at my collection of Chuck Taylors and flip-flops. "Man, I hope they have shoes."

"They've gotta have shoes," Justine says. "But if not, I brought a spare pair of Louboutins."

"And therein lies the difference," I say.

Justine's mom pays attention to these things, makes lists, shops at the best stores. She may not be around most of the time, but the girl stuff gets done. My mom is around all the time but pays almost no attention to the girly stuff. While she and Dad made sure I had a laptop with the most power and speed available and any communication device I could ever need, I was on my own with clothing.

TEN

While we were gone, Mr. Papers decorated the room with more origami animals than I can count. Crickets, frogs, cranes, fish—it's a menagerie. Everywhere your eye rests there is a colorful little animal. So when Justine leaves for her fitting, I grab some paper and try to follow along as Mr. Papers makes a dog. He's actually a very good teacher.

When someone knocks at the door, I contemplate pretending I'm not there. I wish we had one of those eyehole things so I can see who it is. Mr. Papers jumps on my shoulder and grabs my hair like reins, as if he wants to ride me to the door. I open it just a few inches and am both surprised and relieved that it's Bolon. I haven't seen him since the Vimāna ride, although I've heard his voice in my head a few times.

I remember how mad I was after the lava tube chase, how much I never wanted to see him again, but after coming to terms with what I need to do, and the consequences of not doing it, I welcome him with a hug.

There is just something about him.

"How on earth did you find me?" I ask, looking down the hall to see if anyone else saw him.

He laughs as if that's a silly question. "I came to see how you are."

I let him in and close the door. These people might think it's weird that a short Mayan guy in a colorful poncho is making a visit.

"I'm okay, I guess," I tell him. "I mean, this place is pretty amazing."

"Very good," he replies. "And how goes your mission?"

"It's actually going pretty well. Alex figured out how to translate the *Tzolk'in* into hertz tones and then upped them to a frequency called Mosquito Tone that people over twenty-ish can't hear. He embedded all that on a phone app for daily update, and then I put it on the website. Except when you get to the website it looks like it's broken unless you're a kid and can hear the Mosquito Tone directions to the secret site."

"And you're still using the same host server you set this up on?"

"Yep. And I gotta say, they are good! Our hits are going up every hour and we now have more than a million email addresses and the server has never gone down. Let's just hope the *Fraternitas* never tracks it down."

"They won't. Or I should say, they can't—The Council has purchased the server company."

"What? That's amazing!"

"You lead the charge," Bolon says dipping his head. "We

just make sure you can do your job. So what are your next steps?"

"First things first. I have to find Uncle Li. Did you know he stole the Sanskrit books from me?"

"I'd heard that," he says.

"I've known him my whole life and he does something like that," I say, shaking my head. It's still hard to believe. "Anyway, I've got to get those books back. Mr. Papers told me he went to the Dunhuang Caves."

"Ah, yes. That makes sense. Good choice."

"From there, I'm not sure. I guess I haven't planned out that far. I can't really see past why Uncle Li would do this to me. What do you think I should do next?"

"I think you have been doing everything right so far. I can only give you guidance, not lead the way."

"No updates? No, like, situation analysis?"

"I can certainly break down the essence of the situation if that will help. As you know, a culmination of things is happening: this rare galactic alignment that happens once every 26,000 years, the solar system is warming up, and the strongest solar flares in recent history are predicted for 2012. What's more, huge holes are opening up in our magnetic shield, the very thing that protects us from solar flares. This is both dangerous and helpful—you will find that the sun becomes your guide and helper."

"You mean with taking down communications and stuff like that?"

"Yes, and in other ways as well. If ever you come across a problem, try to think of a way the sun could be part of the solution."

"Why the riddles? Why can't you just tell me what you need to tell me?"

"This is what I need to tell you," he replies.

After we look at each other for a moment he says, "Tell me this. Why do you suppose there is so much intrigue about 2012, the end of the Mayan long-count calendar?"

"I don't know," I answer. "Because it's such a mystery?"

"Precisely! It's a mystery, a game. Humans love games; they love to figure out puzzles. If I told you exactly how things would work, where would the fun be? The fun is in the discovery, in the unraveling of mystery."

"So you know how things will turn out?"

"How could I?" he says, smiling wide. "How could I?"

"But the predictions, the prophecies—"

"They mean nothing without human interaction. *You* must change the world."

"So we're on the right track with this sound thing?" I ask.

"Absolutely. Look at tribal cultures—most shamans work with sound because it allows them to transform some aspect of the genetic code. One of the main problems with today's perception is that people assume the process of evolution has ended. As if evolution is a train that has reached the last station on the line. Nothing could be further from the truth! Just because we cannot *see* evolutionary changes that the galaxy triggers does not mean they aren't happening, or won't happen."

"So energy from *out there* triggers switches *in here*?" I ask, hand to my chest.

"Absolutely. Billions of years ago the most advanced system on Earth was a little unit of vibration called hydrogen.

Just one electron orbiting one proton! How did *that* evolve into something that is *aware of itself*? How did simple particles become conscious? How did they evolve to this," he says, gesturing to me, "*without* energetic help or 'programming' from out there?"

"And that's why the *Fraternitas* is jamming the system—so the electromagnetic energy coming from the galaxy gets scrambled."

"Better than almost anyone, the *Fraternitas* knows that evolutionary changes result from three things: the passing of time, things that happen here on Earth, and things that happen to the space in which we float. The *Fraternitas* has been working hard for millennia to control *all* these components."

"And because these evolutionary changes are related to consciousness rather than to our physical bodies, no one really pays attention?" I ask.

"Correct. The *Fraternitas* has done an excellent job of making this kind of thinking seem like New Age pseudoscience. They support mass disdain for anything around this subject."

"That's for sure. Even really educated people like my parents would think it's a bunch of hooey."

"That's why you must communicate this information to young people, before the system beats possibility and wonder out of them. And you must act quickly. The methods the *Fraternitas* uses to try to offset this change are having dangerous repercussions here on Earth."

"You mean with all the tsunamis and hurricanes and earthquakes and stuff?"

"Yes. It's just like when you sneeze from having a cold—

except that when Mother Earth sneezes, millions of people feel it. But when this happens, you glimpse the possibilities."

"What possibilities?" I ask.

Bolon pauses to cough, that wet phlegmy kind of cough that old people have, and then he goes on. "Do you notice what happens every time there is a massive natural disaster?" he asks.

"People come together to help?"

Bolon nods. "The whole world responds with love. All at once all people vibrate in a coherent wave of compassion."

"So you're saying that something good comes out of all that suffering?"

"Yes, but at great expense. What if we all just resonated with compassion without having to lose hundreds of thousands of people in the process? Without the suffering or the fear?"

"But how?" I ask.

"With love."

I laugh. It isn't really the answer I expected. "Come on, that's pretty ... well ... unscientific," I say. I'd like to believe that love conquers all, but seriously?

"Caity, at our most basic level, we are all just vibrations. And there is a measurement for love, which even your most scrupulous scientists will find proof of in your lifetime."

I flash back to the wall of carvings in the secret room at Breidablik castle. When I first deciphered the part of the poem that said, "*Like gravity, love is a force of great might, true power comes when we connect and unite,*" it made no real sense. Now it's becoming clearer.

"I get it," I say to Bolon. "I finally get it."

We sit silently for a few minutes as I process this information. It makes sense. The *Tzolk'in*, the tones, meeting at sites around the great circle—these are all just tools to connect vibrations. To get us all tuned in to the same channel.

"I'm glad you finally see the bigger picture," Bolon says.

"I just hope my days of being chased by thugs in San Francisco and by dogs through underground tunnels on Easter Island are over."

Bolon gets up. "I wish I could guarantee that, Caity," he says. "One last thing. I know this will be difficult, but there can be no more communication with Alex or your parents— no email, text, or phone calls."

"What about Skype?" I ask, already beginning to feel desperate for contact.

He shakes his head. "I'm sorry. You can keep the daily tones going on the website and through cell phones—this is an important part of setting the stage, and they're all coming from one hidden server that we've protected. But other than that, nothing. No communication. They are watching. Keywords are being tagged. We must go dark."

"But how can I do any of the stuff you want me to do if I don't have instructions and if I can't communicate?" I say.

"You can still use postal mail. And you may figure out other ways we have not imagined yet."

Postal mail? I don't remember the last time I sent a letter in the mail. And doesn't international mail take weeks? Months? This is a huge roadblock.

Bolon stands up. "I must go now."

I jump up after him, wanting to keep him longer.

"Goodbye, my friend," he says as he opens the door.

"Will you come to Dunhuang?" I plead before he can leave.

"Perhaps," he says, closing the door gently behind him.

I flop onto my bed and stare at the ceiling. Mr. Papers hops onto my chest with an origami salmon and sets it gently on my forehead.

I get his reference to swimming upstream, but the fact that salmon die once they get to their destination gives me no comfort at all.

ELEVEN

Justine runs back into the room out of breath. "You will not believe what you're about to do, Caity! It's like I died and went to Chanel. You can check out anything—like it's the library of *couture*!"

"Show me, show me," I say, thinking the gown she picked must be pretty slinky if it fits in her purse.

"You can't leave with it! We go there tonight and get dressed, then get escorted to the ball!"

"Did we get famous without knowing it or something?" I ask.

"I know, it's like we'll be going to the Oscars. I'm dying to see what you choose."

"What did you get? I don't want to pick the same thing."

"I want it to be a surprise," she says.

"Shoes?" I ask.

"Oh yeah. And then some."

"Who would donate their fabulous stuff to this place?" I wonder.

"Socialites who can't wear something more than once without being ridiculed."

"Can you imagine? I should be on Socialite Death Row for how many times I've worn jeans and a white T-shirt," I say, glancing at the clock. "Crap, I gotta go!"

"Be nice to Señora Crabcakes if you see her. We got off to a bad start, but I think she means well."

"Well, you're not the one who owns the monkey," I say. "Speaking of, Mr. P. is on the balcony. Would you mind getting him some mango and a glass of water?"

"Only if you don't mind me pretending he's mine and only mine for the hour that you're gone."

"Knock yourself out," I say, slipping into some flip-flops and heading out the door.

———

While walking to *La Administración*, I pass several groups of girls, who all give me the robotic-eye-scan from head to toe. No smiles, no hellos, only judgment. A small group of boys passes by without even the slightest glance. I seem to be visible only to girls, served up for their disapproval.

I sense the danger in all of this. I might just be among the enemy here. I'm in the cradle of just what the *Fraternitas* wants to protect: the Elite. I think about Bolon and his deep belief that I can unify the youth, but reaching these people seems beyond me. We are simply not the same species—it would be like a hamster trying to talk with hummingbirds.

And would they even *want* to change the world? Would anyone here resonate with what The Council wants me to communicate? They're fabulous. They're wealthy. They have everything they want and need. They are heirs to the world the *Fraternitas* controls.

And I am among them. Would they eat me if they found out?

As I pass one of the dorms, I notice Ramón handing a garment bag to the boy I saw through the window last night. He takes the bag from Ramón, has a quick conversation in Spanish, and then runs down the steps. I quicken my pace while doing trigonometry in my head, hoping the trajectory he's on will not intersect mine. His grand presence is too much for me and I feel like I need to run off, like an albino from the hot sun.

"*Excusez moi,*" he says in my direction.

Feeling sure he can't be talking to me, I don't reply and keep walking faster.

"Excuse me," he says again. This time I look over at him, and he says, "Yes, you."

I stop and turn toward him. "Can I help you?" I reply. What am I, a waitress? Why didn't I just say, "Oh, hey there," or "*Bonjour*"?

"I just wanted to say hello," he says in perfect British-style English with only a hint of French accent. Could he get any more cosmopolitan?

"Oh. Well … hello."

"What is your name?" he asks, as he extends his hand to shake mine.

"I'm Caity."

"Julius D'Aubigne," he says. "Please, call me Jules."

Only a very secure teen boy would go by Jules. But then again, what's not to be secure about? Sophisticated beyond his years—check. Handsome—check. Well dressed—check. Seems to speak every language on the planet—check.

"Pleasure to meet you, Jules." I shake his hand, concentrating on keeping my hand firm but not manly. "I'm sorry, but I'm late for an appointment," I say. I'm not trying to play hard to get, I just cannot think of one single interesting thing to say to him, and from the looks of it, this boy eats, drinks, and sleeps interesting things.

"Pardon me," he replies. "Don't let me keep you."

"Thanks. Nice to meet you."

I walk off, but he does not move. When I'm a few feet away he says, "You are not like the others."

I resist the temptation to look back, and instead I pretend I didn't hear him. I don't need to be the pet interest of some rich French kid, no matter how beautiful he is.

Yet as I walk on, I can't ignore the fact that I'm shaky from the attention.

———

When I walk into the cool air of *La Administración*, the receptionist greets me by name. I wonder if there are cameras that match face to name to prompt people to know who we are and when we're coming.

She introduces herself simply as "Vasquez" and I'm not sure if it's her first name or last. She's dressed in the same style of blue suit that Monsieur Didier wears so elegantly and Señora Garza wears so frumpily. On her it looks stylish, which is saying something for a generic, dark blue pantsuit.

"Come along," she says, leading me down a polished-marble hallway lined with heavy dark-wood doors. At the end of the hall is an old-fashioned elevator, the kind with a door like an accordion of metal that you open and close manually. We get in, Vasquez slips a key into a slot next to the letter S, and down we go. We walk out into a hall that looks identical to the one we just left, but the air is a lot cooler.

Vasquez leads me to a non-descript door with a punch-code lock on it. I look away so it doesn't seem like I want to see the code as she taps out the numbers. The door opens with that pneumatic hiss of a subway door. Inside the temperature is different—warmer, dryer. It smells like expensive leather.

I can see why Justine was so excited; this is totally up her alley. Racks and racks and racks of dresses, and a lit-up bookshelf-thing displaying at least a hundred pairs of shoes and a good selection of evening bags. Then there is a glass case with some amazing jewelry. The whole thing is bizarre. Who would donate jewels to a school? What kind of high school builds an archive of fancy clothes? And what is behind all the other doors with keypad locks?

Vasquez gestures to the racks and says, "Please," like she's a hostess who has just laid out a buffet. I kind of wish I had Justine with me so she could help pick out stuff; I'm someone who needs a reference point when shopping. I settle on a Grecian-style dress with lots of draping of fabric on the chest that might add to the illusion that I have more than I do in that department. It's simple and beautiful and surprisingly comfortable. When I come out of the tiny dressing room to look in the three-way mirror, I am stunned. I guess there's a reason *couture* dresses cost so much: they are transformative.

I walk out to where Vasquez is sitting to pick out some shoes and see in her eyes that she is as surprised as I am. She looks up from her texting or whatever she was doing on the phone and says, "*Muy bastante*," before looking back down at the phone.

I thank her and float (in that dress, you can't just *walk*) over to the shoe-display shelf. Most of the shoes are small, but I manage to find an elegant pair of not-too-high strappy silver sandals that will work perfectly. I decide not to use any of their jewelry or evening bags for fear of looking like too much of a charity case. I think my pearl studs will work fine with the dress and I can always stash my key in the yards of draped fabric that are supposed to be my boobs.

Walking back to the dorm, I actually start to look forward to the Spark Ball. I'm nervous about meeting the Beautiful People but excited to debut my new Greek Goddess look. It will be nice to have one last night of fun and freedom before we're back on the hunt for Uncle Li and the *Fraternitas*.

I just wish Alex were here with me. He's the only one I want to impress and he probably thinks I'm snubbing him. I just wish I could do one last Skype with him to let him know what's going on, how I've been instructed not to contact him.

What time is it in Scotland right now? I wonder. *Is he in bed?* I try to picture what he'd look like sleeping, his strong face slack and boyish, the tops of his dark lashes resting on his cheek like a curling wave of delicate spider legs. Does he sleep on his back, open to the world, with one arm up, framing his head? On his stomach with his face buried deep in the pillow? Or does he sleep on his side, his body curled up like a cat while his mind escapes to the alternate world of dreams?

I would love to spend one night watching him, tracking his eyes under the thin skin of his eyelids as they move in response to his night wanderings.

Does he dream of me?

I wish I had told him how I felt about him while we were on the Isle of Huracan. Or, to be more honest, I wished he had told me how *he* felt—that was the only part of the equation where X represented the unknown.

When I get to the room, Justine is on our little balcony with Mr. Papers, who is eating a banana. Papers is so sophisticated that every time I see him with that cliché fruit, I have to laugh.

"I'm not even going to ask about the dress," Justine says, putting a hand up. "I want your choice *de couture* to be a surprise."

"Dress? What dress?" I say. "Oh, you mean the Grecian number I'll be wearing tonight?"

"Caity! I wanted to be surprised!" she says, shaking her head. "But I must give you props for picking that draped-goddess dress. Classic."

"Was every dress you saw burned into your memory?" I ask.

"Can't help it," she replies. "I'm like one of those idiot savants who can't tell time but can play the Hammerklavier

Sonata perfectly after hearing it once. Except my gift is my visual memory."

"Well, tonight should be sensory overload for you then, what with all the dresses and shoes to catalog."

"I am absolutely up for the challenge," she says with relish.

I see her laptop on the small patio table. "So what are you doing now?"

"I'm stalking everyone on our class list, which was in our materials. Do you realize how low-class we are?"

"Yes. Yes I do," I reply as I pick up the class list.

"Seriously, if they're not from some line of nobility then their parents are captains of industry." She pauses to look up at me. "How did we even get in?" she asks.

"Cash money," I reply. "Remember? It makes the world go 'round." I find Jules on the class list and point to his name. "I ran into this guy on my way to the dress fitting. Have you stalked him yet?"

"Absolutely. He is Julius D'Aubigne the Fourth. From Paris, of course. His family has been in the banking business since before the American Revolution. They've donated a *ton* of money to this school."

"Well done, McStalker!"

Justine humbly bows. "My goal is to research every student in our class as well as some upperclassmen before the Spark Ball tonight."

"Rock on," I tell her. "Information is king."

"Actually, according to Wikipedia, our classmate Jordy bin Abdullah's dad is king … "

TWELVE

Vasquez, who is waiting for us at *La Administración*, takes us back down to the *couture* archives where we put on our dresses and prepare to go. Justine's hair is left down with soft, beautiful curls. She helps me put mine into a loose updo, which ends up looking totally effortless even though it takes forty-five minutes and five thousand bobby pins to create.

We look like quite a pair.

I'm glad we planned on getting there an hour late—this seems to be about when people are arriving, mostly as couples. These kids (and I use that term loosely, as no one here looks under twenty-one) are so comfortable in their worldly elegance that any one of them could be walking the red carpet at Cannes or cruising around a casino in Monte Carlo without getting a second look.

Justine and I hoped to get into the ballroom without drawing too much attention, but when we walk in, almost everyone turns and stares. I can feel my face turning bright red. From the corner of her mouth Justine says, "Awkward … "

Boys actually smile and nod but girls look critically at us, turning to one another to make comments. Have these people been together at fancy private schools for so long that they've forgotten what regular teenagers look like?

I follow Justine's lead and walk to the bar, where they are serving sodas and blended drinks, not champagne like they had at the Senior Mixer last night. Unable to trust myself with a white dress and colored liquid, I order sparkling water and lime.

We keep to ourselves, sitting at a small table admiring dresses and boys. No one seems particularly interested in meeting us, which after the last two days of being ignored is no surprise. After an hour or so, kids started dancing to the band, which is playing really good Latin music. During one of the band breaks, when the dance floor clears, we watch a gang of beautiful boys burst through the doors to the ballroom. They roam in a V-formation, like a flock of birds or a school of fish, and the leader, the point man, is Jules.

They weave their way through the small groups that are scattered throughout the room, Jules slapping backs and kissing cheeks as if he were the groom at a wedding. It's kind of irritating to see how people melt when he comes by, and how the school of fish trail behind him.

I look over at him without turning my head so it's not so conspicuous. He's leaning in and talking to Monsieur Didier, as if he's sharing a secret.

"He certainly thinks he's all that, doesn't he?" I say.

"That would be because he *is*," Justine replies. "All that and a bag of Skittles."

I turn my back, not wanting to pay any attention to Jules and his feeder fish.

"He's got to be a total jackass," I say, biting into one of the many hors d'oeuvres I've collected on my small plate. I struggle to swallow when I watch Justine's eyes look above my head, as if someone is by me.

Turning around, I see Jules standing right there.

"Do you kiss your mother with that mouth?" he says with a wicked smile.

"Excuse me?" I say, reaching for my drink to wash down the weird *canapé* I've just chowed down on.

"Please meet Justine Devereux," I say, gesturing to my beautiful friend in an attempt to take the focus off of me. "Justine, this is Jules D'Aubigne."

"*Enchanté,*" he says, kissing the back of her hand. "American, I presume?"

"Canadian," Justine and I say in unison. We've worked hard on our back story and are anxious to use it.

"Oh, how charming," he says. Just then a couple of anorexic girls with jewel-encrusted bangles come up on either side of Jules and slip their arms through his, clearly staking claim.

"Well, it was *mon plaisir,*" he says to both of us. Then he turns to me and says, "That dress is ravishing."

The dark-haired girl on his left laughs and says in a snooty British accent, "It should be! It cost my mother a bloody fortune. She wore it to a *soirée* aboard the yacht of Princess Marie-Chantal of Greece."

I turn so red it feels like my skin might burst open like a tomato in the hot sun.

"You know, before she *donated* it to the school archives," the girl adds, just in case no one within fifty miles understood the point she was making.

Jules smiles and shrugs in that *What can you do? Girls will be girls* way.

Then the blonde girl scrunches up her nose at us and says, "Follow the spark, y'all!" in a pagenty southern drawl.

They steer Jules away, and his feeder fish follow.

I want to cry. If I weren't so mad, I might. I had been prepared for danger, but not for humiliation.

Justine reaches over the table and puts her hand on mine. "Forget it. You know you look beautiful."

"Who *are* these people?" I ask in a quivering voice. "Are they for real?"

"Sadly, they are. Miss Uncongeniality is Arabella Bascom. From Texas. Her dad is the largest military firearms supplier in the U.S."

"Big surprise."

"And Bitchy McBritish Accent is Victoria Ambrose. Her parents own the largest seed company in Europe."

"Shocker," I reply. "Excellent research, by the way. Does everyone's bio come with the words, 'World's Largest' somewhere in it?"

"Pretty much," Justine says.

We try to stay so it doesn't look like the mean girls are running us off, but I can only make it about ten minutes.

When it seems as if Jules and his arm candy are nowhere to be seen, we get up and pretend to be heading for the powder room. We figure there might be a way out down that way and sure enough, at the end of the hallway is a door. We quietly open it and are shocked to find Monsieur Didier and Jules D'Aubigne smoking cigars. We simply cannot win tonight.

"*Mademoiselles* Luxton and Devereux! You're looking lovely tonight," Didier says. "Please meet Julius D'Aubigne."

"We've met," Justine says. I say nothing.

"Ah, *bon*. You know, there have been D'Aubignes at this school since it began," Didier says, slapping Jules on the back. "We might even have to rename the school after your father's last gift," he adds.

Jules waves off the notion.

I'm holding my strappy heels and my feet are getting cold on the stone path. "Well, nice to see you," I say, turning to go.

"Oh, I've spoken to Dr. Clath," Didier adds. "She's quite excited about your itinerary. We've not studied at the Dunhuang Caves yet; it will be a La Escuela Bohemia first."

Justine nods and smiles politely. I raise my fist and with mock enthusiasm say, "Follow the spark!"

Jules and Monsieur Didier raise their fists and both say, "*Siga la Chispa,*" in perfect Spanish.

As we walk away, I hear Jules say, "*Vraiment? Les caverns de Dunhuang?*"

Monsieur Didier laughs and says, "*Oui! C'est très primitive, non?*"

"That's some jackassery of the highest order," I say.

"*Oui,*" Justine replies, lifting up her dress so she can walk quickly. "Now let's go give this stuff back."

Vasquez is still at the reception desk in *La Administración*. We walk in and say hello, but then don't speak at all again until we're dressed in our own clothes and leaving the building. She is a woman of few words, and at this point so am I.

When we get back to our room, we find Mr. Papers again guarding a note that came under the door.

"Again? They don't use email around here?"

I open the envelope and Justine reads over my shoulder.

Departing tomorrow morning. Ramón will come to collect you at 9:00 A.M. Pack lightly; this isn't a fashion show.
Dr. Clath

I feel the skin on my forearms prickle.

It won't be long until I have to face my longtime friend—now my betrayer—Uncle Li.

THIRTEEN

I just pack my laptop, a couple changes of clothes, and some dried fruit for Mr. Papers. Justine has a much harder time packing light, but since she's not carrying a monkey in one of her two allowed bags, she has a bit more space.

We head downstairs at 8:55 and the dorm is silent, everyone sleeping in after the Spark Ball. We're the only ones leaving this early, perhaps the only ones leaving at all today.

Ramón pulls up just as we walk outside. Professor Clath is already in the car, and when she gets out to greet us we get an eyeful of another absurd outfit: the same diabetic-style shoes and elastic-waist jeans from yesterday, but this time the tucked-in T-shirt has a long math equation with a bunch of Greek symbols on it as if it's some kind of inside joke for dorks.

The minute we slide into the car, she hands us each a large folder. "Your dossiers," she says.

"Dossiers?" I ask, taking the envelope from her and then

letting Mr. Papers out of his carrier. Clath recoils and looks at Mr. Papers and then back at me as if I've just let a cobra out of my handbag.

"Oh, I have a monkey," I tell her. "It's okay, Didier knows about it. And he has travelling documents so he's cool."

"I wasn't told we'd be travelling with—" Clath stops speaking and freezes when Mr. Papers leans over to read her shirt and then starts laughing.

"Looks like he got your math joke," I say.

"He can't possibly … " She stops talking when Mr. P grabs a piece of paper from the carrier and starts doing his origami. After a couple of minutes of quick fingerwork he produces a tiny origami pie, which he presents to Clath.

"No," she says, shaking her head. "No way."

"What? What does it mean?" Justine asks.

Clath takes the origami from Papers. "If you read the equation right," she says as she points to her shirt, "the punch line of the joke is *pi*."

"Wow, maybe we can get him to do our trig for us," I say to Justine.

Clath is still shaking her head as if she's just seen psychic surgery or something.

"Here we are," Ramón announces from the front seat.

"Where?" Justine and I ask, confused because we've only gone a few miles.

"We're using the school plane today," Clath says. "It's actually more economical than commercial flights when we have to make more than four connections."

"Sweet!" Justine says, gazing at the plane in the hanger Ramón is pulling up to.

"We can never mention this to my parents," I tell her.

The plane's tail has La Escuela Bohemia's golden star icon and the school's motto, *Siga la Chispa*.

"Follow the Spark, my friend," I say as we get out of the car.

"Follow indeed," Justine replies.

Clath doesn't seem the least bit impressed by the posh plane interior or by the gorgeous male flight attendant named Marco who looks more like a Latin pop star than a guy who serves ginger ale.

We each buckle into a pale yellow leather seat, Justine next to me and Mr. Papers and Clath facing us. There's a table between us.

We barely level out before Clath makes us look at our dossiers. Each envelope has some travel documents, a workbook, and a spiral-bound book about the Dunhuang Caves, complete with history, artifacts, and symbols found there.

"You put this together overnight?" Justine asks, obviously wondering if Clath expects the same level of output from us.

"The Curriculum Team did," she replies. "That's what your parents are paying for—researchers spent the night compiling information about the Dunhuang area and creating a curriculum from which I can teach math, history, philosophy, and art."

"No P.E.?" I ask. "I'm totally missing dodge ball."

"You'll get enough physical exercise, believe me," she replies, adjusting her elastic-waist pants. "There are miles of caves in the areas."

"I was sort of kidding," I say, making a note that sarcasm is lost on Clath.

"Are we seriously going to walk through the entire cave system?" Justine asks.

Clath shakes her head. "That would probably take years."

We start reading about the caves in our workbooks while Marco brings us drinks and snacks. When Mr. Papers comes to sit on my lap and starts eating my pretzels, Marco makes a plate just for him with fresh banana, pretzels, and grapes.

I watch Clath's eyes close and her head bob. Every time it falls to her chest it wakes her up.

"I've been up since four going over all the lessons with the Curriculum Team," she says. "You girls mind if I step back into the bedroom for a snooze?"

"Please," Justine and I both say at the same time.

Once she's gone Marco folds down the table and puts our drinks and snacks on our side tables. He gives us a menu of movies to choose from and then he dims the cabin and shows us how to recline our seats.

This is truly the best school in the universe.

———

Dunhuang is a dusty, dry moonscape. From the air, there is nothing that would clue you in to the fact that this place is special in any way. But we find out how special it is when, not five minutes after we land, we're met by a local guide named Wen. He looks close to one hundred years old, with skin that just drapes over his bones with no muscle or fat in between, and a thin white beard that just sort of gave up after a few inches of growth. Despite his frail appearance, he keeps us going all day long.

The caves are amazing. I was a little worried about having some kind of post-traumatic stress thing happen after the horrors of the lava tube caves on Easter Island, but these could not be more different. Those were craggy and wet and tubular and these are more like carved rock rooms. There's almost no moisture in them, which is what helped preserve all the treasures here.

Turns out the oldest printed book in the world was found here, a book called the Diamond Sutra. There are 492 caves that archaeologists know of, almost 500,000 square miles of painted frescos, and 2,415 painted statues. The stuff that has been stashed here is incredible—paintings, sculptures, more than 50,000 Buddhist scriptures, fabrics, and other priceless ancient relics. And, of course, tons of paintings of the Three Hares.

Wen is excited to talk about the hares, and can recite the number of every cave that has one. But when he tells us that his favorite is in cave number 407, the only one where the hares are running counterclockwise, I just know that's where I'll find a clue about Uncle Li.

FOURTEEN

We part ways with Clath after our tour, saying we'll get dinner in our rooms and meet up with her in the morning. We study maps and memorize the quickest path back to cave 407. Mr. Papers paces nervously while making a series of origami caves and tunnels.

Once night falls, we creep out into the dark. There's a dewiness in the air that wasn't there during the day; a fine, fine mist that falls to the dust, giving off that faint smell of summer rain.

Mr. Papers is getting more jittery by the minute, fidgeting with my hair and moving from shoulder to shoulder. He's as nervous as I am.

We're so afraid of being seen that we don't dare turn on our headlamps until we're in the cave—the cave with the Three Hares going counterclockwise.

I still don't know what I will do if and when I see Uncle Li. It's hard enough to think he'd steal something from me, and even harder to think about him hurting me. But that hasn't stopped me from picking up a large flat rock and slipping it into the pocket of my hoodie, just in case.

Honestly, I really don't know what to expect.

————

The cave has a metal door, which we quietly open and slip through. Only once the door is closed do we turn on our lights.

And there, directly under the painting of the Three Hares, sits Uncle Li—in full lotus pose.

I'm so surprised to see him sitting there in meditation that the years of loving him take over and I run toward him, until the memory of what he did stops me.

He doesn't say anything, just smiles at me in the warm and loving way he has since I was a baby.

"Why?" I ask, looking him in the eyes for an answer.

But he doesn't answer. Instead he stands up and says, "You are right on time."

Mr. Papers hops off my shoulder and onto Uncle Li's. I can feel rage rising from the center of my chest; Justine takes my hand to steady me.

"What are you talking about, right on time? Why won't you answer me?"

"I had to get you here. I had to get you to take the next step," he says.

"You could have asked me to come here—you could have *told* me to come here and you'd have saved me so much time and anger and—"

"Bolon told me you were done. He said you felt you had accomplished what you had to, but that it would be difficult to get you to the next level."

"Well, yeah, but you have no idea what happened to me out on Easter Island because you were *gone* when I got back! I was hunted like a fox! Through caves and tunnels and—"

"But you are here. You are fine," he says.

"So stealing the Sanskrit books was all a big plot to lure me here?"

"The short answer to that is yes. You see, this next part of the unfolding is critical. We needed you to be passionate enough about this to arrange a way to get here, on your own. And I must say," he adds, "you have executed your plan flawlessly."

I don't even know what to say. I just stare at him, hoping this will all make sense.

"If it's any consolation, those books were decoys. Fake replicas. The originals are still safely hidden."

I shake my head. "That doesn't matter. What matters is that you led me to believe that you'd *betrayed me*."

"Caity, I would never betray you. I am your protector, and always have been."

"What do you mean *always have been?*"

"The Council assigned me to you when your mother found out she was pregnant. I hired her to open an old Chinese safe, and befriended your parents so that I could always be close to you."

I'm not sure this makes me feel any better. "You tricked my mom into being friends with you?"

"Caity, if you look in your heart you will agree that I am, and have always been, completely sincere."

I don't say anything, because he's right.

"Remember all the times I'd take you to Chinatown to visit my friends, the herbalists and acupuncturists and Taoist masters?"

I nod.

"You may not know it, but all those visits were lessons by some of the most powerful people in Chinese medicine and metaphysics. Just by osmosis you have probably picked up more information about traditional Chinese feng shui, yin yang theory, and five element theory than many people who study for years."

"But why?"

"Because this knowledge will be essential as you move forward, rebalancing what was put off-kilter for centuries by the *Fraternitas*. Some of the information you won't remember until you need it. For instance, you probably have no memory of studying yin yang theory, yet you could, I'm quite sure, explain most anything in terms of yin and yang."

"Uh, actually, I don't think so," I say. "I don't really remember any real lessons."

"That's because you learned it in context. By listening to our conversations. By asking questions. Let me ask you something. How did you know to look for me here, in cave 407?"

"It had the only image of the Three Hares running counterclockwise—the yin direction. Yin indicates something hidden. I don't know; it was a long shot."

"A long shot, yet absolutely correct. Now tell me this:

you are in the woods and see a vine. What would be a good, quick indication of whether or not the vine is poisonous?"

"If it's winding around something clockwise it's most likely not poisonous, if it's winding counterclockwise it's most likely poisonous," I reply.

Justine drops my hand and looks at me.

"And how can you make that assumption?" Uncle Li asks.

"Because clockwise is a yang direction and counterclockwise is a yin direction. 'Yin' means hidden or dangerous energy."

"Exactly. And speaking of direction, why is it that in sports like track and field, car races, horse races, and baseball, the athletes *always* move counterclockwise?"

"Because counterclockwise is the yin direction and yin is competitive, while yang is cooperative."

"Right again. Now, picture a police car in your head. Which side has the red light and which side has the blue light?"

"Red will almost always be on the left, yang side, blue will always be on the right, yin side," I answer automatically, even though I have never thought about this consciously.

"And knowing that, if you had to bet on two teams who were equal in every way but one team was wearing red jerseys and the other was wearing blue, which team would you wager on to win?"

"All other things being equal, I'd wager on red. The yang team."

"How do you *know* all this?" Justine asks. "I never knew you studied this kind of stuff!"

"I didn't either!" I say, laughing.

"I have been exposing you to all kinds of metaphysical information for years so that when necessary, you can draw from it. Your parents have raised you with the best of Western thinking, very rational and scientific, and I have raised you with the best of Eastern thinking, very subtle and esoteric. A perfect balance of yin and yang."

"Lucky Luckerson," Justine says, elbowing me in the side.

"Since your birth, I have been your protector and your teacher and your friend. And this has been my great pleasure," Uncle Li says, holding his hands together and bowing.

"Now I feel kind of weird," I admit. I can't believe how much I've taken for granted. How much I've been groomed for what is happening now.

"No need to feel uncomfortable. Just know that I always have and always will have your best interest at heart. Now, shall I show you to The Council headquarters?"

Justine and I look at each other and nod.

"Prepare to be astonished," he adds with a wink.

FIFTEEN

With Mr. Papers tucked safely into my backpack, his head out just enough to see, Justine and I follow Uncle Li as he walks quickly and quietly through the night. He takes us to one of the lesser-known caves, what was said in the guidebook to be just a small storeroom for grain. It's said to be sealed on its own with no connection to the larger cave system, so that the grain would stay cool and dry with no drafts.

The cave has been carved out to be square. It's about the size of a small bedroom, but the ceiling is just barely taller than my head. There's nothing in the room anymore, but it still has the bones of a store room; each wall has a carved-out niche with wooden shelves, like bookshelves that are dug into the wall. The ceiling is painted a beautiful dark blue with gold stars, and it features the constellations Scorpio and Sagittarius. Once Uncle Li closes the door to the cave and shines his flashlight on it, it really comes to life, making the gold paint look almost three-dimensional.

"Do you know where the center of our galaxy is?" Uncle Li asks, looking up at the painting.

"Not exactly, no," I say, embarrassed that I don't know this.

"The ancients made sure we could always find it, by having two constellations pointing right at it. Both the stinger on Scorpio the scorpion and the arrow that Sagittarius shoots point right at the Galactic Center," he says, using the flashlight to show us.

"How could they have known that?" I ask.

"That's the eternal question, Caity. How far back does this knowledge go?"

"Seriously, though, how did people with no technology know this stuff?" Justine asks.

"Technology is relative. You may think that a powerful computer is the ultimate in technology, but that is *external* technology. The ancients had very developed *internal* technologies, which we have lost touch with; the ability to tap into the collective consciousness, to tap into the information of the universe. Remember: it's all out there. We just need to tune to the correct frequency."

"I remember Bolon telling me that, too," I say.

Uncle Li bolts the door from the inside and then walks over to the inset shelf at the back of the cave and starts taking off the wooden shelves. Each one has a few wooden pegs sticking out of its back, which fit into holes carved behind them. This system looks like it would be designed to help keep the boards from sagging under the weight of grain bags, but when I see Uncle Li pull out a chain from beneath his shirt with a three-inch-long piece of metal on it, I realize they are more than just holes for support.

Uncle Li starts from the upper left and counts the holes. He stops at 13 and slips his key in. Then he continues to count, stopping at 20 and slipping the key in again. That's when I hear the familiar sound of rock scraping rock and the back of the shelf gives way.

Justine, who has not yet seen my panel that moves nor the door of the tower at Breidablik, gasps. "That is *so* cool!" she says.

Uncle Li makes the "after you" gesture with his arm, but I shake my head. This is no time for ladies first.

He smiles and sucks in his stomach so he can slide through the skinny opening. Once in, he shines the light back so we can see our way through. When we're on the other side, Uncle Li closes the wall up.

I can feel air moving, unlike in the small room where we came from, but I can't see anything until Uncle Li sweeps the flashlight around.

Then I realize that we're on the edge of what looks to be a very steep cliff.

Unable to see how far I am from the edge in front of me, I suck in my breath and press my back to the wall,

"It's okay, really. You're safe here. We just have to get over to the Maglev," he says as he motions to what looks like a small car to the right of us.

Uncle Li walks normally and Mr. Papers skips along as if he's in no danger at all while Justine and I take shuffled baby steps, not wanting our feet to leave what sliver of ground we

can see. Uncle Li opens the back door to this car-like capsule and we get in. He doesn't have to ask us to buckle up;
just seeing the intricate race-car-style seat belts tips us off.
Motioning for Mr. Papers to come up front, he buckles him
in as well.

Once we're all clicked in, Uncle Li puts his thumb to a
small print reader on the dash and headlights come on, illu-
minating the void before us. Then an engine starts humming
and Uncle Li moves what looks like a gear shift.

The capsule slides forward a few feet and then suddenly
we are plunged downward, as if on a roller coaster.

Justine and I both scream—Justine adding some choice
words heard mainly in prison. It only lasts a few seconds and
then we level out. Slowing down by what feels like some sort
of air-braking device, we enter a tube that's barely big enough
to fit our vehicle.

Though surprised, I'm not entirely shocked. After flying
on what looked like a UFO that was built based on ancient
Sanskrit texts, I'm used to weird travel. Justine, having never
been on a Vimāna, not so much.

"What is this thing?" she says, gripping the handle in
front of her so hard that I can see every flexed muscle and
tendon in her arm.

"It's a Maglev," Uncle Li answers, pushing a series of but-
tons as we slide slowly into the tube like we're entering a car
wash. "Nothing new; they've been using them in Asia for
years."

"Oh, this is one of those trains that rides on top of mag-
nets." Mom told me about this; she'd ridden one on a job in
Japan.

"Yes, exactly," Uncle Li replies. "It's just a bit faster than the ones used for commercial travel. Now hold on."

Our heads are pushed against the headrest as the car shoots into the tunnel, but once the first push is over, it's not uncomfortable. Just fast.

"I think the bigger questions is: *where* are we going?" I ask.

Now that the car or train or whatever is on autodrive, Uncle Li looks back at us to talk.

"You are about to go deep into the cave system, far beyond what the archaeologists have discovered, to a city mostly known as a myth. It has been referred to as Shambhala and Shangri-La. It's the home of the Atala Mystery School, where all of the knowledge lost by civilization through the Dark Ages has been kept intact for millennia."

"Right here under the Dunhuang Caves?" I ask.

"This Maglev travels more than eight hundred miles in an hour; we're far from the caves now. Atala is in southern Mongolia—"

"We're going to *Mongolia?*" Justine says with panic in her voice. "Right *now?* Clath is going to freak out if we're not back by morning!"

"We won't be long now. I'll have you back before morning."

"Why Mongolia?" I ask.

"Why not Mongolia? Its terrain and weather make it one of the least desirable places to live. A good place to hide a secret, no?"

"And it's all underground?" I ask, for the first time sort of freaking out about being in this tiny piece of metal shooting through a tube deep beneath China.

"It has to be," he replies.

After what seems like less than an hour, we start to see light coming through the tunnel and the capsule begins to slow down. It takes a few minutes to come to a complete stop because we were going so fast, but as we enter the lighted portion we see the tunnel get bigger and bigger.

We come to a stop at a grove of maples.

"How are there trees down here?" I ask, marveling at the rows of big, green, beautiful trees.

"Simulated sunlight for photosynthesis. It's very simple, actually," Uncle Li says as he starts unbuckling himself and Mr. Papers.

When we get out of the capsule, I'm overwhelmed by the fresh, clean air. There's nothing to indicate that we're in a cave—Justine and I look up, confused about how we can be underground when it looks as though it's a bright but overcast day.

"Cloud generators," Uncle Li says, pointing up. "They help keep the humidity level just right and they soften the look of the artificial lights."

"Incredible," Justine replies.

Papers runs up to one of the trees, climbs it, and then hops from the branch onto my backpack as I walk under it. He's energized in a way I've never seen before.

Uncle Li stops to scratch Mr. Papers. "This is where he was born, you know. I think he remembers it fondly."

"Seriously? Papers was born here?" Justine asks.

"That's right!" I say, "I remember Tenzo saying that."

As we near the end of the maple grove, the path winds through a tunnel just a few feet taller than us. The ground is lit with a softly glowing track of lights, which we follow through a few curves. Just when I'm starting to get disoriented, we round a corner and the tunnel gives way to a massive opening. We are faced with what has to be a movie set: a beautiful underground village built on several terraced levels around a tall waterfall.

Justine and I both stop and stare, and Mr. Papers starts going crazy, running in circles and laughing.

"Welcome to Atala," Uncle Li says.

SIXTEEN

When I was little I used to get a big hollow sugar egg every Easter from our next-door neighbor. It was the size of a really big potato and made of pressed sugar. At one end there was a hole so you could look into the egg, where a tiny scene had been placed. Atala reminds me of looking through a sugar egg at a perfect little Chinese village.

The waterfall anchors one end, and the river it feeds meanders through the village, pooling at some points to make reflecting ponds next to gold, red, and turquoise pagodas that glow warmly with lights. Willow trees grow on the banks of the river between expanses of grass where groups of ducks sit, bills tucked under their wings, asleep for the night.

The side of the cave where the waterfall flows has been terraced to accommodate beautiful pagoda-style buildings that are linked by stairs carved right into the stone. Ferns and moss sprout from cracks in the stone wall.

On the other side of the cave, a few football fields' distance from the waterfall, the rock walls taper down and the water from the river flows into a hole. The thought of accidentally falling into the river and being carried down that hole makes my whole body shiver. Who knows how far beneath the ground we are right now, or how much farther down that hole would take us?

Justine and I are stunned, looking around as if we've just landed on Jupiter.

"I want to live here," Justine whispers.

Uncle Li smiles. "No one lives here for more than a few months at a time. Too much yin; not good for the chi," he says, patting his heart.

He leads us over a carved bridge that crosses the river. At the other side, a small robed figure is sitting on a bench. As we approach, she stands and smiles. It's Nima. We've not seen her since we met The Council members at Muchuchumil Imports in San Francisco. Justine and I run over and hug her.

"What are you doing here?" I ask. "Is everything okay?"

"Everything is fine," she says happily. "I'm here to see you two."

"How did you know we'd be here?" Justine asks. I'm starting to take this kind of thing for granted.

"Access to knowledge is easy," Nima says. "Getting here is hard." She takes our hands and walks us along the river to an open-sided pagoda, painted orange and turquoise with gold trim. There are lamps lit inside, and mats on the floor surround a short table.

Nima motions for us to sit. "Tea?" she asks as she pours four cups. From beneath the table she pulls out a tray of delicate almond cookies.

I accidentally splash hot tea on my lap when Mr. Papers makes a squawk I've never heard before. Looking over to where the noise is coming from, I see two other monkeys that are almost identical to Mr. Papers. They're all holding hands and bouncing in a circle.

"There are *three* Mr. Papers!" Justine says.

I'm dumbfounded. "What the—"

"These are his people," Uncle Li says and Papers throws him a look. "Forgive me; I mean his *monkeys*."

The three of them scurry off before I can get up and meet his two friends.

"They'll be fine," Nima says, "That's Erasmo and Tohil—they believe they run Atala."

"How many are there?" I ask.

Looking at Uncle Li, Nima says, "What, maybe twenty?"

Uncle Li nods and adds, "We can go see the Monkey Center later—"

"Aw!" Justine and I both say at once. "Can't we see it now?" I beg.

They both laugh. "All right, come along."

Nima leads us along the river and we pass several buildings with small groups of people inside. "These are the teaching centers," Nima says. "Currently we are focusing on passing on the Hopi and Tibetan wisdom. Every two months the focus changes and new members of The Council rotate in."

We arrive at the wall where the waterfall is and climb a small staircase that winds up past clusters of ferns and small pagodas jutting from the wall. About halfway up, we enter one of the pagodas, which turns out to be a façade to a tunnel that leads deep into the rock. Lights above come on as we walk, like they do in library stacks at night.

"How do you guys get electricity in here?" I ask.

"We make it," Uncle Li says. "Absolutely clean zero-point energy. We have a small plant about a mile from here."

"What's zero-point energy?" Justine asks.

"It means it doesn't use up energy to make energy. We just harness the fluctuations in dark matter. It's abundant and clean."

"Why don't we use it everywhere?" I ask.

"Because the *Fraternitas* controls the energy supply. If there's no scarcity, there's no profitability."

I start to hear the chatter of monkeys, which is a sound that would make anyone happy. The tunnel ends in a large, clean, well-lit room with lots of trees and tiny hammocks and a large flat rock in the center. It's like a monkey lounge.

One side has a wall of large cubbies, which are obviously the monkey rooms. It reminds me of pictures I've seen of hotels in Japan where you rent a little capsule for the night. Several are sitting in their cubbies, but Mr. Papers and a group of other monkeys are all sitting on the large flat rock, chatting away.

"Seriously, have you ever seen anything this cute?" Justine asks.

"Never," I reply, watching Mr. Papers talk animatedly to his friends. What sounds like random chatter to us must mean something to the other monkeys, because they seem enraptured by what he is saying.

"So they don't do origami with each other?" I ask.

"No, they still communicate with each other in their own

language, but because physically they cannot talk as we can, they use origami to communicate with humans."

"Can all monkeys do this?" Justine asks, gesturing to their conversation.

"Not yet. This is a rare pygmy lineage of Capuchins originally from South America. The first Mayan Elders brought them along when they arrived. Over the years these guys and their ancestors have been modified using electromagnetic frequencies based on those coming from the Galactic Center. Basically, The Council wanted to see exactly what kind of changes DNA would go through as cosmic forces change."

"Looks like it worked!" Justine says.

He nods. "Indeed, they found their predictions were correct; these electromagnetic frequencies start to switch on parts of DNA that are not currently used. In the case of the Capuchin monkeys exposed, it raised their consciousness to a new, almost human level."

"What other stuff can they do?" I ask.

"They've been taught to read several hieroglyphic languages—symbolic picture languages seem much easier than letter-based languages."

"That is totally amazing," Justine says.

"And because they're helper monkeys," Uncle Li continues, "they're taught several ancient methods of defense, including touch paralysis and a very dangerous form of acupuncture."

"Cool!" Justine says, elbowing me in excitement. "Ninja skills!"

"Can we see it?" I ask.

Nima and Uncle Li shake their heads. "Another time,

perhaps," Nima says, gesturing to the tunnel with her hand. "We're going to have to go back to the River Pagoda; there is much to tell you before you must depart."

I could've stayed in the monkey room for days. Weeks. Months.

Just as we're leaving, two monkeys come to either side of Justine and me and jump up on our shoulders to present us with some origami. Justine gets a butterfly and I get the symbol of a snake eating its own tail—the image I'd seen in the water outside Breidablik before any of this even started.

SƐVƐNTƐƐN

"A re you two ready to enter the inner sanctum of knowledge?" Nima asks as we settle back into the River Pagoda.

We nod, completely unsure of what is going to happen next. If aliens walked in right now I'm not sure I'd be surprised.

"This place, Atala, is where all pure knowledge is kept, from lineage to lineage," Uncle Li begins. "Every member of The Council represents an area of indigenous people, and safely passes that knowledge on from generation to generation."

"Why is it so secret? So hidden?" Justine asks.

"Because if the *Fraternitas* had its way, they would kill us all. They have systematically wiped out huge groups of indigenous people either through religious wars, supported genocide, or military action. We're not playing here—this is serious."

"Kill you?" Justine says. "You may have to back up a little for me because I'm not as far along in all of this as Caity, but why would they kill you? What's so dangerous about tribal people?"

"Cultures that still live close to the earth, that still pass along stories from generations before, all have one thing in common: they share a large cosmovision, meaning they all believe that we here on Earth are profoundly affected by what's going on in the sky," Nima says. "Quite simply, they know this is a time of transformation."

"Now the Shadow Government knows this too," Uncle Li adds. "Almost all actions they take are guided by astrological counsel; they just don't want the masses to know this. When you keep the people ignorant, they are easier to manipulate."

"So the *Fraternitas* intentionally keeps this information about precession and cosmic forces a mystery?" I ask.

"The *Fraternitas* wants to keep it a secret, yes, but ironically the story of precession has such a profound effect on human behavior that it has become part of the framework of our lives. In fact, it's talked about by billions of people all over the world every day. It's just in code."

"What code?" Justine asks. "If so many people are speaking in code, how come it hasn't been broken?"

"They do not know they are speaking in code."

"I don't get it," I say.

"How can you talk in code and not know you're talking in code?" Justine asks.

We are clueless, sitting there like two kids on the first day of kindergarten looking at the teacher for answers.

Nima says, "You learned in school that mythology is usually based in *some* reality, usually about the movement of the stars—am I correct?"

"Right, like a way to pass on information about what's happening so people can remember it," I say, happy to finally be following her.

"Exactly. Now, in descending times, when we've just spent thousands of years becoming denser and denser and more materialistic and warlike, we lose this information about how we are changed by the energy around us. So, thousands of years ago people started putting this information in myth so we'd remember it somehow."

"So what's the myth?" I ask. "What's the code?"

"Well, it's different in each culture," Nima begins, "but it starts with the announcement of a virgin birth, then three wise men follow an Eastern star to find God's son born in late December. This person might start teaching at the age of twelve and be baptized at around twenty-eight or thirty. At thirty-three or so, he might die on a cross, only to rise up three days later. Then the resurrection is celebrated during the spring."

"Wait, you're talking about Jesus?" Justine asks. Her parents are big-time Catholics so I'm thinking she might not take this so well.

"The story I was referring to is from a 3,400-year-old inscription on the walls of the Temple of Luxor in Egypt, and in Egyptian writings."

"I'm confused," I say. "That's the same story—"

"There are more," Nima says. "Dionysus of Greece, whose mother was human and father was a god, was celebrated at the winter solstice in the end of December. Dionysus was a traveling teacher who performed miracles like turning water into wine. After his death, he was resurrected."

Uncle Li adds, "Then there is Attis of Phrygia and Krishna of India. Persia, Armenia, and Rome had Mithra. All these myths have some combination of divine birth around the end of December, bright lights signaling the coming of the child, him teaching and performing miracles as a young man, and having twelve followers, and dying in a violent manner, and finally being resurrected and ascending to the heavens."

"Oh my God!" Justine says. "I mean if there is one … "

"I'm not telling you there is no God! I'm not even telling you there have not been Avatars, or enlightened beings like Jesus, born to remind us what we are capable of: Compassion. Peace. Love. Miracles. It's just that the components of these *story-myths* were meant to encode all of the information we need about precession, and then they were hung like a cloak on enlightened beings."

"So I get that they're all telling the same basic story, but I don't see the precession code," I ask. "Like where's the astronomy in the story?"

Uncle Li smiles. "Here's where it gets very interesting. On December twenty-fourth, Sirius—one of the brightest stars in our night sky—aligns with the three brightest stars in Orion's Belt, which have been referred to as the Three Kings. These Three Kings and Sirius all line up and point to the place of sunrise on December twenty-fifth. Of course, the Three Kings also line up to point to Sirius when it rises during the *summer* solstice, signaling the births of solar deities Osiris and Horus the Elder. So, the Three Kings 'follow' the star in the East, in order to locate the birth of the son—or *sun*, to be more accurate."

Justine and I look at each other in disbelief. "What? So these guys all symbolize the *sun*?"

"Yes, the 'Sun of God,' the 'giver of life.' And the son's mother, the Virgin Mary, is the constellation Virgo—Virgo in Latin means 'virgin'—which happens to be the constellation where the sun rises at the end of December. What's more, in Hebrew, 'Bethlehem' means *house of bread*, so the *sun* rising in Virgo, the House of Bread, is the *son* born in Bethlehem."

"Seriously?"

"Then what's the cross and death and resurrection about?" Justine asks.

"After the summer solstice, days become shorter and colder until December twenty-first and twenty-second, when the sun makes it to its lowest point in the sky. This place where the sun rests happens to be in the vicinity of the Crux constellation, also known as the Southern Cross," Uncle Li says.

"So the sun dies on the cross!" Justine says, putting it all together.

"I'm so tripped out right now," I say.

"There's more," Uncle Li says. "Then this strange thing happens—to the eye it looks as if the sun stops moving *at all* for three days, resting in the vicinity of the Southern Cross constellation. Then, on December twenty-fourth, the sun moves one degree north, rising again. So in these *story-myths* the sun dies on the cross, is dead for three days, then 'rises' again to bring light to the world."

"All these myths have another thing in common," Nima adds, "and that's the twelve apostles or brothers which represent the twelve constellations of the zodiac that the sun/son travels around with. This is, of course, the code for the precession of the equinoxes: the sun moves through the twelve constellations annually, and the Earth travels through the twelve constellations every 26,000 years—a full cycle of precession."

"Um, I'm not really sure what to say?" Justine whispers.

"I know. I mean, can we really tell anyone this? Can you imagine the reaction?" I ask.

"This is like burn-you-at-the-stake kind of stuff," Justine adds.

"Though volatile information to be sure, what has always baffled me is how accessible it is," says Nima. "You could get all of this information from a university library. It's just that people prefer not to have their worldview shaken—it's easier to believe what you've been told than to realize you've been fooled. Similar information shows up in almost all cultures, but the *Fraternitas* has done a great job of making it seem like it's unique to the story of Christianity."

"I still don't get why the Shadow Government, the *Fraternitas,* would want to push this," I ask. "I don't see the point."

"Truth resonates," Uncle Li says. "Deep down we all know there's truth and power to the solar fable. By combining the stories of real, powerful people with mythological components, the *Fraternitas* can create a supermyth, one that billions of people will believe century after century."

"And because there's no firsthand account of the life of Jesus, it was easy to layer on a solar fable," Nima adds.

"What do you mean?" I ask.

"Well, the first mention of Jesus in written history was several decades after his death. And the December twenty-fifth birth date wasn't even celebrated until the fourth century. That's when church leaders decided they needed a

'Christian' alternative to winter solstice celebrations that were already happening on December twenty-fifth. They just started folding earlier pagan solstice rituals, like trees and Yule logs, into the Christian tradition. The very first recorded 'Christmas' was the Feast of the Nativity in Rome in 336 A.D., which was designed to coincide with what had been the Roman Festival of the Undefeated Sun."

"So they took all this solar mythology that had been around forever and just put Jesus in the center of it?"

"Exactly," Nima says. "Just as other cultures have done for centuries with Mithra, Attis, and the others."

Somehow knowing all this information terrifies me.

"Deep," I say.

"Vast," Justine replies.

I look at Nima and Uncle Li. "I get everything you're saying—and I'm truly disturbed by it—but if you're asking me to go out and debunk religion, I'm … I'm just not equipped for that."

"You never have to mention a word of this," Uncle Li says. "We just need you to see the big picture. To understand, as you say, how deep and vast all of this is."

"So," Nima says, "let's put this all in context. If at the base of many myths from almost all cultures lies the story of the heavens, including the precession of the equinoxes, wouldn't you agree that precession must have some *profound* effect on us?"

"Ancients knew that with each turn of the Great Year, human life evolved," says Uncle Li. "This makes the alignment of the sun with the Galactic Center, which is what the Mayan calendar is pointing to, even more profound."

"You mean because this alignment is only meaningful to humans?"

"Exactly!" Uncle Li says. "If you were out in the galaxy, you wouldn't notice anything different about 2012."

"Yes, this is a *human* event," Nima adds. "This is about human evolution—an evolution the *Fraternitas* is terrified of."

"And you two will help usher this in."

I stand up and shake my arms out. "I need to cruise around for a minute or something. I'm a little … overwhelmed."

Justine gets up and grabs my hand and we walk out by the river together. Sitting on the edge of the bridge, we dangle our feet over the water quietly moving below us.

"You okay?" Justine asks.

I breathe deeply. How can I answer that question?

EIGHTEEN

I'm not sure I know what 'okay' is," I respond. "It's just so devastating. It was so easy to go about being a kid when I just believed that the people in power had my best interests at heart."

"But would you really rather go back to *not* knowing?"

"I don't know," I say. "I really don't know."

The glow of the pagodas on the far rock wall reflects off the water, warmly lighting the inside of the immense cave. We both sit silently and take in the beauty of the place. I wish I could stay here forever, tucked safely away.

"Are you sorry you came with me?" I ask Justine. I don't look at her because I want her to tell me the truth, not just what I want to hear.

"Not even one single teeny tiny bit," she replies without hesitation.

I squeeze her hand and we sit there until our legs get chilled from the cold water below.

"Come on," she says, getting up and pulling me with her. "We've got intel to gather."

As we walk back over to the pagoda where Nima and Uncle Li wait for us, I feel the earth move slightly under my feet, as if rocks are falling or ground is being drilled. I look at Justine, whose face tells me she feels it too. Filled with the terror of being caught underground as the cave crashes down, we both run screaming to Uncle Li.

"Did you feel that?" I yell as we get closer. I'm surprised to see him standing calmly and smiling.

"It's just the daily movement of the calendar," he says. "Nothing to worry about."

"What do you mean?" Justine says, now bent over trying to catch her breath. "What are you talking about?"

"Come," he says, "you can see from the River Pagoda."

We walk back to where we were sitting before and Uncle Li moves the grass mat from the center of the floor to reveal a square cut into the wood. He slips his finger in a small hole and pulls up a piece of flooring. We look down but see nothing but black space. Uncle Li holds a lantern over the hole and we catch a glimpse of a piece of a massive stone cog.

"Oh! It's like the gears under the tower at the castle!"

"Precisely," Uncle Li says.

"I gotta see this," Justine says, lying on the ground and lowering the lantern to see the twenty interlocking cogs that make up the Mayan calendar system.

"And when one turns, they all turn?" she asks.

"Right, but because they're different sizes, they turn at different rates. Like the one for the *Tzolk'in* turns once a day for 260 days," Nima says.

"The cogs at Breidablik are much smaller than the ones here," Uncle Li adds. "When this turns, you really feel it."

"Are there more of these, or just this one and the one at Breidablik?" I ask.

"There's one more that we know about—in Duluth, Minnesota. These stone calendar cogs have been placed in areas of strange magnetic behavior, almost equally spaced, all at a 46 degree north latitude. Just in this century geologists have identified these three places as having a 'magnetic basement.' But of course the ancients knew about these places."

I throw up my hands and laugh. "So I'm going to assume that the fact that my mom is from Duluth is no accident."

"In the past few months, have you noticed that there are no accidents?"

I nod.

"So if Caity is from San Francisco, it must mean there are some weird things about that city too, right?" Justine asks.

Nima and Uncle Li look at each other and smile. "We would need days to go into that! But soon enough, San Francisco's secrets will be revealed to you."

"And right now we have to get back to the other half of the *Fraternitas'* manipulation tactics," Nima says. "We have talked about the manipulation of the solar myth and the changing of the calendar as a control vehicle, but what other methods do you think the Shadow Government uses?"

"Fear?" Justine answers. "To keep people scared. Provoking terrorism and then pretending like you're the only one who can protect the people."

"Good! And what's the benefit of keeping people scared?"

"You get to keep wars going. You get lots more support

for military funding—and a good chunk of that goes to companies that the *Fraternitas* has interest in."

"Precisely," Uncle Li says. "Fear allows you to control the masses *and* make money. Justifying war is high on the priority list."

"Okay. Now for the big one: How is the Shadow Government engaging in modern slavery? What keeps us working so hard that we don't look up and notice what's going on?"

"Being in debt?" I say. "Working without ever getting anywhere?"

"That's exactly right, especially for what we call wealthy nations. But do you know how it works in the third world?"

Justine and I both shake our heads.

"See, it's a matter of scale. In wealthy nations you can keep *individuals* in debt, in third-world countries you can keep the entire population in debt. This is much easier to manipulate."

"But how?" I ask.

"Take almost any third-world country today. The Shadow Government identifies a country that has resources that corporations need, like oil, and then they arrange a huge loan to that country from the World Bank, the International Monetary Fund, or one of its organizations."

"I thought the World Bank and the IMF were like nonprofits," Justine says.

"They're both private, *for-profit* financial institutions that make themselves look like aide organizations. Basically, they're just massive banks owned by a handful of wealthy people."

Nima adds, "But the money they loan to third- and fourth-world countries generally doesn't go to the country, but rather to big corporations to build infrastructure projects in that country that make it easier for corporations to come in and export goods. At that point, the whole country is left in over-whelming debt."

"For something that wasn't really to help them in the first place?"

"Right. Because the key part of the plan is that the country cannot ever repay the debt they owe; this keeps them essentially enslaved. Then the bank or corporation goes back and says, you owe us a lot of money, so you have to sell us your oil or natural gas or diamonds or gold—whatever resource it happens to be—really cheap. Or maybe they'll build a military base there, or ask for troop support in a war. Or even more damaging, the bank or corporation will take over the country's utilities like electricity or water and sell them to other corporations. Often it is social services like schools and hospitals and prisons that get privatized and sold off."

"So then what was pitched as something that would *help* the country actually ruins it?" asks Justine.

"Exactly. And everything *worth* anything in the country is left it in the control of a group of corporations, banks, or governments."

"But how is that all legal?"

"How indeed?" Nima answers. "As with most things controlled by the Shadow Government, legality has nothing to do with it. Morality has nothing to do with it. This is about control. About world domination."

"I want to make sure I'm getting this," I say. "So the IMF

and the World Bank offer loans to countries, then put the countries into such a big debt that they can't pay it, and then someone steps in to offer to help pay the debt by having the people sell off their resources or schools, power, and water?"

Nima nods.

"It is important that you *really* understand this," Uncle Li says. "Because it is you who will help destroy this system."

We both look at Uncle Li to gauge if he's joking, but he's dead serious.

"Uh, no," Justine says. "I'm out."

NINETEEN

Okay, let's back up here," I say. "I was told that I'd be uniting the youth and creating some kind of global unity or coherence thing that would help with this shift in consciousness. No one ever said anything about destroying financial systems."

"Think of it as releasing, not destroying. And you will have quite a lot of help," Uncle Li says. "But know this: we cannot shift consciousness without also shifting currency— you cannot have any hope for equality and coherence while there is so much rampant oppression. It is the only way to effect *real* change."

I glance at Justine. For the first time she looks absolutely terrified.

"Most of this can be handled at the *Fraternitas Regni Occulti* headquarters in San Francisco," Nima says.

Justine replies, "And the fact that the *Fraternitas* headquarters are just blocks from where we grew up …"

"Coincidence is merely a fleeting glimpse at wholeness," I whisper.

Uncle Li looks at his watch, then stands up. "Dawn is about to break," he says. "We must get you back."

"Wait, what about instructions?" I ask. "Like what *exactly* are we supposed to do?"

"You'll know. Things will fall into place," Nima says.

Taking me by the arm, Uncle Li says, "We've stayed far too long. We must go now."

He pushes a button on the wall, which makes three high-pitched tones. "Summoning Mr. Papers," he explains. "We'll meet him at the Maglev."

We quickly say goodbye to Nima and then make our way through the cave to the tunnel of trees where the Maglev waits.

We barely speak on the ride back; after the download of information we had at Atala, our minds are frazzled. My entire worldview has been shaken. It's a bit like finding out you parents are convicted felons who stole you as a baby.

Nothing can ever be the same after learning all this.

We climb out of the Maglev in Dunhuang, getting a whiff of the dank cave smell that Atala was free from, and walk carefully along the precipice to the hidden door in the grain storehouse cave. Before Uncle Li unbolts the door to let us outside, he pauses.

"What's wrong?" I ask, unable to figure out why he's looking at me long and hard.

"This may have to be the last time I see you for a while," he says quietly.

"What? Why?" I ask.

"We must *never* let the *Fraternitas* find out about Atala," he explains. "Your coming to Dunhuang once with your teacher is fine, but you cannot come back."

"Of course," I say.

Justine crosses her heart.

"You may be under the radar right now, but as you get things moving, the *Fraternitas* may find you. Stay in the light."

I shudder at Uncle Li's warning.

"When necessary, we will get information to you. But you must never try to contact any of us. The Council has survived for centuries because of the circle of trust. Now that you two are in that circle, you must respect it above all else."

Justine and I solemnly agree. I feel queasy knowing that we are on our own.

"Will Bolon still visit?" I ask. "We need *someone* to be there for us!"

"Less and less," Uncle Li answers. "We really must go underground. This is a tense time, and as you know, many powerful souls are here for this shift—both on the light *and* dark sides."

I nod.

"One last thing," Uncle Li says. He pauses for a moment as if to find the right words, and then says, "If I am captured, you must make no attempt at rescue. *No attempt*," he repeats. "Most likely, it will be a trap to catch *you*."

Justine reaches over and takes my hand. We were not prepared for this kind of a talk.

I nod again and Uncle Li comes over and gives me a hug.

Then he holds me by the shoulders and looks in my eyes.

"You can do this," he says. "You *must* do this. It is out of our hands now."

Mr. Papers jumps from my shoulder to Uncle Li's. I see his tiny eyes well with tears as he hugs Uncle Li's neck.

"Goodbye, Caity. Goodbye, Justine. Papers."

I don't reply.

I don't want to say goodbye. I *refuse* to say goodbye. I don't want to leave the safety of this cave. I don't want to know what I now know and I don't want to face what I need to face.

"I have loved you for lifetimes, Caity," Uncle Li says. "Know that we will always be connected."

I nod, because my throat is constricted and I can't speak.

"I must go back to Atala. Could you please put the false wall back before you leave the cave?" he asks.

"Of course," Justine says, taking over for me; I've been made useless by the heavy talk.

Uncle Li gently puts Mr. Papers back on my shoulder. "You remember how to get back to the hotel?"

I nod. If I say anything I'm afraid my voice will crack and I'll lose it.

Uncle Li turns and walks through hole, disappearing into the darkness. Justine and I replace the back wall and the shelves before unbolting the door and sneaking out.

We walk in silence under a blanket of early morning stars. With no city light and no clouds to obscure the sky, it looks like a star traffic jam. The air is dry and crisp and the only sound we hear is the electric buzzing of insects we cannot see.

When we make out the hotel glowing in the distance,

Justine says, "Caity, I don't know if I can do this. After what we heard tonight, I'm just—"

"I know," I say, putting my arm around her shoulder as we walk. "Honest, I know exactly what you're thinking and I feel the same way. But can we talk about it after we sleep? I can barely even focus my eyes."

She nods. I feel guilty about being unable to respond to Justine or even comfort her, but I'm just far too freaked out myself right now to offer any comfort.

Once back safely in our rooms, I take a piece of hotel stationary and write a note for Clath:

> Dear Professor Clath,
> Justine and I are both terribly sick from last night's room service. Can we wait until the afternoon to meet for lessons? We are trying to sleep after a fitful night.
> Your devoted students,
> Caity and Justine

I slip the paper under Clath's hotel room door, flashing back to the last time I did this on Easter Island. After slipping that note to Alex, I had one of the worst nights of my life.

When I get back to the room, Justine is already asleep. Mr. Papers has fallen asleep in my open bag, curled up on a sweatshirt.

Collapsing on the bed, I'm more than happy to escape to a world of dreams. Though I try not to, I cannot help but wonder if that was the last time I would ever see Uncle Li.

TWENTY

A beam of light wakes me from a deep, dreamless sleep. Looking for the source of the light, I see Mr. Papers lifting a corner of the curtain to look out the window. I roll over to peek at the clock; it's one in the afternoon. As I get up to go to the bathroom, I notice an envelope has been slid under our door. The word "Coursework" is written on it in Clath's hand. Ugh. She's not letting anything get by.

Justine is sitting up in bed when I come out of the bathroom, her hair a messy beehive as if she'd been grinding the pillow all night long.

"Just tell me it was a dream," she croaks.

I hand her a bottle of water and say, "It was a dream."

She drinks the whole bottle in a few gigantic swigs and then falls back to her pillow.

"Homework," I say, flashing the envelope. "Let's see what the Pedagogue wants us to learn."

"Wouldn't it be funny if you opened it and it said, 'Write

a five hundred word essay on how the Shadow Government and the Church have controlled the masses by weaving myths with religion.'"

"Almost as funny as if it said, 'Describe how you would change the very nature of humanity by wiping out all third-world debt.'"

We both start laughing hysterically because it's not at all funny and actually too scary to face.

"We're so screwed," Justine says.

"Yup," I agree.

We both stare at the ceiling.

"But it would be pretty cool to be modern-day Robin Hoods," I say.

"Seriously," she replies.

"Right?"

"Right."

"But how?"

"Exactly."

"Are we really talking about this?" I say.

"I don't know, are we?"

"I think we are."

"Crap."

"Exactly," I reply.

I open the envelope to see what kind of evil coursework Clath has slid under our door. Inside are ten photographs of various pieces of art featuring the Three Hares symbol.

On the last one is a sticky note saying, "Now that you've seen it in its original context, please try your hand at decoding."

"I can't believe I forgot to ask Uncle Li about this symbol before we left!" I say, mad at myself for overlooking the main reason we were supposed to be studying at Dunhuang in the first place.

Laying out all the photographs on the floor between us, Justine and I each lie face-down on our beds so we can both look down on them. Mr. Papers comes over from the windowsill and walks up my back to see what's going on.

"What do you think, Mr. P.?" I ask.

He hops off, grabs a pen from the nightstand, picks up one photo, and spears the center of it with the pen tip.

"Hey!" I yell, reaching to grab the photo back. He jumps up to Justine's bed and starts to spin the photo on the end of the pen.

"Does this guy ever stop?" Justine asks.

He looks at us as he spins the photo as if to say, "Seriously? You guys don't get it?"

I try to take in what's happening and then something clicks. "Is it about the spinning?" I ask.

"Is he saying this symbol is about motion?" Justine asks.

"Right! The rabbits represent motion—ever changing, ever reproducing … "

"But what does that mean though?" she asks. "Spinning what? Spinning the center section of the Flower of Life where the ears connect?"

"Oooh, maybe you're onto something. Does something happen when you spin the Flower of Life symbol?" I ask, reaching for my laptop. I open a browser and search "spinning + flower of life."

"Dude, you will *not* believe this!" I say, motioning for Justine to come see. "Look what happens when you spin the Flower of Life—you get this thing called a 'tube torus'!"

"Wait, what? How does it go from the Flower of Life to that donut-like thing?" Justine asks.

"It says here that a tube torus is the spinning, 3D version of the Flower of Life."

"That's totally got to be what the Three Hares symbol is about! Three is a key to the number of dimensions and the running in a circle is a key to the spinning!"

Mr. Papers nods and puts his hands in the air like *what took you so long?*

Since I don't have a printer, I grab my sketchbook and draw what the torus looks like:

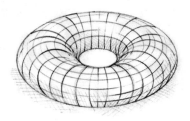

Watching me draw, Justine says, "Okay, so now we get that the Flower of Life makes a tube torus, but one question remains: What's a tube torus got to do with anything?"

I shrug and keep drawing, but Mr. Papers springs into action. I have to put my pencil down to watch because I rarely get to see him do origami this fast—usually his creations are so complex that it takes a while. After just seconds he produces a pink heart, which he gives to Justine, and after a few more seconds he produces a pale yellow star, which he gives to me.

We thank him and he takes a deep bow, as if all has just been answered.

From the corner of her mouth, Justine whispers, "I don't want to offend him, but what do hearts and stars have to do with a spinning Flower of Life or the *Fraternitas* or any of this?"

"I don't know," I whisper back. Once again to the browser. We both watch for what pops up when I search various ways on torus + heart + space + stars. I click on one of the top results.

"No way. Papers is a genius! Listen to this: 'The pumping heart creates a spinning field of electromagnetic energy *in the shape of a torus*'!"

Reading over my shoulder, Justine says, "Freaky—it says this magnetic field of the heart is even stronger than the magnetic field of the brain."

"Isn't it weird to think that we create magnetic fields?" I ask.

"Wait! Look at the result below the one you're reading— the astronomy website talks about the entire universe being a torus shape!"

"*Hearts* and *stars*," I say, looking at Mr. Papers. He smiles so big we get to see every little tooth in his mouth.

"Click on the heart thing! I want to see more about that," Justine says. It's a medical abstract on a U.S. government website about how the heart produces torsion and an electromagnetic field that extends beyond the body.

"Weird," we both say after we read it. Going back to the search results, Justine points to another odd article.

"Click that one," she says. "Something about DNA creating this torsion field, too."

We click through to the site and she reads, "We are all surrounded by a magnetic field that can now be seen and photographed by several medical devices. The torus generated by your DNA and your heart is the same shape as the magnetic torus around the Earth and the sun. From the molecular to the massive, the torus generates a vortex of energy that bends back along itself and re-enters itself."

Then I see something amazing at the bottom of the page.

"That's it!" I say, jumping off the bed and pacing. "That's what Bolon was talking about!"

"What?" Justine asks. "What do you mean?"

Finally, something big is coming together for me.

TWENTY-ONE

ook at the bottom," I tell Justine. "It says the spinning torus creates gravity!"

"It *creates* gravity?" Justine asks, looking at the page. "You mean even at the tiny DNA and heart level?"

"Yes! Do you remember the poem I showed you, the one that came out of the decoded spirals? One of the lines is, '*Like gravity, love is a force of great might*'!"

I grab the computer and pull up the document with the whole poem in it.

"Read that!" I say, pointing to the stanza I'm talking about.

This birth may come like a storm or a dove
The outcome lies in how much we can love
Like gravity, love is a force of great might
True power comes when we connect and unite

"Do you see how this is important to our whole mission?" I ask.

"Not totally," Justine shrugs. "Sorry ... "

"Remember after the first gathering, when I was on Easter Island, you were in Peru, and Chatrea and Amisi were in Angkor Wat and the pyramids? By getting together, being 'on the same channel' so to speak, the energy from our combined hearts or DNA or whatever actually affected physics—that's how we managed to get a reading on the PEAR research equipment!"

"And that's how we got all the animals that are sensitive to waves to be in phase!" she adds.

"So, the sentence '*Like gravity, love is a force of great might*' is totally literal."

"Isn't that weird? That love can be measured?"

"But only if we're all working together instead of against one another," I say.

"And that's where the constant fear tactics come in," she says. "*That's* where the *Fraternitas* works its magic. Keeping people in a state of either fear or poverty. Or both."

"Exactly. Plus, if everything from DNA to the heart to the magnetic field around the Earth, sun, and galaxy all move as toruses—"

"Probably tori, not toruses," Justine interjects. "Like cactus and cacti?"

"Okay, *tori*—then getting our human waves to match the powerful waves coming in from the Galactic Center could be key to making this evolutionary leap."

"Makes total sense," Justine says.

"In the weirdest possible way that something can make sense ... "

"So the big questions are, what is the next step, and what do we tell Clath?"

I put my face in my hands and we both think for a moment. "I'm guessing she'd be pretty interested in what we found," I say.

"Well, yeah," Justine answers, "but how much can we divulge?"

"Just enough," I answer, opening up a Word document. "Just enough for her to help lead us to answers."

In about an hour, Justine and I are able to put together a short paper answering Clath's question: *Now that you've seen it in its original context, please try your hand at decoding.*

The Three Hares:
The Code of the Torus in an Ancient Symbol

By Caity Luxton and Justine Devereux

The Three Hares symbol has been found all over the world, but has never been decoded. The earliest painting of it is from a Buddhist cave in Mogao near Dunhuang, China (600 AD). It was then carried across to Europe on the Silk Road, where it really caught on in England. There it can be found carved in churches all over.

To decode the Three Hares symbol, we started by looking at the one link between the three rabbits: their ears. If you just trace their ears, what you get is a piece of the Flower of Life. The Flower of Life symbol is also found all over the world, in even more places than the hares. It is supposed to be the basis of all things because within these thirteen overlapping circles you can make the five building blocks of organic life: the tetrahedron, cube, octahedron, icosahedron, and dodecahedron (aka the Platonic Solids).

So we looked at the center of the Three Hares symbol and thought about what the hares around the Flower of Life represent: a) SPIN, b) the number THREE, and c) some kind of ILLUSION because though there are three hares, there are only two sets of ears.

Then we looked at what would happen if you applied these three things to the Flower of Life, and that is where we had our Eureka moment! If you SPIN the Flower of Life, you get this interesting vortex shape, and if you make that shape THREE dimensional you get what is called a torus! This shift from the one-dimensional drawing to the three-dimensional torus is the ILLUSION part.

In Math they call the torus the perfect shape and it is now accepted as the model that can be used to describe objects in space.

But this torus, which looks like a simple and delicious cake donut, is not just found in space. It turns out that the muscles of the heart are in the perfect shape to create a torus of energy as it pumps our blood! And on an even smaller level, our DNA forms tori, too. The shape of the Earth's magnetic field: torus. The shape of the sun's magnetic field: torus. Everywhere you look, energy is forming in torus shapes.

But the most amazing part of it all is that the torus energy actually *creates* gravity!

Our theory is that the ancient Chinese, with their well-known thinking on things like acupuncture and feng shui, created the Three Hares symbol to encode this information about how the universe works, from our tiniest building blocks to the largest things in space.

(It only took Western Science ten centuries to create instruments that have the ability to measure the energy from these torus shapes. Way to go, West!)

We both proof the paper and then attach it to an email to Clath, feeling pretty smug.

TWENTY-TWO

"Want to go down to the restaurant?" I ask, as I close my laptop.

"Definitely. I'm starving," Justine answers. "Plus we've got to get out of this bleak room," she says, motioning to the cinderblock walls painted the color of dust.

I open the door and motion for Papers to come along, but he just shakes his head and curls up next to my pillow. All the fun with his old friends last night has worn him out.

The restaurant in the lobby of the hotel is about as bare and simple as our room, and it smells like the funky back rooms I remember at some of Uncle Li's friends' places in Chinatown—of roots and spices and other unknown things. But the hot tea, brought by a tiny Chinese man who smiles big enough to reveal a full set of top teeth yet not one bottom tooth, tastes great.

The menu is interesting. Under the Chinese names of food someone has made hilarious attempts at English translations:

Bean Juice Steams the Spare Rib, Grill Cowboy Leg, Big Bowl Flower Immerses Pork Kidney, and my personal favorite, *White Tree Fungus Braise Pig Heart.*

"Just rice, please," Justine says when the tiny man comes back for our order.

"Two, please," I add.

He gives us a look of concern so I tap my stomach in the universal "tender tummy" pantomime. He fills up our tea cups, flashes a gummy smile, then takes off for the kitchen.

Justine dumps three packets of sugar into her tea and says, "If you had told me a year ago we'd be sitting in a strange little Chinese hotel recovering from a night in a secret city in Mongolia, I'd have called for the friendly straightjacket patrol to come get you."

Shaking my head, I pour myself a third cup of tea. "The weirdest part is that there was no build-up to this. Like nothing in my life led me to believe that I would be put in a position like this, you know?"

"Well, you did have that early ninja training," Justine says.

"I'd hardly call long afternoons in the back of herb shops 'ninja training'."

"Still, you've had this 'protector' your whole life. And your parents are not really standard model."

"True."

"I mean, I can't do any of the stuff you can do on the computer," she says. "You got all that from your parents."

"I'd trade it for your looks," I say, only half joking.

"And that briefcase thing back in San Francisco, that was pure Fiona."

"Huh. I wonder if that's how Mom does it? When we met with members of The Council, didn't Apari say that all that information is registered—we just have to pick up on it? Maybe Mom's ability to 'touch sound' to open safes is really just her tapping into this field of information."

"Whatever it is, it's genetic. So maybe there were signs, clues, what have you."

I shrug. "I guess no sign or clue can prepare you for something as far out of the realm of possibility as what we're in now."

The waiter comes in with a big tray. We each get a heaping bowl of rice, and then he sets another two covered bowls on the table. Pointing to the bowls, he says, "Good for stomach" before bowing and backing away.

I lift the lid on my mystery bowl, then gently set it back down.

"And every time we think it could not get weirder, it does," I whisper.

"Should I look?" she asks with a cringe.

"Not if ye be a lover of frogs," I answer.

We keep the soup bowls closed and focus on our rice, which turns out to be the best rice I've ever eaten in my life. Or maybe I'm just hungry, and happy that it's clean and pure and frog free.

Just as we're finishing up, Clath comes busting into the restaurant like the building is on fire. She looks relieved when she sees us and runs to our table

Sitting in the chair next to Justine, she catches her breath. "You girls," she says, shaking her head. "Unbelievable."

Unable to tell whether she's impressed or angry, I put

my spoon down and take a sip of tea. She just keeps shaking her head. Assuming the worst, I say, "So you think we totally missed the mark?"

"Missed it?" she says, holding up Justine's teacup to the waiter to indicate another. "You blew me away. No offense to either of you, but when we first met I wasn't expecting much. Now I'm very, very impressed."

It's always hard to accept a compliment after a low blow, but we both manage to say thanks.

"I just can't believe no one else has thought of this as an option for the meaning of that symbol," she says, shaking her head. "To come up with such a simple yet elegant solution is just … well … brilliant."

"Wow, that means a lot coming from you," I say, pouring some tea into the cup that our toothless little friend has brought for her.

"I did some serious Internet searching after I read it, looking for others who have made this connection, but it's never been made. You two have come up with a *completely* original solution for that symbol."

I want to give Papers credit where credit is due, but it just seems way too farfetched.

"If you think about it, it makes a lot of sense, though," Justine says.

"Absolutely. Which is why I'm amazed no one else has thought of it," Clath answers, drinking her tea in one gulp. "As a mathematician, I've worked with tori for decades, but even I had not heard that DNA and the heart both work in a toridal fashion. I'd never had a reason to even investigate the tori in relation to biology."

I fill up her cup again, and again she drinks it in one gulp. Her esophagus must be made of stainless steel.

"Waves. It's all just waves," she says as she sets down the empty cup. "Even this china teacup that looks so solid. See, the torus, or the tasty donut as you refer to it, is the only structure in a world of waves that can become coherent and be able to nest inside each other. So yeah, it makes perfect sense that the torus is the underlying energetic structure of the universe."

I look over at Justine, who is folding a sugar packet into a tiny fan. Obviously she is as nervous as I am that Clath will find out that we don't know much more about toruses—tori—than that one-page paper we just wrote.

"So where to next?" I ask, changing the subject. "Where should we go next on our learning tour?"

"We'll spend a full day tomorrow at the caves, get the most out of the place, then I've got this friend I think we need to see. He's at a think tank outside of Cambridge, so we can chalk it up to looking at some Three Hares symbols in Great Britain."

"What's he thinking about?" Justine asks.

"How to get out of his tank?" I reply.

"Stick to symbol analysis," she says dryly. "Clearly that's where your talents lie."

I slide my bowl of soup to her. "Hungry?" I ask. "I haven't touched it."

When she lifts the lid I brace myself for a scream that doesn't come. I look over to see that the contents of the soup have settled to the bottom so it just looks like a bowl of broth.

"Maybe just a bit," she says as she picks it up with both hands and sips.

We look at each other, both biting hard on our lips. Justine motions to the door with her head so I set down enough money for the meal and say, "Well, we better hop on back to the room. We'll pack up—let us know when you want to leave."

Clath takes one more big sip, then sets the bowl down. "I'll go too," she says, refilling her teacup and then gulping it down. "Something odd about that soup."

On the way back upstairs, Clath says she's off to do a bit more exploring. "Care to join?" she asks as we leave her at her door.

"I think we're going to do a bit more research," Justine says. "You know, about *the theory*."

"Of course, yes," Clath says, now taking us completely seriously.

Back in the room, I call up the secret website Alex and I made. Justine and I bask in the tone of the day while looking at the Daylord and number, Ten Ik.

"No surprise that we came up with a totally genius decoding today," Justine says. "The Daylord Ik means it's a mental, agile day that's good for communication."

"And Ten means it's a day of manifestation."

The site makes me think of Alex. Of our time together in the tower. "I really need to get ahold of Alex," I tell Justine.

"We can't risk it. Remember what Uncle Li said? No contact."

"But if we're going to England, we're going to be *right there*. He could meet us."

"We don't even know exactly where we're going," Justine says.

"But we know we'll be outside of Cambridge. Let's just see where the nearest Three Hares symbol is."

I look up the closest example of the Three Hares to Cambridge. "Look, here's one in a church in Long Melford, which is pretty close."

"So how do you get Alex there?"

"I don't know." I bite down on a yellow pencil until my teeth sink completely in, which is freakishly satisfying. Then a brilliant idea floats into my head. "We'll fly him there!"

"How?" Justine asks.

I hop onto a travel site and look at fares to Cambridge. "I'll create an account in Alex's name, book travel, then email it to his account. No one would ever know it was from me."

"And he'll just go? Without any explanation?"

"I think so. I hope so. Let me just find the closest hotel to this church that the Three Hares is in. I'll book him there for three days from now. That will give us all time to get there."

I find a flight and room at an inn near the church, pay with the PayPal account that Bolon gave me, then hit send. Alex doesn't know I can't contact him directly, but he's smart enough to know that if he gets a plane ticket with no explanation, it's got to be from me.

"Done and done," I say, turning off my laptop.

"So are you excited to see Alex?" Justine asks.

I flop back on my bed and stare at the ceiling, wondering how it's even possible for dust to collect on a ceiling. "Let's just say tomorrow is gonna drag like a thousand days," I reply.

"Caves, caves, caves," she sighs. "Like can anything top a Maglev ride to Atala?"

"Nothing short of a stairway to heaven."

———

We suffer through another full day of tours with Wen, which under any other circumstances would have been super fascinating. But all I can think of is seeing Alex and finally being able to talk to him about what is going on.

At the end of a long day, we board the plane. Marco greets us with ice-cold sodas and a snack. I've never been so happy to see a Ritz cracker in all my life. The airplane food we have on the way is better than anything I've eaten since I left Mrs. Findlay's cooking.

Clath has taken quite a liking to Mr. Papers and starts playing some sort of math game with him on the airplane. It involves two origami dice with a bunch of sides on them. Clath writes numbers on each of the sides and then they roll the dice and add them or something. I don't try to follow but it's fun to watch from across the aisle. You can tell Clath is totally enchanted by Mr. P.

Because of time zones, we fly backward in time and land in Cambridge only a couple hours later than when we left China, even though twelve hours have gone by.

We don't even drop our bags at a hotel, just pick up a

car and go straight to meet Clath's friend. You'd think that she would dress up a bit, but no. She wears a T-shirt that says "Mathlete" tucked into her trademark elastic-waist jeans, and has so many fingerprints on her glasses you wonder how she can even see.

TWENTY-THREE

We pass the campus of the incredible Cambridge University, possibly the coolest-looking university in the world. I'm hoping Clath's friend's think tank will be in one of the gothic-spired buildings, and am disappointed when we drive beyond the campus to the city. After some terrifying city driving by Clath, we arrived at a nondescript '60s-looking two-story building. Clath parks and leads us down a side staircase to a basement door. There is no sign, just the number 64 etched on the door.

"What do these people do again?" I whisper as Clath knocks on the glass.

"Serious research," she answers cryptically.

The door creaks open to reveal a jowly man with wiry white hair on both his head and his earlobes, wearing a checkered button-down and a pea-green sweater. He's the classic English researchy guy.

"Clath, my dear!" the man says, holding out his hand. "Lovely to see you!"

Professor Clath offers her hand and says, "The pleasure is all mine, Professor."

We're introduced to Emmet Davis, and find out he's a professor emeritus—which I think means retired—at Cambridge. His specialty was systems theory and now, Clath tells us with a flourish, he's working on a "toe."

"A toe?" I ask, looking around the room at an array of computers and servers that even my dad would be impressed by.

"Shorthand for a Theory of Everything, dear," Professor Davis says with a tea-stained smile.

"I didn't know you could have a Theory of Everything," Justine says.

"It's the holy grail of science!" Clath says, like we're idiots. "To unify all the forces of the universe and be able to express it simply and elegantly as a single model!"

"Any luck with it?" I ask Professor Davis. Clath throws me a look. Now we've both embarrassed her and we haven't even gotten past the doorway.

"Getting closer," he answers. "But where are my manners? Come in, please! Have a seat and I'll get us some tea and biscuits."

Not wanting to give the man a heart attack, I point to the soft carrier on my shoulder. "I have a … monkey," I say. "Should I leave him in the car?"

"Good lord, no," Professor Davis says. "Let the poor chap stay. Only a scant difference in our DNA, in any case. Please, sit. I'll just be a moment."

Justine and I settle onto an old couch with a coverlet on it while Clath takes a tattered armchair off to the side. The coffee table is stacked with technical magazines and note-books.

"Does he live here?" I whisper to Clath.

She shakes her head. "He's actually terribly wealthy. Lives in an estate a few miles away."

"Very British," Justine says. "You can never tell who is loaded."

Professor Davis walks back in with a tea tray and sets it down on the stack of magazines. It sits crookedly and I worry it will fall, but he seems totally unconcerned.

"Well then," he says once we've each been served a cup of tea and a cookie. "What is it you girls are hiding?"

I take a big gulp of tea. "Excuse me?" I say. Justine just looks at me with her big eyes, then looks toward the door as if to say, *Let's run!*

"At your age you don't just arrive at Dunhuang, take one look at the caves, and then write up a document relating the Three Hares symbol to a unified field theory based on the torus," Professor Davis says.

"Is that what we did?" I ask. Clath and Professor Davis look at me like I'm popping off. "Seriously, I'm not being glib!"

"Yes," says Clath. "That is what you did."

"Take me through your thinking," Professor Davis says.

I have to think fast in order to leave out the part about Mr. Papers spinning the photo and making the origami hearts and stars. Instead I tell them that I once saw this program on feng shui that said that *form defines energy*, so I looked at the form to see what the underlying energy would be.

"But then how did you know to connect that to the heart, and to DNA?" Professor Davis asks.

"Lots of Googling and a little luck," Justine says, taking the pressure off me. "Why, are we in some kind of trouble?"

"Not trouble, exactly," Clath says, then pauses. "I'm just trying to understand what you're doing—I sense there's another motive in your coming to La Escuala Bohemia."

"There's no motive; we're just interested in symbols. And myths," I reply.

Both Emmet and Clath are looking hard at us, like we're a piece of modern art that they're trying to figure out. I try not to break out in a sweat, try to remain calm and not let on that we're hiding anything.

"And then there's the matter of the monkey," Clath adds.

"Whatever do you mean?" the professor asks, looking at Mr. Papers, who is sitting quietly beside me.

"He can read math formulas! The little thing can reason—and communicate through origami."

"Rubbish!" Professor Davis says. "Folding paper is one thing, but recognizing math formulas is simply not possible for a Capuchin."

"I'll show you!" Clath says, taking a piece of paper from his desk. She writes down the equation that was on her shirt when we left for China and hands it to Mr. Papers. I can't stop chanting *no, no, no* in my head. I don't want him to show off.

Mr. Papers gives the equation a glance and then folds the paper into the absolute simplest airplane possible and sends it sailing through the air. When it lands in Clath's mess of curls, he squawks and jumps up and down a little like a four-year-old would, making himself look a bit like an idiot. I can't help but smile at his acting.

Clath calmly pulls the paper airplane from her hair and crumples it in a ball.

"Impressive," Professor Davis says with a laugh. Clath looks pissed.

Justine breaks the tension, asking Professor Davis, "Can you tell us what's so interesting about our theory that the Three Hares is a hidden symbol of the torus?"

"Well, for one thing, it's completely unique. The correlation has never been made before you two. Symbols are not really my area, you see, but if this is actually what the Three Hares represents, then it could boost my work a bit. You see, I'm working on a formula that shows that all things, from the smallest particle to the largest system, work on the same gyromagnetic equation."

"You lost me at 'gyro,'" I say.

"He's talking about spin, about the torus," Clath says impatiently.

"Yes. You see, microscopic electrons and black holes move in *exactly* the same way—they have the same gyromagnetic ratio. Extraordinary, really."

"Extraordinary is an understatement," Clath says.

"So Hermes Trismegistus was right with the whole *As above, so below* thing?" I ask.

He nods. "That which happens at the smallest level, also happens at the largest."

"So can you tie this all together for us?" I ask.

"You see, I am swimming upstream with my theory.

Those in academia want to find a unified field theory that works within the constraints of what we already know. Big bang, ever-expanding universe, Einstein's theory of relativity and all that. But I assert that all systems, from the smallest proton to the largest galaxy, work on the same principal: spin. It is spin that creates magnetism, gravity, etcetera. Come, look here," he says, walking over to his computer. He pulls up a 3D model of a donut-shaped torus and then makes it move so we see the outer skin moving up and then going down the inner hole and coming back up the outside edges.

"It's like breathing; the inhale, or contraction, is going down into the center and exhale, or radiation, is coming out of the hole and up. It's all a matter of poles—like two ends of the magnet, one repels, the other attracts. Constant movement, constant flux."

"And where do you see humans in all of this?" I ask, wondering exactly how the suppression of this information is important to the *Fraternitas*.

"We're all part of the system too, of course. When it comes down to it, we're all just nested waves—a torus inside of a torus inside of a torus. But here's where I get pushback from government and academic funding. They will not fund me as long as I support the claim that this system works on the human level, too. And this is why Clath was so keen on getting your Three Hares theory to me—if this symbol is an encoded message about spin on the biological level, it could very well boost my research."

"Do you think there's a conspiracy to keep some of this information quiet?" I ask.

Professor Davis exhales deeply and tugs at a tuft of ear

hair. "Oh, dear. Conspiracy is such a … well … such an *American* term. No offense, of course. But there *is* a tendency to not want to support ideas that show humans are governed by larger forces than just our world leaders."

I would love to spill everything to Professor Davis; he might even be able to help us with some of it. But I just don't trust Clath yet. I'm not entirely sure she wouldn't report us to Didier.

"Well, enough about conspiracy!" Clath says, unable to hide her embarrassment at us asking about it. "There's a stained-glass window of the Three Hares nearby. Emmet, may I use your printer? Research came up with a curriculum for the church while we were flying here. Just need to print it out."

This makes me wonder how much Clath is sending back to the school. "Have you sent our paper back to Research yet?" I ask her.

Clath shakes her head. "No, I hold all your work until the end of the semester, and then we put it together and send it to Testing for approval."

Clath prints out two copies of the curriculum and gives us each one. "Might want to read it on the way," she says.

When I say goodbye to Professor Davis, he takes my hand in his and says, like I'm a respected colleague, "Do keep me abreast of your research, won't you? If I can help publish anything on your Three Hares discovery, don't hesitate to ask."

It's both fun and terrifying to be taken so seriously.

TWENTY-FOUR

We settle in for the drive to Long Melford; Justine and I sit quietly thinking in the back while Mr. Papers rides shotgun with Clath, surveying the scene.

The countryside and the towns are absolutely beautiful. It's hard to understand why there aren't any trashy homes or trailer parks here like all over the United States. Everything has been built sturdily and all the buildings, while all slightly different, work perfectly together.

I poke Justine as we see the sign for Long Melford. I'm tingling all over, like when a local anesthetic wears off and you can feel your nerves firing. We pass the inn where I booked a room for Alex on the way to ours, which is just a few blocks away.

"It's probably too late to see the church this afternoon," Clath says, making a seventeen-point turn in order to parallel park the car in a miniature space. "Let's check in and call it a night. We'll reconvene in the a.m."

The inn where we're staying is more than two hundred years old and although it's very charming, it's doll-sized. I almost have to duck to go through doorways and my feet hang over the sides of the bed. People back then must have been more like elves than humans; it's amazing to think of the physical differences that can occur in just a few hundred years, when you add refrigeration and medicine to the mix.

Clath walks us to our room and says goodbye. I don't even unpack before I grab the hotel stationary and write:

Holy Trinity Church / 8 P.M. Tonight

"I'll be right back," I tell Justine as I write Alex's name on the envelope. "If Clath comes by, tell her I went out to get some Tylenol."

I take the back staircase down and leave from the side door in case Clath went down to the lobby. Then I run at full speed to Alex's inn. Completely out of breath, I try to hand the envelope to the knobby guy at the reception desk and tell him this is an urgent delivery for a guest. He takes out a small silver tray and holds it out it for me, as if he could not possibly touch the envelope with his hands.

Before I run back, I look in the window to make sure knobby guy is really taking the envelope to Alex. When I see him get up and walk with the tray, I sprint back.

Justine and I have a snack in the hotel and wait out the early evening. We get outside just as the last rays of the sun are setting. I start to shiver, both from the cold and the excitement of seeing Alex soon.

The church sits on a hill up from the town, past where

the city lights end. Once it's completely dark, we have to rely on the rising half-moon to light our way.

"Are you excited to see Alex?" Justine whispers.

"Nervous is more like it," I whisper back. "It seems like every time we're apart, I have to start at zero again."

"How do you know that he's not just as excited and nervous to see you?" she asks.

"I don't know—he never seems nervous. He's just so ... so ... ."

"So dreeeeeeeeeeamy?" Justine says, punching me softly on the shoulder.

"Just wait," I reply. "Seriously."

As we get closer to the church, we start to see stones at weird angles poking from the ground. I think at first it might be some formation like Stonehenge, but once we get closer we realize they're tombstones, all askew from the ground moving over time.

"Ew," Justine says, grabbing my arm. "If this place is eight hundred years old, there are some seriously ancient bodies here!"

"Let's run," I yell, grabbing her hand and flying up the hill.

Once past the church graveyard, we slow down to assess the situation. There are no cars outside and only a very dim light burns from inside the gigantic stone cathedral.

"Do churches get locked at night?" Justine asks.

"I don't know," I reply, leading us to a small arched side door. I put my hand gently on the iron knob and turn. Nothing. We walk around back to another door. Locked.

"I guess we'll have to try the front door and take our

chances," I say. The two large double doors to the church are closed, but when I try the handle, it moves. Slowly opening the door just a crack, we both poke our heads in. Papers squeezes his whole body through and runs in. I don't want to yell for him, but I also don't want to lose him in this enormous church, so Justine and I follow.

It seems to be empty. It's dark, except for the glow of offertory candles, every statue and pillar making a sinister shadow. As we walk to the front of the church to be sure no one is there, we hear, "Pssst!" from a dark corner.

"Alex?" I whisper, following the sound.

"Here," he says, emerging from a tiny side room devoted to a statue of some dark figure.

Just the sight of him—his messy hair and his wide shoulders under a Navy pea coat—makes me happy to the core. I cannot see him without also feeling that kiss, his faint stubble, his pine scent. As soon as I reach him, he gives me a huge hug. My nervousness melts. His hug feels like getting into a warm bath after skiing.

Papers breaks our hug by jumping up on Alex's shoulder and wedging himself between us so he can fully squeeze his neck.

Justine puts out her hand and offers it to Alex.

"Alex, this is Justine, my best friend in the whole world."

"'Tis a pleasure to finally meet you!" he says, taking her hand and then bowing deeply.

"Likewise," she says, blushing at his bowing. Her eyes dart over to mine and I give her the look that says, *I know! Can you believe he's for real?*

"So you made it," I say, starting the obvious.

"Well, when a bloke receives a mysterious plane ticket and hotel reservation in his email, he's bound to show up."

"Did you have to explain where you were going?" I ask. "I mean, was there anything anyone would be suspicious of?"

"Nae, Thomas helped me cook up a story about going fishing with one of his old seafaring mates. As long as I show up with a few cod from the market, I should be fine."

I look at Justine, and she's as mesmerized as I am by the accent. What is it about a Scottish accent that turns plain English into something entirely delicious?

I nudge her to break her stare.

"How are my parents?" I ask. "Do they seem okay?"

"Aye, they seem fine. Gran says a new group just booked a trip so they have some business to take their minds off their loss—of the house and of you."

"And Thomas? Everything good with him?"

"Thomas is still on high alert. Not leaving the castle for a moment and keeping a close eye on who comes and goes from the island. He still fears retaliation from the *Fraternitas*."

"Well, I hope you know I haven't been ignoring you— they said it was super critical that we no longer communicate by cell or Skype or even email. That's why I had to see you in person. I just don't know how we'll exchange information with no phone or computer."

"I wondered why you went dark!" he says.

Justine immediately imitates his rolled Rs on "dark." We both look at her and she puts a hand to her mouth. "Did I say that out loud?" she asks. Alex just laughs.

"Yeah, we can't use any digital communication. So we have to figure out some other way to plan stuff."

"Oh, there are ways around that!" he says, shrugging like it's no big deal.

"What do you mean?" I ask at the same time that Justine says, "How?"

"My mates and I have a system with the Breidablik School email. See, very few of us have computers at home so we have to use school computers. But 'sent' email is checked, and outside email is not allowed. So to get 'round it, we all memorize each other's passwords and check each other's drafts folders. If you see a draft email with your name as the subject, you know it's yours."

"That's brilliant!" I say, so loudly that my voice echoes through the church.

"Aye. Since it's not sent over the server, the school never sees it. The same system would work perfectly for what we need."

"So we just open a new Gmail account that we all have access to and only write email as drafts?" Justine asks.

"Aye," Alex says. "If it never leaves your inbox it can never be traced."

"It's genius. Somehow I'll get the username and password to Uncle Li and Tenzo, and you can get it to Thomas, then we'll all check it every day in case we need to communicate. The *Fraternitas* will never see it."

"So now that email is settled, want to tell me why I am here?" Alex asks. "I suspect it has something to do with the Three Hares?"

Justine looks at him like he's psychic.

"He saw the hares on the false wall in my room," I explain to her. "And on my key."

"Before I left, I read up about the town I was being mysteriously sent to. Turns out Long Melford is famous for this church, and this church is famous for its stained glass—including one window that features the Three Hares," Alex says. "Wasn't a stretch to put it together."

"Write-ups of this church always talk about the Three Hares, but it's weird that there is no mention of it being a symbol that started in China."

"Aye, all mentions I saw relate it to the Holy Trinity," he says.

"So where is it?" asks Justine. "Let's find those hares."

"The site I read said it's above that door, under the stained glass of Our Lady of Pity," Alex says, pointing across the church.

We each grab a candle and head in that direction. Because it's pitch black outside, we can't see much of anything until we get right under the window.

Then we see it.

"Look! It's tiny!" I say, pointing to the small circle under a series of three really big stained glass windows.

We move a chair over to the window so Alex can hold a candle up and illuminate it, but even he's not tall enough. Papers jumps from the chair to Alex's shoulder, grabs the candle, and then hops up to a ledge, shining the light on the stained glass.

Finally we see it clearly.

TWENTY-FIVE

Justine's eyes light up. "Oh, wow—that's so weird. It's not just the Three Hares in the window. Look what's rising up over the right side of them."

"Is that the *sun*?" I ask. "Unbelievable!"

I quickly pull out my sketchbook so I can get every detail down.

"Look, the hares are going counterclockwise, the yin direction, because the other half of the window, the sun, is yang. This is what Uncle Li would call a complete Tai Chi—a perfect balance or whole."

"A whole what?" Alex asks. "I think you two have made a leap I don't know about. What's the sun got to do with the Three Hares?"

"This window symbolizes everything we've just discovered. This leap in human evolution has to do with two things: what goes on in the sky, and this spin—this torus energy that unites everything. This one window combines both concepts!"

"Torus energy?" Alex asks. "As in torsion?"

"Exactly!"

"In Dunhuang, when we looked at the Three Hares really closely," Justine explains, "it became clear that it was a symbol about spinning the Flower of Life in three dimensions."

"You're saying if you spin a 3D version of the Flower of Life you get a torus?"

"You actually know what a torus is?" I ask.

"Of course; it's like a donut."

"Right! Neither of us knew that. Crappy American education."

"And what does torsion have to do with anything?"

"It has to do with everything! From a teeny proton up to a black hole, everything spins and creates torsion energy. And that includes DNA and—most incredibly—the heart."

"The heart?"

"Yeah," Justine says, "the seven muscles of the heart are situated perfectly so that when they squeeze blood through your body it creates this vortex of magnetic energy in a torus shape."

"And can you guess what that vortex creates?" I ask.

"Rainbows? Unicorns?" Alex says. "Look, you're beyond me now."

"No, just stay with us for a moment. This spin creates *gravity.*"

"So DNA creates gravity? The pumping of the *heart* creates gravity?" he asks.

"Every tiny thing, every speck of dust, every planet in orbit, every galaxy—they all spin. Which means gravity is a byproduct—energy is the expansion, gravity is the contraction.

Constantly, over and over and over again. Nothing is ever lost or gained, only transformed."

"So we humans are affecting the gravitational field?"

"Yup," confirms Justine.

"Now think about that line in the poem in the hidden room that says, '*Like gravity, love is a force of great might, true power comes when we connect and unite*,'" I say. "Something happens when we're all on the same wavelength, connected by thought or intention or place—or all of those things."

"So all of this is connected? The Mayan calendar, the precession, the Three Hares, this new theory about torsion energy?" he asks.

"Totally," I answer. "These are all pieces of the same puzzle. All things that lead to this supposed transformation."

"And all part of what the *Fraternitas* is bent on stopping?" he asks.

Justine and I both nod.

"And have you seen or heard from them lately?" he asks.

"We've been totally under the radar. No email, no phone calls, no texting," I say. "And there's not one single sign of the *Fraternitas* knowing where we are."

Justine knocks on a wood pew for luck and I follow her lead.

Alex looks back up at the small circle of stained glass that says so much in such a little space. "Do you reckon they knew what they were drawing here, the original artist?"

"Probably a code that only those in the know could understand," I answer. "When it's here with the sun, the artist just *had* to know what it meant. Plus, the Three Hares are going counterclockwise, which is super rare. Only a small handful of hares in these symbols go counterclockwise."

"All that ying-yang stuff is lost on me, but I'll take your word for it."

"Yin, Alex," I say with a soft push to his shoulder.

A whoosh of air blows through the building, making the fire of the candles wave and dance. Instinctively, we all hit the ground and army-crawl to the door. Alex pops his head up to see if it's clear and then opens the door for us. I didn't think I could run any faster than I did running up through the graveyard, but I do. My feet barely touch the ground as we run through the dark night to the warm glow of town. Mr. Papers keeps up with us, which is pretty amazing considering his age.

Once in town, we ditch into an alley and wait to make sure we weren't followed. We're all doubled over, gasping for breath.

After a few minutes, we realize no one followed us and Alex walks us to our place. I'm not at all hungry but I can't bear to say goodbye to Alex, so I suggest we have dinner in the little restaurant of our hotel. I figure if Clath comes down it will be easy enough to explain Alex away as a guy we just met.

Justine, being the best friend in the whole world, eats her soup in record time and then yawns and says she's going to hit the hay. I eat as slowly as humanly possible to let these last moments linger. Over tea and dessert, I fill Alex in on what we learned on our trip to Atala, careful to never mention the place itself.

Just as I'm trying to figure out in my head what saying goodbye will look like, Clath comes in to the restaurant with a tray of dishes. She looks at us with a furrowed brow and comes straight over.

"Feeling better, Caity?" she asks suspiciously.

"Yes, finally better enough to eat. Dr. Clath, this is … I'm sorry, was it Roger?"

"Robert," Alex answers.

"Nice to meet you," Clath says. "You from here?"

Alex shakes his head. "On holiday with my family."

"We were both eating alone so we started chatting," I say.

"Well, I see you're all finished now, so I'll walk you up. I was just bringing my room service tray down. The shepherd's pie was unbelievable."

I reluctantly get up. This was not the goodbye I wanted.

"Thanks for the chat, Robert," I say, offering my hand. He shakes it and gives it a secret squeeze.

"Pleasure was all mine," he says.

Then there's nothing I can do but turn and walk away with my prison warden.

Just as we're about to reach the stairs I feel a hand on my shoulder. "Miss, you forgot your receipt," Alex says, handing me a piece of folded paper.

When I get to the room I immediately unfold the paper to see what it says. It's an email address. We'd forgotten to decide on a name and password so he'd jotted one down:

Username: Creid.Rùn@gmail.com
Password: FuaighCruitheachd

Justine looks over my shoulder. "Random," she says. "Like we'll ever remember that."

164

"I will," I say clutching the paper to my chest. "It's Gaelic for *Believe love connects universe.*"

"That is the most romantic thing I've ever heard!"

"It's carved into the tower at the castle, in twelve-foot-high letters made of cups and rings."

"Was Professor Davis just talking about cups and rings?"

"Yep. They're symbols found all over Scotland that no one has been able to explain. But I think, like Professor Davis, that they're pictures of toruses."

"*Tori,*" Justine says with a smile. "Like cacti."

I burn the piece of paper in the bathroom sink so it never falls into the wrong hands.

Then, falling back on my bed with a sigh, I close my eyes and recreate our goodbye—with much less Clath and her drugstore shoes and much more kissing.

TWENTY-SIX

I wake up in a sweat, panicked about something I can't put my finger on. My heart beating too fast to get back to sleep, I roll over and look at the clock. It's five in the morning and still pitch black out. Could I sneak out and try to find Alex's hotel? No, after the lava caves under Easter Island, the thought of being alone in the dark without anyone knowing where I am freaks me out too much.

Justine and Papers are still sleeping soundly, so I decide not to turn on the lights or TV. I grab my laptop and open my email. Though I'm not allowed to send outgoing mail, I always check for any incoming email from school. There's a new message sent by a random account I've never seen. The subject line says, "UNCLE."

Uncle Li?

This unnerves me since we're not supposed to be communicating. Shaking, I open it up. The message says, *I log in to a safety site at least once every twelve hours. If you are receiving this email, it is because I was not able to log in and it was automatically sent. Proceed with caution on your path. As always, follow your heart—the heart is known as The Emperor for good reason. Li*

"Oh *no!*" I say. "No!"

"What the—" Justine yells, sitting up in bed.

I show the email to her, my mind spinning too fast to hold a thought.

"What do I do, Justine? Tell me what to do!" At this point I'm walking around and shaking my hands like they're covered in flies.

"First, you need to calm down," she says. "Sit down. Let's talk this through."

"I don't know what to do—I have no way of getting in touch with Bolon or any of the other Council members! They appear when they need me, but not the other way around."

"Then all we can do is wait."

"I can't wait. I can't!"

I rummage around my bag for my phone. Though I know I'm not supposed to, I call Uncle Li's number.

"Caity, think this through."

"It's the only way," I say, blocking my number and calling Uncle Li.

Each of the three rings in my ear seems louder than the one before. And then a voice.

"*Hallöchen, frauline.*"

The sound of Barend Schlacter's fake-cheery voice makes my whole body contract, like a dry heave.

"I'll go to the authorities," I say, sounding more like a kid on safety patrol than I want to.

"And how do you know *we* aren't the authorities?" he replies.

I have no answer for that.

"Really, who can you trust?"

"I'll find someone," I say. "I have proof that you exist! I can put the pieces together for—for someone."

"And this is worth to you the price of your dear Uncle Li's life?" he says. "Because that is what it will cost you."

"How do I know he's still alive?" I ask.

"I will put him on the phone."

"He has to answer a question I ask so I know it's not a recording."

"Fine, one question. Ask him what day it is and then you will know he is alive."

"Okay."

"You are now on speaker phone. Ask your question."

I put my phone on speaker too. Justine and Mr. Papers lean in to hear.

"Uncle Li, it's Caity," I say. "Can you tell me what day it is on the Mayan calendar?"

"Hello Caity," he answers in a shaky voice. "I'm a bit confused about the Gregorian date but on the Sun Shield calendar—forgive me, I mean the Pieces of the Sun calendar—I believe it is Eight Ahau."

"Are you okay?" I ask.

"Rise iron mug!" Uncle Li shouts. I hear a thud and then Schlacter screaming, "Do you *want* me to kill you?" at him.

Then the phone clicks off of speaker and Barend Schlacter comes back on. "Fool."

I look at Justine—it seems like she might start to cry.

"What do you want? What can I do?" I beg. Hearing Uncle Li so confused has weakened me.

"You know what we want," he says. "The books. The Sanskrit books."

"But I don't have them. I have no idea where they are."

"Well, you'd better find them then, yes?"

"I'll try," I say.

"No, you *will*," he replies. There's a moment of silence I don't know how to fill before he says, "*Guten tag*," and hangs up.

I have to consciously focus on not throwing up.

"What do I do?" I ask Justine.

She just shakes her head and says, "We are so in over our heads."

"I don't think he's okay. He was totally confused—it's nowhere near Eight Ahau."

"I know. It's weird to hear him so disoriented. And what was the 'Rise Iron Mug!' thing about?"

"I have no idea," I say. "In all the time I've known him I've never heard him mention an iron mug."

Mr. Papers hops over and grabs some origami paper. I don't know if he's building a distraction or an answer, but we watch closely. It's complex, with lots of folding and stacking.

Out of the blue, Justine jumps up. "Wait, what if those were clues?" she says. "What if his mistakes were deliberate?"

"You mean the date?" I open my laptop as Justine writes down exactly what he said. "And the name of the calendar. Instead of calling the *Tzolk'in* 'Pieces of the Sun,' he called it the 'Sun Shield' and he gave the date as Eight Ahau."

"You could be totally right!"

Wondering how anyone figured anything out before the Internet, I put *sun shield* and *8 Ahau* into the search engine.

"Bingo!" I say as the results pops up. "Uncle Li was talking about Pacal the Great! The famous ruler of the Mayan city of Palenque was called 'Sun Shield' and 'Eight Ahau'!"

Mr. Papers comes over holding the creation he's been so deliberately making—a 3D image of what I'm looking at on my computer screen: the Temple of Inscriptions at Palenque where Pacal is buried.

"Palenque?" I ask Mr. Papers. He nods vigorously, then goes over to my suitcase and starts rummaging around.

"What's he looking for?" Justine asks.

I shrug. There's no telling with Papers.

He finally pulls out the old leather-bound Grimoire and brings it to me. This book of decoded symbols helped me decipher the poem back at Breidablik, so I carry it with me to keep it safe, but I'm not sure what it could do for me now. I look at each page, turning it every way possible to try and see what Mr. Papers wants me to see, but I find nothing new. I shrug at Mr. P. and he shakes his head in disappointment.

"I honestly don't get the Grimoire thing—I don't know what Papers wants me to see," I say. "But obviously we're on the right track with Palenque. That's got to be where he is."

"Then that's got to be where we go," Justine says.

"What do we tell Clath?"

"Let's find a symbol to decode or a myth to study there," she says, leaning over and pointing at my laptop. "What about Pacal's tomb? That's a pretty famous carving. There must be something in there that we could study, yeah?"

"What about the iron mug thing? What did he say?"

"He said, 'Rise iron mug!' like a command."

I try searching it and only come up with cheesy mugs you can buy and engrave. "Nothing," I tell Justine.

"Maybe it will make sense as some point," she says. "As much as any of this can really make sense," she adds.

"Yeah, maybe there's some kind of iron mug at Palenque. But for now we need to get Clath and make tracks to Mexico, ASAP."

"But what about the books?" Justine asks. "How are we going to get Uncle Li back with nothing to trade?"

"I really have no idea where the books are. Uncle Li never told me; he just said they weren't at Dunhuang. We just have to trust that Palenque will either have the books or him—or maybe both! I mean, Uncle Li's fake mistake on the date and the name of the calendar can only be interpreted one way."

Logging in to the new Gmail account, I write an email message to Alex, explaining what's happened. I promise him I'll check in to the account once a day with an update, and beg him to please get some information on where the Sanskrit books are. Then instead of hitting send I just save it to the drafts folder. That Alex is one clever boy.

Unable to just sit around, I start packing up again. "When do you think Clath gets up?" I ask Justine, who has crawled back under the covers.

"I don't know, but it's 'o-dark-thirty and we haven't had a decent night's sleep in a while. Can you at least try to rest?"

Out of respect for her, I get back into bed. But I can't possibly sleep knowing Uncle Li is out there somewhere with *them*. I try to tap into information, try to pick up something about where he is, but I'm too worked up to get anything.

Instead I just lie there stiffly, like a fallen totem pole. After a while, my mind drifts and I see the letters R I S E I R O N M U G float through my mind. They swirl like tiny kites in the air. Then it hits me: It's an anagram! It really spells something else.

I lean over to the open laptop on the nightstand and search for an anagram engine. Clicking through the first one that pops up, I put all the letters in. About 80 possible word combinations are returned, but I know the answer when I see it: GRIMOIRE SUN.

It's physically painful to have to lie there and not wake Justine again. For the first time I understand what it must be like to be an obsessive compulsive hand washer or a Tourettic person who thinks their head might explode if they don't shout some random word.

So instead I reach for the Grimoire, once again scouring it for something related to the sun. I find nothing. Then I start really looking at the symbols in the Grimoire and thinking about the anagram. Each one of the seven decoded symbols has a letter under it, which gets me thinking about anagrams. What if there's a message here, too?

I put the seven decoded letters, V A Y D C I N, into an anagram engine. When I see the first word that pops up I laugh out loud. DAVINCY. What is this, a Tom Hanks movie?

It's phonetic but spelled wrong, but in this case there isn't a way to indicate how to use two letter Is.

Would da Vinci have anything to do with this? He was kind of into science so maybe it has something to do with the spinning vortex and gravity thing. I search da Vinci + torus expecting a long shot at most, and am astonished to see the first thing that comes up is an article on da Vinci and the Flower of Life. I click through to see two pages of drawings he did of the mathematical properties of the Flower of Life and, even more incredible, a drawing of it *spinning*! He totally knew that when you spin the 3D version of the Flower of Life you get a torus, the underlying structure of everything.

I'm still amazed at the mystery of the Flower of Life. How can one design hold so much information? Unable to remember what the poem in the hidden chamber exactly said about it, I open up my sketchbook to refresh my memory.

You know of the hares and their unity knot
Now find what the Flower of Life sits atop
It holds sacred knowledge from tribes of the earth
Wisdom essential for new world rebirth

It's all starting to come together. The pieces, the clues. More than five hundred years ago, Leonardo da Vinci was playing with this knowledge—knowledge the *Fraternitas* worked hard to suppress.

Can one girl, her best friend, and a monkey really change all that?

TWENTY-SEVEN

When Justine finally wakes up, I practically explode with words, telling her about the two anagrams. She, too, has to look at the Grimoire, but she doesn't see anything related to the sun either. The da Vinci thing kind of freaks her out.

"So you think we should mention this to Clath?" she asks.

"You mean in case it's important for Professor Davis?"

"Yeah, I mean, he was pretty interested in finding old references to the spinning Flower of Life that make a torus, and da Vinci is like the godhead of stuff like that."

"Can we somehow work that into why we need to go to Palenque?" I wonder out loud.

"Maybe we should just wrap it up into the Three Hares stuff to make that paper more interesting."

"I still don't know what angle we're going to use for going

to Palenque. I wonder if Didier is on alert for students traveling to any Mayan ruins after the whole email thing."

Justine laughs. "Man, if he even knew how many people he got to visit the website after his little tantrum in the auditorium!"

"Seriously."

"Well, old myths are part of our secondary study—we could use that as a reason to go to Palenque."

"Actually, that's perfect. We won't even mention the calendar; we'll just go to study their old, old myths."

Justine and I write a note to Clath saying we'd like to go to Palenque, adding some choice bits about how this was the place our parents were most interested in us studying. All I can think about while I'm writing the email is Uncle Li and his cryptic pleas for us to go to Palenque. This has to work. It has to.

We slide a note under Clath's door and then shower and start packing. After we're dressed, I open up the curtain to a clear blue sky and the three of us wince from the brightness. Chattering, Mr. Papers runs to my bag and pulls out the Grimoire I've just packed.

"What's he doing?" Justine asks as we watch him walk to the windowsill.

"I can never tell," I say.

Papers has the Grimoire in a shaft of sunlight, loosely opened so the pages fan themselves out. He's staring at the book like a cat watching a mouse that it's about to pounce on. Justine and I move closer but still can't tell what's going on.

Suddenly he opens to a particular page and holds it to

the sun. Sensing what's about to happen, I run over to see it. Lines start to appear, first faintly, then darker.

I remember back to Bolon telling me that if I ever had a problem to solve, look to the sun. I kind of thought he meant metaphorically. I can't believe I didn't think of this.

He hands me the book to hold in the sun and then goes to grab the Palenque origami he made.

"This is Palenque?" I ask, pointing to what looks like a map. He nods.

Justine has not said a word. I think we just blew her mind.

"Justine, hold this open while I get my sketchbook. Who knows if this is like a one-time thing or what!"

Justine sits on the windowsill and holds the book while I sketch the map of a hidden tunnel and room under the ruins of Palenque.

"You know we still have to go up to the church with Clath and pretend we've never seen that stained glass of the Three Hares," she says.

"Yeah. We can make it quick. On the way up there we should tell her we've already formed some opinions based on a photo we saw and that seeing it in place will just be a good double check."

I finish drawing out what we found in the Grimoire just as the shaft of sunlight moves. In moments, the lines fade back and hide in the paper fiber.

Clath's knock at the door startles us. I quickly put the sketchbook and Grimoire away as Justine answers the door.

"Got your note about Palenque," Clath says without so

much as a good morning. "Fine plan. Love that you girls are always thinking about what's next."

"We just need a minute to pack and we'll be all set," I tell her.

She rolls her suitcase in and sits at the small desk. "Great. I'll just wait here, then."

Justine and I carelessly stuff our things into our bags as Clath tells us that she's called the pilot to meet us at the local airport so we don't have to drive back to Cambridge, which feels like a huge relief. The sooner we get to Palenque, the sooner we can find Uncle Li.

Out trip to the church goes as smoothly as Justine and I had planned. Clath seemed impressed with our interpretation of the odd addition of the sun into the Three Hares symbol, immediately texting Professor Davis with the information. "He was very impressed by you two," she adds, as if it's the most shocking fact ever.

We settle into the plane for a very long flight. Since we're using a small plane we can fly right into the small airport by Palenque, but we have to stop for fuel twice along the way. Clath tells us that once we're in Palenque, we must plan an itinerary for the next few weeks because the school is not going to look favorably on much more inefficient, spontaneous travel.

————

After being in Scotland and England, so far from the equator, Palenque looks bright. Burn-your-eyes bright. We drop our stuff at the hotel, including Mr. Papers, whom I don't dare take out of the carrier. I hear that howler monkeys are all over this place and I'm afraid he'll get attacked. So I set him up in our room with a fresh papaya and a bottle of water before we meet Clath and our guide back in the lobby. Clath has planned for us to take a general tour this first day to get the lay of the ruins, then says she'll do more one-on-one stuff the rest of the week.

The ancient city of Palenque is enormous. It's hard to believe the Maya could build such amazing things with just measuring cords and rough tools. And the tomb where the great ruler Pacal is buried is a feat of engineering. They built the massive tomb so that it could never be removed by setting it in a burial chamber and then building the temple over and around it. Only a skinny staircase led in and out of it so that Pacal and his tomb would never be able to be carried out. To this day, he rests there, unlike so many others who were uprooted and put in museums, most often in countries not their own.

We pass Pacal's tomb in the Temple of Inscriptions and cross a stream to a group of smaller temples. When we get to the Temple of the Sun, I watch the hair on my forearm stand on end even though it's more than 100 degrees here. Something is beneath this place. Something we need to find.

There are far too many people here to try the door that's marked in the Grimoire. As much as it sends a chill through me to think about, we will have to ditch Clath somehow and come back here at night.

At the end of the day, we part with our guide and walk out the back way down a path by the river. It's beautiful and quiet and timeless. I stop to investigate the ruins of what were houses—stone walls still in place but missing roofs—cobbled together like hives. One of these stone structures has a staircase, which I want to climb so I can see what's down the hill on the other side. As I approach it, I spy a mound of tiny fire ants. This sparks an idea.

After I quietly cover the mound with leaves, I ask Clath to take a picture of me and Justine. It's evil, but I figure it's the only way. I call Clath over and ask her to take a photo of us on the top of the staircase. She stands just beyond the hill of biting ants, so I ask if she'll move a little closer. Then I ask her to take another, and another, and another step.

It must take a minute to feel the nips, but once she does she starts jumping around like she's walking on hot coals. Justine and I rush over to help her, but the ants are everywhere. She has to take off her socks and shoes and walk into the river to get them all off.

She scratches her legs the whole walk back to the hotel. We ask if she'd like to go to the restaurant with us, but she says no, she's got to go back to her room and take some Benadryl to stop the itching. *Perfect*, I think. Nothing makes you sleep as soundly as a dose of Benadryl.

At the hotel gift shop, Justine and I buy a detailed map of Palenque, a couple of flashlights so we have backups, two candles, and a lighter in case our backups need backups. There is no way I'm going to be stranded in that place in the dark.

We wait until eleven (when it seems that the staff is no longer walking around the grounds) to make our move. This time Mr. Papers refuses to be left behind, and he attaches himself to my shoulder.

It's only about a quarter of a mile to the ruins, but the

thickness of the trees block out any light from the sky. The eerie sound of howler monkeys—which is much more like jaguars roaring than monkeys—has my heart jumping like beads of water in a hot pan. Mr. Papers has his arms *and* legs around my neck so tightly it feels like I'm wearing a knotted scarf.

We decide to jog to make this all go faster—there's something about the pace of walking that makes you feel less in control, like you are at the mercy of whatever might be out there.

When we see the sign for the entrance to the ruins, we peel off the road and into the jungle. There's really no way to completely enclose the ruins of Palenque; they just sort of end in the thicket of forest. There are guards in areas where people can drive up, but since we're walking through the woods and crossing the stream to get in, we can remain unseen as long as we keep our flashlights low and pointed down. The dirt is well packed and the brush is not that thick—thankfully, decades of archaeologists traipsing around have made the jungle surrounding Palenque pretty easy to get through.

We cross the shallow stream that we had scoped out earlier in the day, which puts us behind the Cross group of temples. From there, the ruins are set in a large, open grassy area with no high trees to block the bit of light coming from the night sky. We turn off our flashlights and walk quickly to the base of the massive *El Palacio*, The Palace, with its high tower that intrigued us this morning. Before we follow the map and go underground, we can't resist standing where great Mayan kings stood centuries before gazing up into the sky.

Once we're around the back side of *El Palacio*, we find

the small door that leads to the pitch-black tunnels that twist their way up and around the inside of it. In the tunnel, I turn the flashlight back on. The temperature drops in the stone passageway and all noise is blocked out. The only thing we hear is our own breathing.

Pausing at a massive slab—the very slab where Pacal would have lain down and meditated in the cool air when it got too hot outside—I put my hand to the flat stone and feel it sucking the warmth from my own body, as it did his.

A tiny staircase leads us to the flat top of the building, the highest place you can go without walking up the stairs of the tower set atop this structure. Turning off my flashlight, I emerge from the dark to a dome of stars. Not one cloud blocks the sky.

"Unbelievable," Justine whispers, moving her head in all directions to see the sky.

"I wish there was a way to see it all at once," I say.

I grab her hand and we walk to an area where there is a recessed rectangle. The guide told us that back in the day this was filled with water, like a rooftop pool, so astronomers and kings could watch the movement of the sky in its reflection. We take the steps down into the pool, now empty with its bottom covered in short grass instead of water.

Lying on our backs on the grass and looking up, we try to take it all in. Mr. Papers finally relaxes his grip on my neck and lies beside us on the grass, gazing up. As these billions of stars burn light years away, the sky looks like it's throbbing.

"What a trip, to be seeing the same thing Pacal saw centuries ago," I say, more to myself than Justine.

"It's not so hard to believe, you know."

"What?" I ask.

"That we are all connected. That all of this is just one gigantic organism."

"I know. How can we *not* be affected by where we are in relation to these massive fiery things?"

"I think if more people looked up at the stars, we'd all be better off."

We stay there for a while, both mesmerized by how the pulses of light we see above us seem to be synchronized with the sound of the jungle, which is humming with night sounds.

"Are you afraid of what we'll find in the hidden room?" Justine asks.

"A little," I admit. "I guess I'm afraid of what we *won't* find—I'm not sure what will happen if I can't get those books."

"Well, I guess we'd better go find out," she says.

Silently, we walk back down the way we came up and then over a small bridge from *El Palacio* to a group of three temples that face each other—the Temple of the Sun, the Temple of the Foliated Cross, and the Temple of the Cross. I was drawn to the smaller one today, the Temple of the Foliated Cross, because it's tiny and wonky and a little overgrown with weeds. But it's the more spectacular one across from it that we climb.

At the top, in the back corner of one of the tiny chambers, there's a small chink in the rock. This is the door marked on the map. I cannot bring myself to stick my finger in it, so I use the end of one of the long candles I bought in the gift shop. When Justine sees the wax crumble, she pushes me away. "I'll do it," she says, sticking two fingers into the dark hole. After feeling around for longer than I ever would, she manages to move something. One of the thick stone panels that I thought was a wall rotates just enough to reveal a very skinny, very dark staircase.

"Mr. Papers?" I say, handing him a flashlight. "Would you?"

He looks at me and rolls his eyes. Instead of taking the cheap tourist flashlight I was offering, he reaches for my big metal flashlight and shines it down the opening. No snakes, no critters—so far so good.

Since Justine bravely stuck her fingers in the hole, and Papers is going first, I suck it up and follow. I have to turn sideways to even fit, and once I get a few feet down, I can no longer see my feet; the staircase is too narrow and steep. I just feel for each step. Justine has her hand on my shoulder and is feeling her way behind me. After about twenty stairs, we reach the ground. We are under the *Templo del Sol*, the Temple of the Sun.

The space widens just a bit, enough for us to walk side by side. Having memorized the map, I know we have to follow this tunnel almost the whole distance of the base of the pyramid in order to reach the room.

Neither of us is talking; we're both breathing heavily and walking as quickly as we can. The farther we go, the more panicked I'm feeling about getting stuck down here. Just as I fear I might start hyperventilating, the tunnel turns. Right after the turn is a stone door. Mr. Papers gives it a push and it rotates open, this time to reveal a smaller door covered in silver and decorated with glyphs.

I pull on the handle, shocked to find the room behind it already glowing with light.

TWENTY-EIGHT

Bolon is sitting on a small stool in the corner of this room, every inch of it lined in gold.

"*In lak'ech*," he says, standing up to greet us.

Justine grabs my hand, digging her fingernails in with fear.

"Hi, Bolon," I say, giving him a huge hug. This is *exactly* who we need to see right now.

Justine swallows a couple of times as if her mouth has gone completely dry with the shock, and then comes over to meet him.

"Wow, I'm not sure I actually believed you existed," she says as he hugs her.

"Maybe I don't," he replies with a smile. "Who is to say?"

"Well, I'm really glad to meet you, even if you do talk in riddles."

Justine and I look around, dumbfounded by the gold everywhere we look.

"Is this real gold?" I ask.

"It is, yes."

"It's so beautiful," Justine says. "May we touch it?"

"Yes, of course. Just don't press too hard on the glyphs. This gold is quite soft."

Every inch of the walls is covered in Mayan hieroglyphs and drawings. I gently touch a wall, surprised to find it's not cold. The beauty is overwhelming, yet I can't fully appreciate it because of the weight of the secret I'm keeping.

"Bolon, I have to tell you something," I say. My voice gives away the fact that it's not good news.

"What is it, Caity?" Bolon asks with concern.

"They have Uncle Li," I blurt out. "Barend Schlacter has him and I don't know where. But they need the books and I didn't know what to do, except to come here."

For the first time since I heard about Uncle Li, I start crying. Maybe I felt I needed to be strong until I could transfer control to someone else. Bolon puts his arm around my shoulders and I lean into him, into the familiar scent of wood and fire and spice that seems to be at his core.

"We sensed he was missing," Bolon says. "But did he not instruct you to stay out of it should something happen to him?"

I pull back and look at Bolon. "Yes, but—"

Justine says, "You mean we're supposed to just … leave him?"

"No good will come of you two being captured, too. Let The Council handle Li. You need to focus on your mission."

"Honestly, this has gotten so complicated, I'm not really sure what my mission is," I say, wiping my eyes with my

T-shirt sleeve. When Mr. Papers sees me do this he hops up on my shoulder and dabs at my tears with his tiny hand.

"It is simple: Unite the youth and overthrow the *Fraternitas*," Bolon says. "Those two things will allow the transformation to happen so that all humans can flourish in peace."

"But what about all the other stuff? The torus from the Three Hares embedded in the Flower of Life, the fact that this is what makes gravity, the poem at Breidablik, precession, the calendar … "

"All tools and parts," Bolon answers. "Just as you could not make a car without specific tools and parts, you cannot create the world you want to see without all these."

"It's all sort of coming together for me," Justine says, "but the DNA part is what's a mystery. Is our DNA somehow going to be all different?"

"Not different, just changed," Bolon says. "Here's an example: scientists have just done DNA testing on a very, very old species of fish. What they discovered shocked them: these fish did not *develop* DNA that allowed them to move from water to land. The genes needed to make arms and legs were *in them* the whole time."

"They were carrying around the instructions for arms and legs the whole time?" I ask.

"Exactly. All the instructions were there, it was just the switches that were turned off. This confirmed what the ancients have all known: there is *infinite* potential inside of us. All that is needed for transformation is a switch, of sorts."

"So there are the genes that make our bodies and other genes that are switches?" Justine asks.

"Yes, there are genes that are switches, and still other

genes that give the switches on and off orders. It is these switches that are so receptive to the high-energy particles coming from the Galactic Center and the sun."

"And that's what will change us?"

"If we can get a clear signal. And that requires the two things I mentioned first: getting out from under the control of the *Fraternitas*, and getting the youth united in a real, coherent way."

"Coherent in, like, the wave sense, right?"

"Yes, we must get back in sync with the nesting waves that pattern the universe," he says. Then he walks over to the center of one of the gold-paneled walls. "This is the same design that is on Pacal's massive tomb lid in the *Templo de las Incripciones*, which has confounded archeologists since it was discovered a few decades ago. What do you see here?"

When I first researched Pacal, I saw this image and read that a lot of people think he's in some kind of spaceship. "It's hard to shake the spaceship thing from my mind," I say.

"Try," Bolon replies. "In light of all that you have learned, try to look at it with fresh eyes."

I stand before it and fuzz up my eyes so I stop seeing details.

I try to think like Uncle Li—when he does feng shui analysis, he always says "Form Defines Energy." He says that by looking at a form, you can predict its energy or movement. I can see why people would think Pacal is in some kind of spaceship; he's reclined in a container and looking up. But then I notice that the sides of this thing he's in are drawn to show that they are in motion. Once I see it that way, it looks as if Pacal is being sucked in—or through—this thing.

I run my fingers up the side of the thing that he's in, and follow the momentum. He's falling into a hole, a victim of gravity, but below him it looks like energy is flowing out again.

"A torus!" I yell. "This is a cross section of a torus!" Gold seems to absorb sound in a weird way, so my voice sounds strange and loud and powerful. "Look, Justine—don't you think the walls of this show him being sucked in?"

"Totally! And the bottom shows the energy shooting back out and up. Just like being sucked into a donut hole and then pushed out the bottom."

"Is that right, Bolon? Is that what this carving is about?" I ask.

Bolon smiles and nods. "This is about *above and below*, the big and the small. All things at the smallest level follow this energetic torus pattern when we live naturally, unobstructed. And where is the energy centered in this carving?"

"The exact center is right between his two hands," Justine says.

"Which, according to feng shui, means that's where the source energy is," I add. "He's definitely doing something intentional with his hands."

"If you had to guess, what would you say?" Bolon asks.

"It looks like expansion and contraction, the same energy that the torus produces."

"Very good. What Pacal is doing with his hands is called making *mudras*."

"Oh, right!" I say. "Some of Uncle Li's friends taught me *mudras* when I was little. All I can remember is the meditation one, probably because I saw Uncle Li do it a million times."

"Wait, what's a *mudra*?" Justine asks.

"It's like a symbolic hand pose," I say. "It's from India, but Buddhists use them, too." Digging out a piece of paper and a pencil from my backpack, I place it over the picture and gently take a rubbing, making sure I don't press too hard.

"*Mudras* are powerful things," Bolon says. "This very ancient practice was recently researched and it was proved that these hand gestures stimulate the same regions of the brain as language."

"Wow! I love that science is now testing out ancient practices," I say, amazed at being able to see the picture come to life on my blank paper as I rub.

"I seriously don't get how all of this stuff is now being proven by science," Justine says. "It's freaky how much they knew about the body and space without instruments or computers."

"When you are in sync with time and space, sometimes those things are unnecessary. They were able to tap into areas of the brain we have yet to unlock. But that is where you two come in, isn't it?"

When I'm finished, I place the paper with the rubbing

gently in my notebook so it won't get smudged. "Wait a sec, can we go back to Pacal's hand *mudras*? Are they really ancient Indian *mudras*?"

"They are, yes. His left hand is in *Sarpasirsha,* male snake energy, and his right hand is in *Kapitha*, divine female energy. Again, he is teaching us how the universe works. The snake is expansion, radiation, waves. The divine feminine is attraction, gravity, pulling in."

"And growing out of the center of these things is the great tree," I say, finally seeing the whole picture. "That's the symbol of the Milky Way, right?"

"Yes. Our recycling center. Pacal is shown descending into the mouth of the earth monster only to be shot back out through the Milky Way. As you know, every atom in your body has at one time been part of star stuff, and will be again. We are ordered, or put together, by the great consciousness. And it is time for our consciousness upgrade."

"*If* we can overcome the *Fraternitas*," I say.

"*When* you overcome the *Fraternitas*," Bolon replies. "Once this energy is in balance, once we are able to resonate completely, unfettered by the 'noise' the *Fraternitas* is putting out, then we will grow to our full potential."

"I can't even think about taking down the *Fraternitas* until I get Uncle Li back. But we need those books. We assumed they were here because of something Uncle Li said about The Sun Shield and Eight Ahau."

Bolon stands up and walks to a corner where a gold box sits on top of long, highly decorated legs. "Come here," he says.

We walk over to the box and see a beautiful design of a

stylized butterfly. I instantly recognize it as the butterfly made by the core days in the *Tzolk'in*. When he opens the box, I see something astonishing—the same bird I've seen on the ceiling in one of those hidden-room dreams I have.

"I've seen this," I tell Bolon. "This was in the dream I had about finding a room in a house I'd lived in forever. There was this peacock head with a crystal light fixture for an eye."

"That wasn't a peacock, it was a quetzal."

"A quetzal?"

"It's a sacred bird to the Maya. It symbolizes freedom because it's one of the few birds that will die in captivity. You have heard of Quetzalcoatl, yes?"

"Yeah, he's the guy they call the Feathered Serpent, right? It's even mentioned in the poem on the wall of the castle: *'The butterfly will emerge in three different ways, At the source, at your core, and by way of the days, Called feathered serpent when spoken of in code, Connected to all by the great white road.'*"

"So the Feathered Serpent is a butterfly!" Justine says.

"Precisely. The Butterfly, or Feathered Serpent, is a symbol of transformation."

"And if the poem is right, this happens at the source, the Galactic Center. Your core, or your own DNA, and the days—what's that, like the transformation of time?"

"A new reckoning of time," Bolon says.

"What's the great white road?" Justine asks.

"The Milky Way," Bolon and I say at the exact same time.

"Jinx!" I say.

Justine hits me on the shoulder. "Don't say *jinx* in a place like this—are you crazy?"

"Oops, sorry … "

"The serpent has always been a symbol of DNA, of your inner coil. The fact that it is given wings is symbolic of the freedom, the switching on, of new DNA. We must let it fly, give it no limits, not hold it in captivity. That is what we mean by the return of the Feathered Serpent."

Bolon reaches into the gold box and pulls out something bundled in leather. Closing the lid, he places the bundle on top of the box and gently unties the leather cord.

Inside are two thin books covered in the most beautiful iridescent violet covers I have ever seen. Could these be the books the *Fraternitas* is willing to kill for?

TWENTY-NINE

So these are them?" I ask, not really believing I'm seeing what I'm seeing. "The Sanskrit books?"

"They are," Bolon says. "There are many decoys out there, but this is the last real set in existence."

"What is this made of?" Justine asks as we both reach out to touch one of the hypnotic covers.

"It's a unique combination of tree fiber and mica. Wood and mineral."

"And I have to give these to Barend Schlacter to get Uncle Li back?"

"No!" Bolon says. I've never heard him so emphatic. "No. I will deliver decoys to Barend; he will not know the difference until he takes them to be translated."

"What's in these real ones?" Justine asks.

"This is a collection of information known through the ages, collected and guarded by a group called The Nine Unknown Men. If this information gets into the hands of the

Fraternitas, we will never be free. It must stay protected at all costs."

"Like what kind of information?" I ask.

"Information on technologies that make pure water cheap and plentiful, details of how a collective consciousness on the planet will work, instructions on healing with sound and light, a sort of 'space travel' based on non-locality, how to extract clean energy from dark matter using this knowledge of spin—or tori; the list goes on."

"I don't get why this information is hidden!" I say. "This could change everything."

"Yes, it could. But this technology also has dangerous negative uses," Bolon explains. "And the people in position to exploit it, the people with the money and power to do so, will be looking at how to use this information to control the masses, not free them."

"Do the *Fraternitas* know any of this?" Justine asks.

"Unfortunately, yes," he says. "But only tiny pieces discovered from combing ancient myths. The *Fraternitas* and other aggressive nations have bits of this information. If you look at the list of projects going on in Governmental Black Operations, all are related to information contained in these two books."

"Well, then there's only one thing to do," I say.

Bolon looks confused. "What do you mean?"

"We have to publish this," I say. "Worldwide."

"But then the *Fraternitas* has access to it," Bolon says.

"Yeah, but so will millions of other people who can actually use this information for good!"

Bolon looks at me as if he's trying to figure out whether or not I'm joking.

"We'll start distributing it through our underground network so that they get a head start. I can email it to every kid who has signed up for the calendar tones. We're up to over a million names."

Bolon looks like he's just been tasered. "Are you serious?"

"About what?" I ask. "The number of kids we can contact or that I want to send this information out?"

"Both," he says.

"Totally. I mean, I know this is above the heads of a lot of these kids, but some would absolutely know what to do with this information. We can publish it on the hidden website that you can't get to unless you can hear the instructions in the super-high frequency, which means that only people twentyish and younger can hear it."

"She's right," Justine says. "If the *Fraternitas* is not the only one with the information, then they can't control it. I mean, if this was the *sole* reason the Internet was invented, it would be worth it!"

Bolon's look softens. "You may have a point. We've just spent so many centuries guarding this information that it's frightening to think about putting it out there."

As he pulls at his chin, his eyebrows furrow. "I'd always thought of placing it directly in the hands of the few people who would do the most good."

"Maybe we *are* the ones who can do the most good."

Bolon smiles.

"At least that's what you've been telling me this whole

time," I say. "That it's kids who are going to lead this revolution."

"You mean *evolution*," he says.

"Right—kids will lead the *evolution*. But we have to get this information out there. Hiding it is just what the *Fraternitas* wants."

"I suppose you have a point."

"Seriously, this is information for the world, yeah?"

"It is. But the prophecy says that it cannot be used for good until a shift happens."

"But what if releasing the information is part of the shift?"

He shrugs. "It's an excellent point, Caity. Really. It's just going to take a moment to get used to the idea."

"Think about it—lots of people that signed up for the calendar tones have .edu addresses. If college students repost this to their college groups, imagine what could happen! Getting this kind of information into the hands of kids who are at big research schools can totally fuel new projects!"

Once he really absorbs what is happening, Bolon agrees. "Okay. But first you must translate, which means finding a scholar you trust implicitly."

"Tenzo," I say. "Tenzo can do it."

"Alright then," he says, tying the books back up in the piece of leather. He hands me the package. "I trust you will know when the time is right."

When I take the books, all I think is, *I should not be the one in charge of these.*

Bolon looks me in the eyes and says, "Yes, you should."

After closing the gold box, he blows out the candle that

lit the room. "We must go," he says, leading us back through the dark tunnel and up the tiny staircase. He doesn't use a flashlight, so we don't either. When your senses are on high alert, it's amazing how much you can perceive without any light.

The smell of fresh night air mingling with the dense air of the tunnel as we near the exit makes me think of Uncle Li. Makes me wonder if he is in some dank cell somewhere, under the hold of Barend Schlacter.

"Do you think he's okay?" I ask as we walk out into the open air.

"I am not sure," Bolon says. "I will try my best to get him released. It breaks my heart, but it is what we all knew might happen when we joined The Council."

"Is it worth it?" Justine asks.

I was thinking the same thing, but was afraid to say it out loud.

"If you knew of all the atrocities indigenous people have suffered at the hands of the greedy, you would agree that the answer is yes," Bolon says. "It is easy to sacrifice one's self if it is for the benefit of millions of others."

Justine doesn't look at me but I know what she's thinking.

Will we have to be sacrificed, too?

Bolon walks us through the jungle to where we can meet up with the road. Before he leaves, he holds onto my shoulders and looks me right in the eye. His dark skin glistens like a child's in the night's dim light, but his eyes seem old and tired.

"We are so proud of you, Caity. Stay on the white path and speak the truth. Release the Feathered Serpent."

"When will I see you again?" I ask. "I don't know where to go next."

"It is time for a talk with *your* council. With the hundreds of thousands of young people who are ready to change the world."

"Here? Here in Palenque? But I'm not sure I can get it together that quickly ... "

"You will," he says in that way he has. "I will make sure the gate leading to the observation tower at the top of The Palace is left open. At sundown when they close the site, sneak up there and close the gate behind you. They will never look up there when they clear the grounds. You will get a good signal from there—a good signal in every way."

I glance at Justine and she just shrugs, as if to say, *Don't look at me, I'm not the one telling you what to do.*

We say goodbye to Bolon at the edge of the jungle. As we walk a few steps down the road I hear "*In lak'ech,*" but by the time I turn around he is no longer there.

"Dude," Justine says as we walk back though the dark.

"I know," I say, feeling the full weight of what's in my backpack.

THIRTY

As we walk back to the hotel, we plan tomorrow's talk, agreeing that the best way to do it would be a live streaming audio. That is, if I can get Alex to build me some kind of application that takes my voice and translates it to Mosquito Tone.

By the time we get back, it seems like even the jungle has quieted down. I can feel my mood lighten as my sense of safety increases on the paved lit paths through the hotel grounds. The lights in our cabana are off, but by the light of our porch I see someone sitting on the railing outside our door. I grab Justine's arm and stop.

"What's up?" she says, looking around for the reason I stopped.

"Don't worry, *amies*," comes a voice from the porch. "It is just me, Jules D'Aubigne."

This does nothing to calm my nerves.

We walk up to our cabana and Jules extends his hand. "*Mon plaisir*," he says as he shakes both of ours.

"Wow, what are you doing here?" I ask. This doesn't come out very friendly, but I'm really confused. Plus I'm distracted by the way he smells. It's not as strong as cologne, maybe a hair product or a face lotion or something. Whatever it is, it's incredible.

"Same thing you are. I'm studying," he says, hopping off the railing.

"Studying what?" Justine asks suspiciously.

"The Mayan calendar, of course," he answers.

"Didn't Didier say we weren't supposed to study that?" I ask, sounding like a playground tattletale.

He waves the thought away. "For what my parents have given this school, I can study whatever I want," he says. "Beside, who says he has to know?"

"Doesn't your Pedagogue have to clear this stuff with the Research and Curriculum departments?" Justine asks.

Jules laughs. "What is it with you two? I don't understand why you are so interested in my studies. Can't we just have a nice chat?"

Justine uses her key to open the door, and Mr. Papers scurries in, unseen by Jules. "I can't stay awake one more minute," she says. "Caity, chat all you want."

I look at his face carefully to see if there's any trace of disappointment. I'm assuming it's Justine that Jules wants to spend time with. Instead, he smiles and says, "*Bonsoir.*"

"Shall we sit?" he asks, gesturing to the two rocking chairs on our porch.

Out of sheer curiosity, I say, "Uh, sure." Having seen a

fist-sized spider on the porch earlier, I run my flashlight over every inch of the chair before I sit down.

"So what were you two girls doing out in the jungle at night?" he asks with a smile. Every time his rocker moves I get a whiff of his amazing scent. I'm sure I smell like BO and the salsa I splashed on my shirt at dinner. Lovely.

I hug my backpack, not wanting to have it out of sight or mind. "Just a little night walk around the grounds. Lots of amazing sounds in the jungle at night."

"I've been waiting here for the better part of three hours," he says. "You must have circled the grounds a hundred times."

"How about you don't worry about what we're doing and we won't worry about what you're doing?" I'm getting a little irritated.

"Fair enough," he says.

We make small talk for a while, in which I get to finally use all the facts I'd made up about my Luxton heritage. I must say, I'm pretty good at weaving that tale. I'm absolutely bone tired, but the fact that I'm sitting in the dark with Jules D'Aubigne keeps me wired.

After a while the sounds of the jungle shift noticeably. Not long after that, the light changes. I hate seeing sunrise when I haven't slept; it's incredibly depressing.

"It's almost sunup," I say. "I suppose we should get a little sleep before we start our day."

He nods and stands up, then reaches down for my hand. In one fluid movement, he pulls me up and into him. Since I'm still hugging my backpack, it ends up between us, so he takes it and sets it on the chair.

I am not moving. I am not breathing. I am not thinking.

I am only there, being held closely by this tall handsome creature who smells like everything good in the world rolled into one single scent. He lifts my chin and then puts his lips on mine. My heart fires like a round of caps.

Oh, no.

When he steps back he says, "I've wanted to do that since I met you." Then he leans down to pick up my backpack and hands it back to me.

"Uh, thanks," I say. I hold it tight to my chest and watch him walk off into the dusty morning light.

I can't possibly tell Justine about this. I can't tell anyone. Maybe it was a dream. Or maybe if I think of it that way it will become one.

Too distracted and buzzed to sleep, I leave a message in the draft folder for Alex, telling him I've been instructed to do another talk. I ask if he can build some plug-in application for my microphone so that my voice is translated into Mosquito Tone and also ask him to post something on the hidden website about another gathering tonight at 8 p.m. Palenque time, along with corresponding time zone times.

I am fully aware that I am asking him to do all this stuff for me right after I have kissed another boy.

No, he kissed me.

It doesn't make sense. Jules D'Aubigne could literally get any girl in the world. What would he want with me?

When I finally lay my head on the pillow I am out, and fast. When a knock on the door wakes me I'm disoriented, not sure where I am or how long I've slept. Justine sits up, looks at the clock, and then goes to the door. It's Clath.

"Hello, girls," she says, walking in. "Thought I'd let you know I'll not be going to the ruins today. After yesterday's standoff with the *hormiga roja*, I'll be seeing a local doctor and keeping my legs sterile."

I feel both terrible and relived. "Are you okay?" I ask.

"I'll be fine. I just need to get a cortisone cream and make sure none of these look infected. Doesn't hurt too bad, but it itches like the dickens."

"Sorry," I say. "Anything we can do?"

"Just your schoolwork," Clath says. "I thought the lid of Pacal's tomb was mighty rife with symbolism from the Mayan creation myth. Maybe you could take a crack at finding some correlations."

"Definitely," Justine says. She can tell I'm biting my lip so I won't laugh. "It's definitely … uh … rife."

"Let's plan to be back at it tomorrow at oh-nine-hundred."

When Clath leaves, we both start laughing. "Oh my God, do you think her head would explode if she knew what we did last night?" Justine asks.

"Totally. How perfectly is this all working out, with her staying here today?"

"Except for the surprise visit from Monsier D'Aubigne, it's been smooth sailing," she says.

"Oh, he's harmless," I say.

"Really?" she replies. Looking me dead in the eye, she asks, "You don't think he has an ulterior motive for being here?"

"What do you mean?" I wonder for a moment if Justine is jealous that we stayed out there together and talked through the night.

"It just doesn't add up, that's all."

"I know what you're thinking—that there's no way he would come here just because *I'm* here."

"Caity, that's not where I'm going with this."

"Can we just stop talking about it?"

"Fine," she says curtly, and rolls over to face the other way.

Getting up to shower, I feel the tension in the air. This is not resolved.

Justine sleeps, or at least pretends to, while I keep checking our website. Finally, I see the update announcing the talk tonight—meaning that Alex has read the draft email. I log in to the shared account to see if he's written back.

> Caity–I've been thinking about you a lot lately, wondering where you are and what you are doing. I'm glad to hear you are well. Updates have been made to the website and I've created a little app that should translate your voice into Mosquito Tone in real-time. It's in a zip folder attached to this mail.
> Good luck. Looking forward to hearing your voice, even if it is in the frequency of a blood-sucking insect. Cheers mate, Alex

After last night's kiss, my heart sinks when I read this.

I spend what's left of the day doing research, updating the website, and generally planning for the talk tonight. Justine seems distant and I hate that I let a boy come between us in any way. While I'm in the room on the computer, she's by the pool. I tell myself that sometimes a little space is a good thing.

Mr. Papers is hard at work on some origami projects but when I look over at him, he hides his work in a hotel stationary envelope. He's never done this before, but I respect his privacy so I don't pry.

Justine comes back around four, seeming more relaxed. She says she'll be all ready to go right after she showers. We need to take the bus to Palenque, go in like all the other tourists, and then stash ourselves in the observatory tower in *El Palacio* until the place closes.

Even with all the work I've done today, I'm still not sure I know what I'll say.

We make it to the door of the tower on top of The Palace and then wait for crowds to thin before we check the wire gate. Once we're alone, we try the gate, which has been left unlocked like Bolon promised. Quickly closing the gate behind us, we scramble to the top and hunker down so no one can see us. We still have an hour or so to wait. Mr. Papers has been inside my backpack—we didn't think they'd let him in here with all the howler monkeys around—so I unzip it and let him out. I see he has brought the hotel stationary envelope with him, stuffed with flattened origami.

We sit on the floor and look at the stone walls that go up about five feet. Above the walls are windows, which we need to avoid. It's kind of soothing to be deprived of sight but still be able to hear everything that's going on below us. Throngs of tourists—most of them speaking foreign languages— milling about, howler monkeys starting their early evening communication, trees blowing in the lazy breeze. Slowly, the human sounds quiet down while the jungle sounds get louder.

Well after we hear the last voice, I'm still too nervous to peek over the edge to see if it's clear. I whisper to Mr. Papers to do it; though he doesn't look like a howler he's still less conspicuous than a red-headed American girl. He hops up to the ledge and looks all around, at one point even curling his fist and holding it to his eye like a scope to get a clearer view. When he motions for us to stand up, we do it slowly and stand just tall enough to peer over the edge. It's completely clear.

The dark comes quickly once the sun sets behind the tall trees that surround the ruins. I look at the time on my laptop—7:45. *Just fifteen minutes to gather my thoughts.*

"Would you like me to wait on the steps below?" Justine asks, sensing how nervous I am. "I know how weird you are about this being a 'performance.'"

"Honestly, it has nothing to do with you. It would just be weird to do this with *anyone* watching."

"I totally get it," she replies, holding out her hand for Mr. Papers. He shakes his head and holds up his envelope. "I guess he's got info for you."

I laugh, which feels nice. I don't remember laughing all day.

Despite the tense day, my best friend descends to sit in the dark ruins below me so that I will feel more comfortable. My heart swells with love for her, and that swelling reminds me of exactly what needs to be done. When it's a few minutes before eight, I set up and rig my flashlight so my face is somewhat lit.

At eight on the dot, I start the live streaming video, hoping that Alex's app is translating it all into Mosquito Tone.

THIRTY-ONE

ello again, friends," I begin, pausing just long enough to pretend that the world is saying hello back. I feel that coldness at my core that I remember from last time I did one of these, and quickly visualize myself as a funnel, collecting information and condensing it out the other side.

"This time I'm coming to you from an ancient Mayan city deep in the jungle. If you hear something like the roar of a jaguar in the background, that's just the howler monkeys. This is truly a place full of mystery and wonder. But I guess it's turning out that there are many places of mystery and wonder on this planet of ours.

"Last time, I told you about this force of corruption that's controlling the world—controlling the money, the wars, the trade, even our bodies. And I said we can change that.

"We are the most powerful group to inhabit this planet in recorded history. There have never been as many people under twenty living at the same time before. We hold in our hands—actually our hearts—the power to change this course of corruption and the course of our own evolution.

"I have been told that *everything* is consciousness. That we shouldn't keep asking how our brain evolved to a level of consciousness because the real question is, how did consciousness evolve our brain? It is freaky, when you really think about it. I mean, how did what started as a cluster of hydrogen atoms eventually become a human that is conscious of itself? And why? What is the next level? If we apply the *As above, so below* theory, then each little part has to look like the whole. We are moving from just being humans who are aware of our own selves, to a bigger collective organism that is aware of itself."

I wonder for a second if anyone is listening and then decide it doesn't matter. What matters is that I tell the truth.

"The Mayan *Tzolk'in* calendar that follows human cycles is 260 days long. That's a fractal of 26,000, the number of years it takes the Earth to get back to the very spot where the sun will rise on December 21, 2012. This means that the 260-day human calendar is a fractal of a larger human calendar. What started as individual consciousness 26,000 years ago could evolve into a collective consciousness now.

"I know this sounds weird, like we'll all move as one blob or something, but that's not what it's about. It's about realizing that we are, and always have been, connected. It's about using that connectedness for good."

Mr. Papers riffles through his envelope and takes out five small origami suns. I scratch behind his ears, and smile to thank him for helping guide me.

"We are entering the cycle of the Fifth Sun. The first

cycle was of feminine energy and was ruled by fire, the second cycle was of masculine energy and earth ruled it. The third cycle was feminine and air ruled it, the fourth cycle—the one we're ending now—was of masculine energy and water ruled it. The fifth cycle, the one that starts in 2012, is a cycle of harmony between masculine and feminine and ether will rule it. Ether is different from air—ether is the stuff that space is made up of, what is called 'dark energy.' It comes through us, in us, around us. I think this is fascinating because we spend the majority of our time online sending and receiving information through the ether. But ether is not being used just for good. Superpowers are spending untold dollars working toward using our upper atmosphere as a weapon and a shield; they are trying to harness the power of ether to block the energy coming to us from the Galactic Center.

"This Fifth Sun ruled by ether is where we will all connect as our consciousness becomes like the thinking layer of the Earth. There are now enough human brains to connect as one—through the ether. When this comes about, a shift will happen. This is what the Shadow Government is so afraid of.

"We are all, every one of us, just a cluster of vibrations. Nothing but energy. So how can we *not* be affected by the electromagnetic energy coming from the galaxy? After 26,000 years, our sun is once again rising in line with the center of the galaxy on winter solstice of 2012."

Next Mr. Papers takes out an origami ring. With one pull it pops up into a 3D donut, a torus.

"The black hole at the center of the galaxy is putting out more energy than we can even fathom. The calendar the Maya tuned for humans, this *Tzolk'in* calendar, was called the 'Pieces of the Sun.' Now I finally get why—because these cycles of sunspots, which are very literally 'pieces of the sun,' are what infect us with information, with consciousness. These sunspot cycles are like accelerators for whatever energy is coming from our galaxy. The year 2012 just happens to be the time when the sun rises in line with the center of the galaxy *and* we have solar storms at their maximum. Think of the energy from the galaxy like a powerstation and the sun as a power transformer that delivers the energy in a way we can consume it. This is the energy that will change us, if we allow it.

"All these ancient sites that have these mysterious old symbols of the Flower of Life and the Three Hares, these are places that hold knowledge about how the universe works—subversive knowledge that those in power don't want us to know. Even da Vinci has drawings of this, of the Flower of Life spinning and turning into a torus. This donut shape is so important on every level, from microscopic to universal. Electrons and black holes move in exactly the same way! Isn't that incredible, and yet at the same time kind of obvious? We are all just spinning energy. The trick is to spin in unison, in coherence.

"That's why we need these daily hertz tones, these vibrations that reverberate. We must become one—and I don't mean we are one in the woo-woo sense; I mean it in the physical sense.

"So maybe what the Maya meant by 2012 being 'the end of time as we know it' is merely the end of time as a linear thing. If we are truly linked, if you can be everywhere at once, then is there time? Is there space? Or is there only flux and flow?"

I see Mr. Papers looking in his envelope for something. Then he pulls out a flattened star, pops it back into its 3D origami form, and holds it on his hand like an offering. I nod.

"The oldest stories around are the stories of the stars," I say. "Years from now, even little children will think it's crazy that we didn't factor cosmic forces into evolution, that we thought we were untouched by the energy around us. It's like us looking back to when people insisted the world was flat, and if you sailed too far away you'd fall off. Crazy talk! Because where things are in the sky matters.

"The corruption is deep, and it's wide. These people are brilliant. They know how to piggyback disinformation on truth. But there are cracks. Look around—the breakdown is everywhere: banking, politics, churches, corporations. What the *Fraternitas* has put in place can't hold. So they're scared and they're raising the stakes with more conflicts, more wars, more exploitation of poor people."

Next Mr. Papers pulls out a dollar, folded into the shape of a heart. A perfect piece of communication.

"We have to do a mass shift of money, just as we shift our consciousness. This is key, because only by releasing people from the bondage of the *Fraternitas* can we allow for the kind of personal freedom and love necessary for this transformation, this shift.

"There, I said it: LOVE. Love is what it will take. Remember that donut shape I was talking about, the torus? Science can now demonstrate that the muscles in the heart make a torus-shaped energy field when it pumps. The stronger the feelings of love, the stronger the field gets. How beautiful is that? Now do you see why it's so important for the *Fraternitas* to keep us in a state of fear and panic? So that our waves cancel each other out.

"We are all part of a vast universe expanding and contracting as it spins. The expanding part creates energy, radiating light and energy outward; the contraction part creates gravity, holding on. On every level, it's just one big in-and-out breath. We, like all other things in this universe that spin in this way, *create* gravity!

"There is nothing we cannot do. We are full of infinite creativity, infinite possibility, infinite love.

"Connect now, this moment, with a feeling of love. Love for a person, for a pet, for a parent. The *Fraternitas*, the Shadow Government, has been trying to keep us off balance for thousands of years. But we're finally at a place where we can take that power back. That power is within each one of us—it is literally in our hearts.

"These are rough and magical times, as the masters say. Be mindful, be heartful. And above all, remember: *we* are the ones we have been waiting for."

At that I click "stop" on the video stream and close my computer. From where I'm sitting, I can see a patch of sky through a window above me. I breathe deeply, trying to hold a memory of every sense—the moist, warm air; the smell of roots and trees and river water; the hard, cool stone against my back; the sight of tiny sparkling pinpricks popping through a flood of violet sky.

And for less than a second, so short a time I don't know

if it's real or an illusion, I see forms disappear and all I see is pulsing energy.

I feel it, I really do.

I feel the swell of whatever it is. Unity. Collectiveness. Oneness. It comes over me like a tide of energy, swirling, lifting my own energy with it.

"Did you just feel that?" Justine asks from below. Her voice sounds tiny and far away.

I stand up and walk down to her.

"That was amazing," I say. "I totally felt that."

"It was like being in a washing machine of energy for a minute, swirling and tumbling with the other clothes!"

"Is it over now?" I ask.

"Or are we just used to it?"

Mr. Papers shakes his head and makes a wave motion with his hand.

"Let's get back so I can listen to the recording," Justine says. "I didn't even get to hear anything! What did you say?"

I can't really remember. It's weird how stuff just sort of comes through me.

As I'm stuffing my laptop into my backpack, we hear the loudest howler monkey concert in history. All of a sudden they are all howling together, which sounds like a pack of lions all roaring at once. Mr. Papers jumps into the backpack with the laptop and burrows down.

"We gotta get out of here!" I say, zipping the pack almost closed and grabbing Justine's hand. We run down the stone steps as fast as we can, then down through the tiny, pitch-black staircase that winds through the base of the palace. For some reason it's ten times scarier than when we snuck in, maybe because the howlers are still going crazy with noise. When we finally exit the palace ruins, we sprint down the wide open grass to the back exit. Just as we're gaining speed, Justine stops abruptly.

"What?" I ask "What's wrong?"

"Wait. There's no one after us; just chill for a minute. Look up. We may never be here again. I want to remember this as a magical place, not some place I was scared of."

She's right. I look around at the ruins: the stately Temple of the Sun that hides its golden secret, the Temple of the Foliated Cross all wonky and beautiful, the grand Temple of Inscriptions fit for the king who is still entombed beneath it.

We look up at the stars and can almost see them rotating in the sky.

We are wondrous beings in a wondrous land.

THIRTY-TWO

The alarm goes off at 8:00, which we figured would give us enough time to eat and jot down some ideas for Clath, just to make it seem like we studied all day yesterday. Before I hop in the shower, I check my phone and see that I have a new text.

And then I read six little words that change my life: *Li is dead. You are next.*

"No!" I scream. "No!"

There is a hollowness to my voice, like it's been processed through a digital music program to remove all the human-ness. I fall to the floor and put my face between my knees. I have never felt anything like this.

Uncle Li is dead.

And it's all my fault for not getting to him soon enough.

Justine comes over and grabs my phone. After reading the text, she crumples to the ground next to me.

"I didn't think they'd do it. How could they do it? I thought they were bluffing!"

Justine just shakes her head and stares at the wall. "Caity, we have to call someone," she says flatly. "We have to call the police, or the FBI, or—"

I shake my head. "Justine, we do not know who to trust! We can't call the FBI! We can't call the school, we can't even tell Clath. Don't you see? *There. Is. No. One!*"

"Then what do we do? Just sit and wait to be next?"

"We have to disappear," I say. "It's the only way we'll be safe."

"Disappear? Like 'witness protection plan' disappear? Forever?"

I have to think this through for a minute.

"No. Not forever. Just until we get things under control. We both have to leave tonight—we'll get tickets and go. But you *cannot* go back to San Francisco, not right now. You need to go somewhere safe—not home."

"What? We have to split up? I can't leave you!"

"We *have* to. There's no other choice. They'll be looking for me, not you. But if you go back to San Francisco with me, they'll hunt you down too."

"I don't have anywhere else—"

"What about Princeton?" I say.

Justine closes her eyes and thinks for a minute. "I guess … "

"Actually, it's perfect—you can go stay with your grand-father and check in on Tenzo. Wait! You can take the books to Tenzo for translation! They're not safe with me."

"But where will you go? Where is it safe for you?"

"I have to go to San Francisco."

"*You* can't go there either!"

"I have to, Justine. It's time."

"For what?" she asks. "Time for what, Caity?"

"Time to take down the *Fraternitas*."

Justine looks at me as if all my teeth have just fallen out.

"I'll be fine," I say, sucking up my composure. "But first we need to get you out of here."

She nods, then points to Mr. Papers, who is in the corner making something that takes great care.

"What's he making?" she whispers. I shake my head. Whatever it is, he wants to do it in private, and he's taking his time to make it just right.

Looking online, we see a direct flight to New York leaving in four hours, so we book a seat for Justine. She starts packing up her stuff while I look for a flight for me. I find one to Los Angeles late tonight, with a connection to San Francisco.

We make paper covers for the Sanskrit books to keep them protected and to hide them from prying eyes, and then load them in the very bottom of Justine's backpack. I'm a little nervous about letting them out of my sight, but I also know this is the only way.

Just as I finish getting my things packed, Mr. Papers comes out of the corner. He's holding an origami version of what looks to be Uncle Li, lying in the middle of this big beautiful lotus blossom. It's his finest work yet, and his saddest. Walking slowly over to my bag he removes my spiral notepad and then rips the back cover off. Justine and I are both waiting to see what he'll do with this piece of card-board. After gingerly pulling off the shreds from where it was released from the spiral coil, he sets the piece flat and begins folding. A few moments in, I see what he's making: a box to protect his creation. Once the box is constructed, he puts the lotus and Uncle Li inside it and then sets it in his carrier. Apparently he has plans for it.

We decide that the safest way for her to get around will be public transportation—the subway from JFK to Grand Central Station, and then the train up to Princeton Junction. Staying lost in the crowd seems the most obvious—and com-forting—move.

I walk with her through the grounds to the lobby and we both wait outside in the muggy air for a cab. When one pulls up and I realize we have to say goodbye, it feels like my heart is being put on a skewer for roasting. How could I have brought her into this?

She grabs my hand and says, "Stay safe. Please don't do anything crazy."

I nod. "You know where the draft emails are, right?" I ask her. "Check there daily for updates."

"Okay. And when Tenzo finishes with the translation, I'll post them there."

"Lose your phone, okay?" I say. "Neither of us can have them anymore."

She nods. As I move to close the door she says, "Caity—"

"I know," I say. "I know."

I close the door because dragging this out is painful. As the cab drives away, she leans her head out the window and says, "Follow the spark, y'all!" sounding just like Arabella Bascom.

I want to run after the cab like a dog, but instead I just stand there watching the car get smaller. When it turns and I can no longer see it, I feel my chest constricting. I can't take a full breath. I have to lean back to get more air in my lungs, and my mouth is so dry it feels like I've gargled with dust.

Next door to the hotel is a little convenience store, so I walk in to get a soda. While I'm back at the fridge case, I see a kid stick a bag of chips inside his pants and then shuffle toward the candy. That's the guy I want to have my phone. Walking up to the counter, I set my phone just out of sight of the woman at the register, then pay and leave. As I walk out I look back and see the kid discover the phone—it's as good as gone. I hope he burns all my minutes up while Barend Schlacter tries to track me down through it.

Guzzling the orange soda in just a few swigs makes my eyes water and my throat burn, but the physical pain is relief from what I've been feeling.

How do you live with the knowledge that you were responsible for the death of your oldest friend? By the time I get back to the room, I realize I have no other choice. I have to tell my parents.

I have to have them help me finish this.

The only thing I can't figure out is how to reach them without tipping off the *Fraternitas*.

Think, I tell myself. *What's the lowest-tech method to reach my parents without it being monitored? Phone and texting are out, Skype is out, emailing is out. Is IM monitored? Probably, if it's going over the Internet. What about a telegram? Do they even do telegrams anymore?*

Then I get it: *FAX!* Fax is old school, and if I write kind of weird or backwards or something then it will be completely unreadable by any program that's trying to scan handwriting. And since it's just going to the Breidablik fax number, no email names will be involved.

I run back into the hotel lobby, borrow two pieces of paper, and take them to the ladies room. There, on the counter, I look in the mirror while I write on the page, so the letters are backward. It's kind of hard to do, and low-tech as far as code-breaking goes, but at least the letters won't be read by scanners. In a messy, backwards hand I write:

> M & D,
> In trouble, need to see you. Call houseboy for details.
> Meet at the K.D. in 48 hours.
> Love, C

Putting just the fax number on the cover page, I hand the sheets to the man behind the desk and ask him if he can send it immediately. He's engrossed in this game show with big-breasted women wearing too much makeup and too few clothes, so he only glances at the paper for the number before dialing it and sticking the pages in. While the fax rolls through the machine he goes back to watching his TV show. I have to "ahem" when it's done to get the papers back, which he grabs and hands to me without ever taking his eyes off the TV program.

Back in the cabana, I write a note for Clath.

Dear Professor Clath,
Please don't be mad but we decided to take the early
bus to the Bonompak Ruins. We're working on a new
theory and will share everything tomorrow morning
at breakfast.
Your devoted students,
Caity and Justine

After placing this outside her door, I run back to my room and immediately buy tickets for Alex and my parents. I do this in Alex's name so the receipt goes to his email, which will hopefully trigger him to look in the draft folder of our shared email account.

Then I write a draft email to explain what has happened with Uncle Li and say that I'm not safe. I tell Alex my parents will be calling him and that he should go right away to the castle to talk to them.

For the first time, I allow him to tell them as much as he wants and needs to.

And then I type the words, "I love you." Because it's true. And because if anything happens to me—regardless of whether or not the feeling is mutual—I would want him to know it.

THIRTY-THREE

Sitting alone at the airport feels weird and lonely. Even Mr. Papers seems depressed; all he wants to do is stay curled up in his carrier with his homemade box of origami. Without him or Justine, I have nothing to distract me from the huge hole left in my heart.

I wonder if Alex has told my parents yet, wonder if they are freaking out—or worse. What if they won't help me? What if they take me to juvie or lock me down in some kind of military school? I seriously would not blame them. I have to toughen myself up to handle their supreme disappointment when they find out all that's happened.

And along the supreme disappointment lines, Clath will be freaking out when we don't return from a day at the Bonompak Ruins. That one was actually cruel. She'll be furious, but I doubt she'll tell Didier—she'll be too scared to tell him that she lost us. I'm guessing we have two days before all hell breaks loose.

Right before we board, I connect to the airport Wi-Fi and check our shared email account. My hand shakes a bit when I click on the drafts folder, after how I ended my last email draft. The weird thing is, I don't regret it.

There is one new draft from Alex.

> Dear Caity—I don't have the words to express how sorry I am to hear about Uncle Li. I am terribly worried about you, though I reckon you will keep a level head until we can arrive.
>
> I know firsthand what a loss like this feels like, and nothing can ease your pain. But you may get some comfort in knowing that website hits go up almost 10% a day. We are now pushing daily tones to more than two million phones! If you haven't had a chance to check Tenzo's reports from the random number generator, you should—they are showing a steady upward rise like they have never seen before. Tenzo said usually an event will spark a coherence spike and then it will go away, but this data is showing a steady increase.
>
> Please keep your wits about you and hold tight until we can reach you. I am on my way to talk to your parents now.
>
> I cannot lie; I am terrified to tell them everything.
>
> Alex

Not one mention of the last three words that I typed? Ouch. I accidentally groan out loud.

My flight number is called so I pack up my computer and take a peek at Mr. P., who is still curled up in his carrier, leaning on the origami box. He looks up at me with his glossy round eyes, closes them again, and then sets his little head back on the box.

Once I'm in my seat and I see the flight attendant close the door, I'm finally able to relax. I've gotten on without being found and, at least for the next few hours, I can feel completely safe. Once at our cruising altitude, I look out the window at the vast jungle below and wonder how many Mayan villages we will fly over. How many Daykeepers are out there counting the days, performing ceremonies, keeping the world intact?

With few passengers on the flight, I'm the only one in my row. I set Mr. Papers' carrier on the seat next to me, slip in a couple of pieces of dried fruit and a bottle of water, and give him a little scratch behind the ears.

Does he blame me as I blame myself?

Mentally and physically wiped out, I fall asleep within seconds of resting my head against the cool plastic of the plane window. I only wake up when the wheels hit the ground.

I have to run to catch my connecting flight, but thankfully it's short and within an hour and a half, the San Francisco cityscape comes into view.

Seeing the blinking light at the top of the Transamerica Pyramid makes my heart thump in my chest, and I feel rage burning in me. How dare the *Fraternitas* set up headquarters in the very building everyone associates with San Francisco! How dare they scheme their plans of mass control from my backyard! How dare they take the life of my oldest friend.

I try to push the hatred from my heart and look over my beautiful city, remembering all the great memories I have here. And how many more I hope to make.

———

I have the whole day to wait until Mom and Dad and Alex touch down at the airport, and I hadn't given much thought as to what I should do. I don't feel safe going to Muchuchumil Imports now that Uncle Li is gone—who knows if it has been discovered? It seems like the only place I'll feel safe is locked inside a hotel room.

Once I'm through customs, I look for an open family bathroom, then sneak in and lock the door. Letting Mr. Papers out to stretch his legs, I sit on the little plastic bench and log on to the Internet. I want to find an airport hotel and pre-pay with Bolon's PayPal account so all I have to do is pick up the key—someone my age paying cash for a hotel room might raise suspicion.

Once that's done, I motion for Mr. Papers to get back in the carrier. He walks slowly over and steps in. This is really starting to worry me—he's lethargic and hasn't done any origami since he made the lotus with Uncle Li resting on it.

I hope seeing Alex will perk him up. I know it will perk *me* up.

———

The motel is scrappier than it looked on the Internet. It's an old stucco two-story building with doors that open right outside, dirty from years of being in the path of jet-fuel grime. The whole thing gives me a bad vibe, but I check in anyway.

I have to pull Mr. Papers out of the carrier. His fur is all matted and dull, so I give him a little cat bath with a warm washcloth. After a few minutes, he's looking sharp again. When I finish, he looks at me dead in the eyes and puts one little hand on each of my cheeks. I seriously would not have blinked if he'd actually spoken to me.

Suddenly he looks over at the door, his eyes widening. Terrified, I whip around in time to see the doorknob turning. Before I can move, the door opens and Barend Schlacter stands before me. Right behind him—like a tall, evil shadow—stands Donald. I haven't seen him since Easter Island. It still freaks me out that he's the carbon copy of good, kind Thomas.

I know I should run or scream, but I can't do anything but think, *No one in the world that I care about knows where I am.*

I could disappear forever and they would never find me.

"You are looking well, *frauline*," Schlacter says, walking over to me. He has no sense of personal space and stops just inches from my face—so close I can smell his nasty breath and see oil glistening in the pores on his nose.

"What do you want?" I ask, backing away. "You've already taken my oldest friend—what more could you want?"

"The books, dear. The books."

"I don't have them anymore, honest."

"You're lying."

"Seriously, you can look though my things! I don't have them."

"Donald, guard the door, will you?" Schlacter says, not taking his eyes off me.

The coward won't even look at me. He just says, "As you wish," and walks toward the door. Seeing my room key on the table, he slyly pockets it and steps outside. Cretin.

"Go ahead and look. Tear the room apart. You won't find them because I don't have them!"

Schlacter makes a quick grab at me and gets both my hands in one swipe. I pull them away and he slaps me so hard I see white spots. While I'm dazed, he grabs my hands again and binds them together tightly with a plastic zip tie.

I can't help the tears that roll down my cheek. The pain, the shock, the fear of dying alone in this dingy room—it's all too much.

"Sit," says Schlacter, pushing me to the bed.

He pulls out the desk chair, turns it around, and straddles it.

"The books are in the mail," I say. "I mailed them to Scotland. Go there if you want to intercept them."

He just shrugs and pulls a small roll of dental floss from his chest pocket. He pulls out a huge length, enough to strangle me.

"I don't believe you," he says, slipping a few inches of the floss between his two capped front teeth and running it back and forth.

"Look around," I say. "Search the place!"

Watching him floss is enough to make me vomit, so I turn my head down. I see something move beneath his chair and realize that Mr. Papers is quietly inching away behind him. Thinking he's trying to escape, I try to keep Schlacter engaged.

"Like I said, you won't find them here. They're in the mail, priority international. They'll be there in a couple of days."

He pulls the floss from his mouth and flicks the debris

into the air. "Do you want to know how I killed him? How I killed your dear 'Uncle' Li?"

I can't speak, so I just shake my head. I wanted to provoke him so Papers could get away, but now he's completely deflated me. I have no voice to use.

I keep my head down but can see movement through my curls. Mr. Papers is slowly climbing to the top of the dresser behind where Schlacter is sitting.

"Look at me!" he barks. "I want to see your face when I tell you what his last words were."

I look up in time to see Mr. Papers reach inside his tiny vest and pull something out of the seam. I can't tell exactly what it is—a tube of some kind? A straw? He brings this small thing to his lips, walks a few paces to his left so that he's directly behind Schlacter, and then blows. I don't see anything, but something must have hit Schlacter because he screams "*Autsch!*" and reaches to the back of his head.

He's pulling hard at whatever Papers stuck in him, but he can't seem to get it out. Then Papers fires another one, and Schlacter falls forward onto the chair back that he was leaning against.

That's when I see the two needles sticking out of the back of Barend Schlacter's skull.

THIRTY-FOUR

Mr. Papers hops over to the bed, still holding the tiny tube. I watch as he walks up Schlacter's back and pulls one of the two needles out. Sticking it back into the tube, he then tucks it all back into the inside of his vest seam.

When he motions to the door with his head, I hold up my hands. "You have to get these off," I whisper. "Donald is still out there."

Mr. Papers leans over my hands and with his sharp little teeth starts gnawing at the zip tie. He's almost made it though when Donald opens the door.

We both look up at him, guilty. When he runs toward me, I wince and cower, certain he's going to kill me. Stopping immediately before us, he reaches into his back pocket and pulls out a large pocket knife.

This is it.

"Please, Donald. Please don't," I beg. "I'll tell you where the books are. I'll give you anything you want."

He picks up Schlacter's hand and feels for a pulse.

From the corner of my eye, I see Mr. Papers slipping his hand into his vest for the tiny needle and blow tube.

Donald reaches over, picks up my bound hands, and slips the knife under the chewed-up zip tie. With one easy pull, my hands are free.

I look up at Donald, and he smiles. Turning to Mr. Papers, he says, "Put that thing down, mate. I'm here to help."

"But—"

"I know," he says. "I reckon you have no reason to trust me, what with my history and all." He twirls the knife so that the handle is toward me and offers it. "Take it, lass."

Mr. Papers is still in the shadowy corner with the tube to his mouth, at the ready. But Donald doesn't go after him. Instead, he reaches into Schlacter's pocket and takes out two zip ties and his phone. "Keep this too if you'd like," he says, tossing me the phone. Then he binds Schlacter's hands and ankles.

I stand to see if he'll stop me, but he doesn't. Instead, he fishes around for Schlacter's wallet. "I must go get him a room so we can get him out of yours," Donald says. "I understand if you don't trust me and need to go, but at least let me get this horses' arse from your room 'fore you leave."

"I don't understand," I say. "Why are you helping me now?"

"The bigger question is, why haven't I been helping you for years?"

"But you're with the *Fraternitas*!"

"Not in any meaningful way, and not any more. Was

never promoted from Tyro. I should've known they were just using me."

He seems so different from the Donald who was with us on Easter Island. I sense that he's telling me the truth and I have a ton of questions for him, but all I want at this moment is get away from Barend Schlacter. "You're right; we can't leave him in my room. I'll wait here while you go get a room with his credit card."

Donald turns to Mr. Papers and says, "Monkey, you're in charge. I'll be back in a jiffy." Papers jumps off the desk and stands on the bed facing Schlacter, the tube to his lips and ready for action.

I'm right by the door, with my hand on the doorknob, just in case Schlacter wakes up and freaks out. I'm not really sure what kind of state he's in—I see his chest going up and down, but he's out cold. I just don't know for how long.

I want to run, but if Barend Schlacter dies in my room, it will be the end of me. I have no idea what Papers did to him, but I can't chance having the San Francisco police connect him to me.

I try to run a scenario in my mind where Donald is playing me. Would he give me a knife? Would he sacrifice his relationship with Barend Schlacter and the *Fraternitas* to get something from me? To get the books?

Possibly. Absolutely.

"How can we test his loyalty?" I ask Mr. Papers. He puts up his finger as if to say, "Just a moment," and then closes his eyes to think. When he opens them again, he grabs a piece of origami paper from his carrier and folds two origami books.

"What, pretend we have the books?"

He nods.

"And if he shows interest we'll know he's after something?"

Papers nods again.

"Brilliant."

I can't help but scream when the door to my room opens. I'd forgotten for a moment that Donald had my key.

"Go to the room to your right, lass," he says as he hands me a key. "And make sure no one is looking before you open the door."

I look outside and there's no one around, so I open the door next to mine, prop it open with the ice bucket, and then go back to help Donald. He's managed to get Schlacter over his shoulder. I look outside to make sure it's still clear, then we run next door.

Donald flops Schlacter down on the bed in the new room. I'm kind of freaked out that one needle is still stuck in his head.

"Is he in a coma or something?" I ask.

"Or something," Donald answers. "Looks like the needle hit him square in the Wind Mansion."

The fact that Donald has this kind of knowledge freaks me out. "I've got to get out of here," I say, running back to my room.

Donald follows. "Wait, lass—one more thing. I know no apology will do, but I must tell you how sorry I am for what I've done."

He looks so much like Thomas that it's hard not to instantly trust him again. I have to actively put my guard up.

"Just tell me one thing: did you try to save Uncle Li?"

"Aye," he says, putting his hand on his heart. "God's honest truth, I did not think Schlacter would kill him. I snuck food and drink in to Li. He's the one who turned me, really. Once he explained the big picture, I just couldn't defend what I was doing."

"Then why couldn't you save him?" I ask, voice cracking from the weight of the words.

"Schlacter did it. A young person in the *Fraternitas* reported that you'd had another one of your chats with the kids, and he was outraged. See, you've made him look like a fool to the *Fraternitas*—he'd told them you were no threat."

"That's the only good news I've had in days," I say, opening the carrier so Mr. Papers will get in.

"They all underestimated you. No group understands the power of the cosmic forces at work more than the *Fraternitas*—the potential for a leap in human evolution is a most terrifying notion to them. How could they control the masses, control the money, control the power if these changes happen?"

"And they think they can just distract us with fear and war and poverty and use places like HAARP to control the atmosphere?"

"It's worked so far, lass. The only ones who really believe there will be a leap in evolution based on where we are in the galaxy have been indigenous peoples—Native Americans, Aborigines, African tribes—basically those being killed or oppressed by governments, corporations, and banks."

"And the *Fraternitas* is behind all of this?" I ask, already knowing the answer. I just want to hear Donald say it.

With a deep and sorrowful nod, he says, "Aye."

"And now they want me?"

"At first you were just on their radar, but in no way a threat. Barend Schlacter wanted to find you himself because you made him look bad. He was never going to be more than a Praetor, just as I see now I was never going to be more than a Tyro. No one but those who share bloodlines are allowed to move up."

"How did Schlacter find me here, of all places?"

Donald points to my backpack. "A tracking device was slipped into your rucksack at Palenque."

"What? How could that be? I was never out of sight of my backpack."

"Someone slipped it in."

"Who?" I ask, racking my brain to remember anyone suspicious who was ever near me on that trip.

"None other than the heir to the head of the *Fraternitas*."

"What? Who is the heir to the *Fraternitas*?"

"The Magister's son. The person who will rule the *Fraternitas* next when the Magister dies."

I'm baffled. "How did he get to my backpack? Who is he?"

"A lad by the name of Julius D'Aubigne."

THIRTY-FIVE

I gasp so loud the noise I make even scares me.

"I can't be in this room anymore. I have to go," I say, almost hyperventilating.

When I think back on the kiss with Jules, I want to vomit. He took my backpack from between us. That must have been when he slipped the chip into it. I hate him. I hate myself for falling for it.

I try to pull myself together so I can get out of this room.

"Can I help at all, lass?" Donald asks.

Unable to trust anyone now, I still can't tell if he's playing me. I decide to tempt him with the books to see if he bites.

"Mr. Papers and I are going mail the books to a friend to keep them safe. Do you want to come?"

"Oh, berries! You're not carrying those books, are you? You've got to get them off your person as soon as possible."

"Do you want to see them?"

He puts his hands up as if to push me away. "Nae. For

the better part of the last few decades those books have fueled in me an awful evil. They're yours now—as it should be."

"Did you ever show them to the *Fraternitas*?"

Donald shakes his head. "I don't think they ever believed I really had the books. Tried to learn Sanskrit myself so I could decipher them, but never quite got it. I could read just enough to know they were important. I knew if I showed the books to the *Fraternitas*, they'd take them; I wanted to have the upper hand."

I decide not to tell him that the books he had were decoys. "Why them? Why would you betray your whole family and The Council for the *Fraternitas*?"

"It started as youthful hubris. I found it hard to believe my own father would give me up, have me living with the staff, just to protect these books. Imagine you found out that your parents chose some books and a fanciful tale over you?"

"But there was so much more at stake."

"I see that now. But then, as a lad, I couldn't see it. I left with the books, made inquiries, and eventually fell in with the *Fraternitas*. It's extremely difficult to get in even at the Tyro level; it's a very tightly controlled group. Only 'cause I said I was a Mac Fireland did I even get an ear."

"So they knew about you, about the castle."

"It was because of me that Hamish was killed—the men who came to the castle went because I told them where it was. I'll have that blood on me 'til my death."

My eyes well up. "That wasn't Hamish. That was my friend Alex's father."

Donald just looks up at the ceiling and shakes his head.

"I don't know what to say, really. I have no way of making amends for what I've done."

From inside the carrier, Mr. Papers holds up an origami version of the Transamerica Pyramid.

"I know one way you can make amends," I say, taking the building and handing it to Donald. "Get us in here."

"Aye," he says.

Donald helps me find the tiny RFI chip that Jules put in my backpack to track me. It was in the left pocket.

"Stupid!" I say under my breath as I remember back to the kiss and how Jules touched my backpack twice. What a fool I was to think that he was interested in me. What a bigger fool I was to even consider him over Alex.

We leave the sketchy hotel and I flag down a taxi. With the RFI chip in my palm, I lean over the open passenger window. As I ask how much for a ride to the city, I secretly drop the thin chip into the window well. The cabbie says he can't go north; he can only take a fare south because he's heading back down the peninsula. *Perfect*, I think as I watch him drive away with the tracking device.

We head to the BART Station for a train to the city. I still have several hours until I meet my parents—enough time to work out a plan.

We decide to go to Pier 39 because it's a huge tourist place and we can easily blend in. It's a perfect day in the city—crisp but completely clear. No longer seeing this place every day, I'd forgotten how beautiful it is.

Picking up a dozen of my favorite homemade donuts, we head to the end of the pier, back where there's a great view of Alcatraz Island. I admit to Donald that I don't have the books, and he doesn't even ask where they are. Instead, he tells me everything he knows about the *Fraternitas*, and we discuss what we could do at the Transamerica Pyramid. By the time the light starts fading and the nerves about seeing my parents kick in, we have a plan.

Now I just have to trust it will work.

We say goodbye and part ways, each of us in a different taxi, both of us with daunting tasks ahead.

I ask the cab driver to take a side street so there's no possibility of driving by the charred ground where my house used to be. I didn't even take proximity to the house into account when I told my parents to meet me at K.D. (our name for the otherwise nameless Korean deli a few blocks from our house). It's like I can't believe it's really gone unless I see it with my own eyes, but I also can't handle seeing it with my own eyes.

Though I've probably sat at the grimy plastic tables in the back of this convenience store and deli a thousand times, it feels completely different right now. After all that has happened, I feel like a stranger in my own neighborhood. The Korean deli people would freak if they saw a monkey, so I keep Mr. Papers' carrier zipped up.

I have time to spare, so I open up my laptop and check the secret drafts folder, hoping there's something from Justine. She hasn't let me down.

Caity – I hope you're with your parents as you read this, safe and secure. I'm with Gramps now. Made it here with no problems at all. I was able to meet with T and give him the two "items" that I was carrying. He is working on it as fast as he can, literally day and nite. By the way, he says the whole coherence thing is blowing their minds at the lab. Apparently whatever you and Alex cooked up with this daily tone thing is making all the random number generators in the world start to not be so random anymore. He was trying to be positive about the whole thing but I could tell he was scared. I think he's worried that someone in the Fraternitas will get their hands on this data and figure out what's going on. I have to say, I'm a little scared too. Don't worry tho, I'm not going to do anything crazy. For the first time, I'm really enjoying being with my grandpa.

I'm still thinking about your talk. I'm not really sure how you know all that stuff, but it's pretty amazing. Love you, Justine

I immediately write a new email to leave in the draft folder.

J – You're going to make me cry if you keep being this nice! I'm glad you are safe with your g-pa, and that you got the "items" to Tenzo. I'm dying to see what they say. I had a run-in w/BS, but Papers took care of him. New developments on the side of evil: Donald has flipped and is now helping me. I'm waiting now for parents and Alex to show up, and I'm so scared about what they will say and do. I love being home again. I guess I should put "home" in quotes. Still haven't been able to drive by the charred remains, but knowing it's so close by is really helping me build up the confidence to do what I have to do. If we are lucky, tomorrow the world will be a much different place.

I love you, J. You're the best friend anyone could ask for.

Saving the email, I close down my laptop and look at the clock on the shiny mint-green wall. They could walk through the door at any time.

I fiddle with the Korean condiments. I don't think I've

ever been this nervous to see my parents—I have no idea how they're going to react to me. I've never disobeyed them or gotten in trouble or even gotten below a B in school. To go from an incredibly well-behaved child to the scheming girl that I've become is pretty severe.

I'm not sure I would forgive me if I were them, but I have to at least make them understand what's at stake.

THIRTY-SIX

ecause I'm sitting in the back of the store, I see my parents before they see me. Dad walks in first, with purpose. Mom is behind him with tired eyes—but as she gets closer, I see it's not lack of sleep, it's because she's been crying. Surely, over worry about me. Alex, glancing around nervously, is trailing after both of them.

When I stand up, they finally see me.

They both run over. *They still love me.*

I'm caught in a huge squeeze. Being compressed has never felt so good.

Dad pulls back, puts his hands on my shoulders, and says, "Oh, are you in a world of trouble."

"I know," I say, looking from him to Mom and back again. "Probably more trouble than you even know."

I finally make eye contact with Alex, who's standing behind my parents with his hands deep in his pockets. He's looking sheepish—I wonder if my parents were hard on him.

He gives me a tiny smile and then looks back down at his shoes.

"You know Alex had nothing to do with this, right?"

"We understand he was not the instigator," Mom says.

"But he *was* aiding and abetting," Dad adds.

"I take all responsibility," I say. "I forced him to do everything he did."

"You can take responsibility," Mom says, "but at least give credit where credit is due; that daily tone phone app Alex made is incredible."

"Isn't it?"

"Brilliant," Dad says, ruffling Alex's hair.

"Where's Justine?" Mom asks, looking around.

"She went to her Grandpa's house where she'll be safe. I didn't want her here, with all that's at stake."

"And where does the school think you are?"

My grimace says all.

"You didn't tell them?" Dad says. "You just went AWOL?"

"Yeah, but our Pedagogue won't even notice until ... " I look at the clock on the wall. "Well, soon. Okay, I know I'm in huge trouble, I know doing all this without telling you was wrong, but can we just focus on what we need to do within the next few hours and then deal with punishment?"

"Let's sit and figure it out," Dad says, raising four fingers to the deli guy. They only serve one thing here: a freakishly good Korean barbeque sandwich. The deli guy, who's seen us here a million times, never acknowledges that he knows us. Either he has that weird kind of short-term amnesia or he's just not a people person.

We get drinks while the deli guy puts the sandwiches together, and then sit to eat.

"So," Dad says, "will you please tell us exactly why we are here?"

I purposely take a large bite of sandwich so I can buy myself a little time.

"How much do you know?" I ask, still not sure I can tell them about Uncle Li.

"Alex has filled us in as much as he could," Mom says. "And we've read the information you put up on your hidden website—after Alex divulged the real URL. Smart to give directions to it in Mosquito Tone!"

"He also translated the audio file of your speech at Palenque back into a hertz range we could hear."

"Did you listen to it?" I ask, thinking back on all I talked about and wondering if I said anything incriminating.

"It was incredible, honey," Mom says. "The entire time I was listening I was wondering who you were—and how you knew all of the things you were talking about." Instead of pride in her voice, there is a tinge of sadness. Maybe she feels like she doesn't know who I *really* am.

"I'm the same person," I say. "It's just—"

"You don't have to do that," Dad says, interrupting me. "*We* need to expand; it's not that you have to shrink. There's greatness in there," he says, tapping my forehead.

Mom smiles and nods, but I can still sense a bit of disappointment. I suspect it will be a long time before she can get over all the betrayal.

"So we understand the basic concept. What we don't understand is the inherent danger. Alex said you were in danger, yet we still don't really know who the enemy is. Who or what is this 'Shadow Government'?"

"The big problem is that the enemy is *everywhere*," I say. "At the highest levels of world government, military, business, banking—the people making the rules and making the money."

"And these people are after *you*?"

"Yes," I answer. "And probably you guys, too."

"How do you know?" Dad asks. "Have they threatened you?"

"Worse," I say, setting my sandwich down. I've completely lost my appetite despite not eating all day. It's time for the truth. It comes out as a whisper. "They've hurt Uncle Li."

Mom and Dad both go white. Neither one says anything.

"Remember Barend Schlacter?" I ask, barely getting the words out before losing it. I put my arms on the table, lay my head down, and start crying. Neither of my parents moves; it's Alex who puts a hand on my back.

Drying my eyes with the deli's small, scratchy napkins, I take a few breaths through my nose. "It's bad," I tell them. "Uncle Li is … *gone*."

It's freaking me out that neither one of them is saying anything. They're just staring at me.

"It's not your fault, mate," Alex says, breaking the awkward silence. "These people are mad!"

I look at my parents. "Will you guys say something, please?" I beg. "Ground me until I'm forty-eight, tell me you're sending me to a military school—just say *something*!"

Dad shakes his head and breathes in deeply, like he's just woken up from drifting off. "I'm sorry, Caity, I just—"

"We're just trying grasp the enormity of the situation," Mom says. "I thought we were sailing into rough waters, not a tsunami."

"Why Li?" Dad asks.

"He's been my protector—assigned to me by The Council, the only group out there that knows everything about the *Fraternitas*."

Mom looks at me sideways. "My meeting him to unlock that old Chinese safe—not a coincidence?"

I shake my head.

"There's so much to tell you guys, but right now I need your help. Can you help? *Will* you help?"

Both of them nod. Mom dries her eyes with a napkin, Dad's chin is quivery.

"Thank you. We need to do this—it's time to go to the pyramid."

"The pyramid?" Mom says.

"The Transamerica building. The pyramid. Headquarters for the *Fraternitas Regni Occulti*—the main puppet masters behind the Shadow Government, and the group that Barend Schlacter works for."

Dad wipes some barbeque sauce from his chin. "My God, they have an office? Right here?"

"Smack dab in the middle of San Francisco."

"And exactly what are we going to do there?" Mom asks.

"Well, here's where it gets tricky," I answer.

Mom looks at Dad and shakes her head slightly, as if she's almost given up on me. "Tricky hard or tricky illegal?"

"Um, kind of both," I say, wincing.

THIRTY-SEVEN

Deciding that I'll explain on the way, we all get in the rental car and head for the pyramid. Alex and I sit in the back and Mr. Papers gets out of his carrier to sit on Alex's lap. It's nice to see him perking up again after how down he was.

I don't give them all the details for fear they'll pull out, but I lay out the basics: Donald is going to get us into the *Fraternitas'* headquarters so we can get into their computer systems and make some ... *modifications.*

Alex has filled them in on Donald's back story, the fact that it's he who is actually Dad's uncle, not Hamish. But they are all, including Alex, shocked to hear that he will now be helping us.

"How do you know it's not a trap?" Alex asks, rightly suspicious of Donald.

"If he'd wanted to trap me, he could have—I was alone in a sketchy hotel room and even baited him, but he didn't waiver. Even Papers trusts him. But either way, we still get into the *Fraternitas* headquarters, which is all that matters now."

I set the scene: Donald will meet us in the parking garage and will take some video of us "captured." Then he will call the Magistrate and tell him that he will bring us all in if the floor is cleared of all staff. This will be fairly easy since it's nighttime and most staff will have left.

Donald had explained to me how rare it is to have the Magistrate here. He thinks it's because of my last talk at Palenque. Jules showed them how to access it and once they listened to it, they were enraged.

"They're very keen on getting you into their offices," Donald had added.

Dad pulls into the parking garage. "All the way to the bottom, last possible space," I tell him. "That's where we wait."

I'm surprised to feel Alex's warm hand grab mine. I give it a squeeze and look over at him. I feel bad for having put him in the awkward position of having to deliver the news to my parents and travel with them halfway around the world. This whole thing has taken him out of his element and made him quieter, shyer. I hold tightly to his hand as we wind our way down through the dim parking lot. We get to the last space, but Donald is not there.

"Wait here?" Dad asks, cutting off the engine.

"Yep," I say.

Mom unbuckles her seat belt and turns around in her seat to look at me. Alex gently lets go of my hand and pulls his own hand back to his lap before she can see.

"Now that we have some time, please fill us in on what exactly we'll be doing here," she says.

I give it to her straight. "It's two things, actually. We need to jam the frequency transmitters in the U.S., Norway, and Russia that are messing with our atmosphere, and then make the IMF and World Bank erase the debt of third-world countries."

Mom and Dad both do the cartoon double-take.

"What did you just say?" Mom says at the same time Dad says, "Excuse me?"

"I know, I know," I reply.

"Do you, Caity? Do you?" Dad says. "You're talking about *mayhem*. Undoing decades of—"

"Decades of corruption," I interrupt. "Decades of the richest people on Earth preying on the poorest. Decades of intentional, perpetual slavery and intentional messing with the ionosphere and magnetosphere."

"How can you even know all of this?" Mom asks. "What can you know about the *magnetosphere*?"

"From The Council. Uncle Li and others have been teaching me. You know deep down that you can't deny what I'm saying—no one can deny this, no one who has been paying attention."

Mom looks like she could use a Barbie knee to crack.

Dad is chewing so hard on the side of his cheek that I expect to see a hole appear.

"What's been happening is the opposite of love," I say. "And it has to stop."

Dad says, "Even if I agree that it has to stop, I don't think you see the mass havoc it will create."

"But the havoc is there already! We're just shifting to a different kind of havoc. You guys both know that all systems reorganize after chaos—it's Science 101. We just need that chaos to produce a good reorganization instead of an evil one."

"And somehow this is all part of the Mayan calendar?" Mom asks.

"The Maya had super-advanced knowledge of how *where* we are in the galaxy affects *who* we are as humans. They knew a shift would happen, leading up to and following the year 2012. Unfortunately, the Shadow Government knows this, too—and wants to stop it. Because free, enlightened people are hard to control."

"So tell us what you want us to do," Mom says. "How will you help this happen?"

"A couple of ways. The first thing is the third-world debt. We'll need you and Dad to figure out a way to get into the IMF and World Bank systems."

"Caity, I've done programming work for World Bank, and even then I didn't have access to their system."

"What happened to Angus 'I can hack anything' Mac Fireland?" I ask. "Besides, we're doing it from the *Fraternitas'* side. Since not all the loans are bogus, we're just tapping into the ones that the *Fraternitas* is involved with—and Donald tells me they're linked in their computer system."

"And the frequency transmitters?"

"That one is actually easier. Uncle Li explained it to me. They all reboot after a shutdown, so we just need a quick piece of code that redirects them to a different satellite after blackouts."

"These places have backups for their backups—they'll never have a complete blackout," Dad says.

"They will if a massive solar storm hits."

"Oh God, that's right—there's some connection between 2012 and sunspots?" Mom says. "One of the Berkeley alums mentioned that."

"Yep, the solar flare cycle is like every eleven years, and 2012 could bring some of the biggest ones in modern times. Some sunspots are the size of Jupiter, shooting billions of tons of energy toward the Earth. The Council knows how to predict solar flares and then they can switch on their hidden satellite."

"Hidden satellite? How can a satellite be hidden?"

"I don't know, Dad. All I know is that they have a satellite that's protected from the solar flares, and when the other ones have blacked out, they'll switch it on."

"So when all the other satellites go down, you plan on just bouncing the signal over to another satellite from—what planet is it on?"

"I know it sounds crazy, I *know*. You just have to trust me. Once we get into the *Fraternitas'* headquarters it will all make sense."

"If we ever get in," Mom says, looking outside her window. "Wait, is that … Thomas?"

We all look out the window to see Donald walking toward us. I open the car door and say hello, and then Mom and Dad get out. Donald shakes everyone's hand. Alex doesn't look him in the eye as he shakes his hand. I wonder if he's still freaked out by him, or if he feels guilty for drugging him on

Easter Island. Donald even shakes Mr. Papers' hand as he sits on my shoulder.

There's an awkward silence while we all stand around, so I say, "Okay, what's next?"

"I reckon we should take the video in the stairwell, where there's some light," Donald says. Then he pulls five handkerchiefs from his coat pocket. "Got to make this look realistic, all apologies to you."

"You're going to gag us?" I ask, thinking maybe I'm being played after all.

"Have to. But I won't bind your hands, I'll let you just hold them behind your backs so it looks like you're bound."

"Fair enough," I say, following Donald to the stairwell.

Donald lines us up against the concrete wall, careful to place us out of sight of any writing. This looks like it could be a cell anywhere. He puts Dad and Alex in the back and Mom and me up front. We all take a handkerchief to tie around our mouths like gags, then we put our hands behind our backs. We try to look as miserable as possible. I only have to think about losing Uncle Li to be sobbing.

Donald turns on his phone video and starts taping. "Here they are, Magistrate," he says. "Clan Mac Fireland and the lad who was helping Caitrina execute her plans." Then he reaches over and roughly pulls my gag down. "Anything to say for yourself, Caitrina?" he says. I shake my head, still crying. "She's ready to give up her secrets," Donald says. "Should be a *very* easy interrogation, I reckon."

At that he stops the video and tells us we can remove our gags. I'm shaking from even pretending to be captured.

"Need you to stay put for a moment while I go out to send this video. Can't get a good signal down here," he says.

We spend a tense few minutes pacing in the small concrete space, and freeze when we hear the elevator coming back down.

Donald walks out. "It's done," he says. "The Magistrate is clearing everyone off the floor; there were only a few staffers left there anyway."

I open my backpack for Mr. Papers and then zip up the top, leaving just enough room for his tiny hand to reach though and unzip the bag if he needs to.

We silently get on the elevator and take it up to the main floor of the pyramid, then transfer to another elevator. Donald uses a key code to get access to the floor the *Fraternitas* is on. I look over at Alex and see beads of sweat on his forehead. I wonder if he'll even speak to me again, once this is all over.

The speedy elevator going so high up plays with my stomach. I have to breathe deeply to keep calm for what's ahead. Finally the elevator slows, dings, and stops. Though I know almost anything could happen when those doors open, I'm truly shocked at who I see standing right in front of me when they do: Jules D'Aubigne.

THIRTY-EIGHT

Draped over one of the expensive-looking modern chairs in the waiting area, Jules lifts a hand and says, "*Quelle surprise!*"

I walk out looking at the floor. I can't bear to look him in the eye. Donald pushes at us like he's herding sheep until we're standing in a tight group in front of Jules.

"*Père, ils sont ici!*" Jules yells, casually checking his phone as we stand before him. I carefully set down my backpack behind Dad. As I glance down, I see Mr. Papers' fingertips reaching through the small hole.

"*Bonsoir!*" comes a voice from a dark hallway. When the speaker reaches the light, I can't help but gasp a little. He looks so much like Jules they could be brothers. Even now, with hatred for Jules burning inside me, I see his face as a work of art. And his father's, even more so. Age has added color and depth to his face, and fullness to his jaw. Their suits are the same cut and style, and they hold themselves in that indescribable European way that tells you they are wealthy and entitled.

"Quite a beastly little crew you have there," the older D'Aubigne says to Donald. "You didn't think to bind their hands?"

"Couldn't really be seen guiding four cuffed people up the elevator now, could I? Besides, who needs cuffs when you have one of these?" he says, reaching under his coat where a gun is hidden.

D'Aubigne nods. Turning to us, he puts his hand on his chest and says, "I am Claude D'Aubigne, thirty-third Magistrate of the *Fraternitas Regni Occulti*." He delivers this like he expects us to bow and curtsey, or kiss his ring.

We all just stand there, hoping Donald will do something with his gun like he said he would.

Claude D'Aubigne comes closer to us, close enough for him to reach out and touch my hair. "Rough around the edges," he says, looking at me like I'm a piece of livestock he's considering buying. "Funny that a girl such as yourself should wind up with this much power."

I don't want to look at him, but if I look down or away, he wins. So I stare into his eyes, which are the blue of a glacial lake.

Jules gets up from the chair he was lounging in and walks lazily over, as if having four captured people brought in is an everyday occurence.

"She's a quirky little thing, isn't she?" he says to his father, now standing right next to him. "With quirky little ideas."

I can't help but shake my head.

"What?" Jules says. "Please, feel free to speak."

"I tell the truth," I say. "My quirky little ideas are the truth."

"What is *true* has no bearing," Jules says with a scoff. "Those elders have played you for a fool. You are the mouthpiece for a dying group of simple people. You and your little calendars and tones; do you think they have any power over the technology that we have in place?"

"What are you so afraid of?" I ask. "To want to live in a world run by the Shadow Government, you must be afraid of something."

Jules smiles and glances at his dad, who is standing with his arms crossed looking amused at this debate.

"Why yes, I am terribly afraid of something: poverty. Why should I have to give up my power, my money, my status?"

"You didn't even earn it," I hiss. "You just inherited it."

"And you—have *you* earned the right to do what you're doing, or did you inherit it?"

That hurt.

"You're living out of balance," I say. "It can't be sustained. Don't you see that? I don't care how awesome it is to have all that power and money—eventually it will come to an end. And I think that will be a lot sooner than you expect."

"I pity you," he says, looking at me like he wants to hit me. "You will fail. You will fail spectacularly."

Just as I'm trying to think of a comeback, I hear the familiar sound of Mr. Papers and his little tube. The first needle hits Claude D'Aubigne, who gasps and reaches back to feel what's stuck in his head before falling to his knees and ending up face-down on the ground.

"*Père!*" Jules screams, leaning over his dad. "*Père!*"

He doesn't seem to notice the long thin needle sticking out from the base of Claude D'Aubigne's hair. "Donald, help—" he screams, before he too is hit with a needle. "What is that?" he says, walking in circles and trying to pull the slippery little needle out of the back of his skull. It takes a few seconds before his eyes roll back and he falls forward onto one of the fancy modern lobby chairs.

I glance over at my parents, who are clearly not prepared to see what they've just seen.

"Did Papers just kill them?" Dad asks, his face chalky.

"Nae, just hit them in the Wind Mansion—bit of ninja acupuncture," answers Donald. "They'll be out for a spell."

"Is it safe to leave them here?" I ask. "Or should we hide them away?"

"There's an interrogation room on this floor," Donald says, walking over to the reception desk and foraging around in one of the drawers. He pulls out a roll of packing tape. "We can lock them up there."

"An interrogation room? Who would they interrogate here?" Mom asks.

Donald and I both look at Mom like she's a child. "Seriously? Mom, you have *no* idea who we're dealing with here."

"Help me bind them," Donald says to Alex and Dad. They both nod and bend down to help. Once Jules and Claude's arms and legs are bound, Donald props them up against the wall. Mr. Papers checks all their pockets, pulls out cell phones and cardkeys, and hands them to me.

"Let's go see if we can get into the interrogation room, shall we? May need your lock-picking skills, ma'am," Donald says to my mom, who grabs my hand and pulls me along with her.

Dad and Alex stay with Jules and Claude D'Aubigne, though with all the packing tape we've used, there's no way they could get free anytime soon, even if they did come to.

Donald leads us through a maze of hallways and stops at a room that says *Interview Suite* on it. "Ever seen one of these?" he asks, gesturing to the keypad lock on the door.

"Piece of cake," Mom replies, kneeling down in front of the keypad. With her face as close to the door as she can get it, she looks intently at every key. "Should only take two tries," she says, pushing four numbers. We listen for a click, but nothing. "If it wasn't that, it has to be this," she says, punching four numbers again. We hear the magic click.

"What a keen gift you have," Donald says.

I'm always astounded by her talent. "How did you know the numbers?"

"Simple human patterns," she answers. "Everyone presses very hard on the first and last number, almost as hard on the third number, but pretty light on the second number. Security in this office is through the roof, so this keypad is probably just for internal use. Without high risk, the code would rarely change. I just looked at what keys were a skosh more worn. The only thing I had to guess on was which was first and which was last."

I'm more impressed than ever.

There's nothing in the room but one metal chair. The walls are made of dark, one-way glass and the faint smells of cigarette smoke, coffee, and pee hang in the air.

"Lovely," I say.

"I guess 'Interview Suite' is a euphemism," Mom says, using the chair to prop the door open. "Well, this is a perfect place to put them."

I tap on the glass to make sure they can't break out. It's so thick it almost feels like stone.

Shaking his head and looking at the ground, Donald says, "Ah, the horrors that have gone down here."

I don't even want to know. I just want to keep moving so we can get out of this place. "I'll go back and get them," I say.

I run back full-speed through the hallways, because they're creepy with a capital C, and then lead Dad and Alex back to the Interview Suite with Jules and Claude. There's something really, really satisfying about seeing Jules D'Aubigne and his dad being dragged along the floor in their five-thousand-dollar suits. The Magistrate has been taken down. For now.

They prop both of them up against the wall and Dad double checks the tape on their wrists and ankles, then rips the tape off their mouths.

"Wouldn't want anyone to suffocate," Dad says. "We need them alive for when the authorities come."

I don't have the heart to tell Dad we don't know what authorities to trust.

"Come with me then," Donald says as he closes the door to the Interview Suite. "You'll want to see the server room now."

He walks us through the maze of hallways to a door with a card-key sensor on the outside. I hand him the keys that Mr. Papers scored from the D'Aubignes. "Server room requires two keys so no one can ever get in alone," Donald says as he swipes one card after another. When the door opens, Dad smiles. A room full of humming servers is his happy place. He sits down at a computer, but Donald pulls him away.

"After all I've done, I'm taking the fall for this, not you. Tell me what to type and I'll do it."

Dad shakes his head. "We only have a few hours; there's no way I could do this remotely. Fiona and Alex, I'll need you to go wrestle up some laptops, hack in, and come back to help me write these programs. I'll start by getting the lay of the land here."

"But you think it's possible?" I ask. "Can it be done?"

"Anything is possible," Dad answers.

I look at the time at the bottom of the screen. "Donald, what time do we need to be out of here?"

"Five thirty in the morning at the latest, lass."

"Okay Dad, that gives us about ten hours. What do you think?"

"We'll do what we can here, but when dawn comes and we need to get out, we'll take the servers with us. If what you say has been happening really has been, we need to take these to the CIA."

"What? We can't do that! You don't realize how infiltrated this Shadow Government is—they have people everywhere! They'll just take the servers, smile, and hide them. And then most likely kill us."

He pulls out his phone. "Not if we have someone there we trust. I'll call Scott Dilazzaro, my old friend at the *Chronicle*. I'll have him meet us in the lobby at 5:30 tomorrow morning to help escort the servers to the CIA. He can call in other reporters, or anyone else he feels could help."

"But isn't Scott, like, the technology editor?"

Dad points to the rows of servers. "Is this not technology?" he asks.

He dials the number and fills Scott in. Apparently Scott has some good ideas of his own that Dad seems to like. Hanging up, he says, "Well, there will be a film crew along as well! Scott's part of a PBS documentary on why the San Francisco Bay area has always been at the forefront of technology. Pretty handy coincidence; this way he doesn't have to tip off another news outlet, but he can still get everything on tape."

Mom and Alex walk in with laptops and fistfuls of different cords. Dad connects them all together and then says, "Commence the hack!" as if he's telling NASA he's ready for blastoff.

Alex looks at me, terrified, and shrugs. "I don't really know what to do," he says to my parents as they both tap away at their keyboards. Mr. Papers jumps on his lap as if to console him.

"Watch and learn, son. Watch and learn," Dad says. "I'll let you know when I need you."

Donald and I have nothing to do. He looks at me and motions with his head to follow him out.

"What's up?" I ask, once in the hallway.

"I want to show you something," he says. "Something not very many people will ever see."

THIRTY-NINE

Donald leads me to the elevator and we go to the forty-eighth floor, which is as high as the elevator goes in the building. Because the pyramid is so tapered at that point, it's not nearly as big up there as you'd think and one glass conference room takes up the entire floor. Donald walks over to a special door that he opens using Claude D'Aubigne's key card. Inside is a metal staircase, which we climb for several stories until we reach a platform. A metal ladder above us stretches straight up, farther than I can see.

"You first?" he asks.

"No way," I say. "Uh-uh."

"It will be worth it. You have my word."

"I'll only go if you go first."

Following Donald up the metal staircase, I consciously talk to my hands with every rung. *You can do it*, I say. *You have a strong grip*. We climb at least ten stories on this straight ladder before a hole appears at the top. Donald climbs up through the hole and then reaches down to help me up. I am too afraid to let go, so I hoist myself up. We are in a tiny round room, a room so small we can't stand upright, completely encircled in glass.

I can feel the building swaying with the wind. It's difficult to believe that we're not going to blow right off in this little bubble. We can see the entire city aglow beneath us, and out past the glow is the glossy black bay. It's absolutely beautiful.

Donald sits on the floor facing Fisherman's Wharf and the bay, so I sit too.

He unbuttons the cuff on his long-sleeved wool shirt to massage his wrist. That climb was an arm-burner. I catch a glimpse of the outside of the FRO spiderweb tattoo that I'd seen on Barend Schlacter.

"You have one, too?" I ask.

"Aye. It's like a brand. You get it when you're initiated into the *Fraternitas*."

"Is this symbolic of the web of deceit that they weave?"

"More than that, lass. The spiral represents the inherent spin energy of the universe, but nature's way is to spin it clockwise. In this symbol, the web gets spun counterclockwise to show man's dominion over this force. The twelve sections represent the twelve signs of the zodiac that the Earth travels through as it moves through the Precession of the Equinoxes."

"That's creepier than I even imagined."

"I reckon I'll have something pretty drawn over it soon," he says, rolling his sleeve back down.

"Pretty spectacular view you have here," I say.

"It's more than just pretty. Are you ready to hear the secrets of Tlamco?" he asks.

"Is that what they call this little clubhouse?"

"No, it's the name of the city that sat here thousands of years ago."

"Before San Francisco?"

"Far before. Do you know of the Great Circle around the Earth? The way many of the world's most mystical and powerful places are connected by circles?"

I nod. "Bolon told me about it," I say. "It's amazing how many magnificent old temples were located along the Great Circle."

"Tlamco, or San Francisco, shares a similar relationship. Do you happen to have your sketchbook on you?"

"Always," I reply, pulling it out of my sweatshirt pocket.

Donald uses the pencil I keep in the spiral coil of the book to draw part of a globe.

"Look here, lass. If you draw a straight line from the massive temple at Angkor Wat to the mysterious Nazca lines in south America, and then draw a circle around it, San Francisco sits right on that great circle."

"Seriously?"

"Aye. And if you divide the miles from San Francisco to Nazca by the miles from San Francisco to Angkor Wat, you get exactly 1.618, also known as Phi—the Golden Ratio. This is a very sacred place on the Earth, with very powerful energy. It is no mistake that you were born here."

"And no mistake that the *Fraternitas* is headquartered here?"

"Aye. Not only in this city, but in this building in particular."

"What's so magical about the building? The fact that it's a pyramid shape?"

"It goes much deeper than that. Look down. Do you notice that all of the streets in this section of the city are on a very precise square grid? There is only one exception—the only diagonal street is Columbus, the street that runs from Ghiradelli Square to this pyramid. The angle of that street is *directly* in line with the Great Circle that links San Francisco, the ancient land carvings at Nazca, and the temple at Angkor Wat."

"No way! That's incredible!"

"It doesn't stop at that, either. Some powerful math is encoded in this very building. Tell me, how many days in the sacred *Tzolk'in* calendar?"

"Two-hundred and sixty."

"You know how tall this building is? Exactly 260 meters."

"What a—" I was going to say coincidence, but I know better by now.

I don't know if it's the swaying of the building or the incoming knowledge that's making me feel dizzy, but I have to put my palms on the floor next to me to keep from spinning.

"Did Li ever teach you the correlation between DNA and the Chinese I Ching?" Donald asks.

"You mean that they're both based on the number 64?"

He nods. "Yes. Always been a profound connection there, with the number 64. Now take a guess at how many meters tall this spire is, atop the building?"

"Sixty-four?" Now I have chills on top of vertigo.

"Aye. See, this building, symbolic in its shape of a pyramid, encodes the two things central to Mayan cosmology: the 260-day human calendar and the 64 codons in our DNA. It weaves together two ideas central to the evolution of our species by representing both time and our human makeup."

"So whoever built this building had to know this stuff?"

"Likely it was someone on the planning commission—it was the city that told them it could not be as high as the architects had designed it. It had to be 260 meters. Could've very well been someone from The Council on that planning commission. They're headquartered here for good reason as well."

"So this building was originally a place of good power?"

"Oh, yes. Once the pyramid was finished, it was covered in crushed quartz, giving it its sparkly white color as well as the awesome transmission power of a huge quartz crystal. See, this is precisely why the *Fraternitas* have moved in—they've been harnessing the power of this building's sacred architecture and crystal composition to further their plans."

"You've just blown my mind. I can't believe I've looked at this building thousands of times and never realized any of this."

"It works on a more subtle level, lass. But it's had its influence over this part of the world for a very long time. It's also no coincidence that Silicon Valley—which could also be called Quartz Valley, for that is what silicon is—is the leader in technology focused on the power of the quartz crystal, the heart of all computer technology."

"And the *Fraternitas* has been sucking the same energy from this place?"

"The wealth that they've accumulated since moving into this building has been astounding. They now have more power than ever in the worlds of military, banking, and world government."

"Not after today," I say.

"I reckon not. They never figured you'd understand the power of the true Holy Grail."

I turn to look at Donald. "What do you mean?" I ask. I've heard about a lot of weird stuff, but no one has ever mentioned the Holy Grail.

Donald reaches for my sketchbook again and makes a simple drawing. "Recognize this?" he asks.

"What, two spirals?" Then I see what it really is. "Oh! It's the inside of a torus!"

"Aye. The Holy Grail isn't the golden cup of lore, it's a map to the basic structure of the universe, from the largest thing to the smallest thing."

"And this is what the *Fraternitas* has been trying to block in us?"

He nods. "But you found the key. One of the most powerful creators of this force is the human heart. If you can manage to get the largest generation of kids ever on this planet to all put out coherent waves of love, you will be able to overcome all the imbalance the *Fraternitas* has worked toward for centuries."

"Is that really what the Holy Grail is? A symbol of vortex energy?"

"'Tis. And the Flower of Life, the Three Hares, also both ancient symbols of this energy. If we understand nothing else, this can guide us to a new way of living. 'Parently in those Sanskrit books lies the key to how to work with it."

"Oh! That reminds me—I need to check in on Justine and Tenzo. He's translating them for us."

"Sure hope he's trustworthy," Donald says. "And well guarded."

A gust makes the building sway and we both grip the handrail until our knuckles are shiny and white.

"Best head back then," Donald says weakly. He's gone gray and waxy-looking from the swaying. I just hope he can make it down that ten-story ladder.

Climbing down is infinitely harder than climbing up, because you're looking at the space below you and seeing how far you could fall. By the time we reach the platform, my hands are calloused and achy from gripping so tightly.

Now the elevator seems like a safehaven. I'm almost afraid when it dings for the thirty-third floor. What if something happened while we were gone? I can't even guess how much time has passed. It almost seems like we went to outer space and back.

The floor is quiet. Winding our way back to the server room, we're relieved to see Dad, Mom, and Alex all tapping away at their computers.

Alex glances at me with the look of someone who has just hit a home run. "I'm hacking, Caity! I'm hacking! I just learned how to Daisy Chain!"

"Sweet! What's the plan of attack here?"

"A nice combo plate," Dad says. "A Trojan Horse, some worms, and a few multi-functional viruses. You know, back when

I was doing some work for the World Bank, the programmer in charge was a bit of a jerk; he kept telling us that his cryptography was Deep Magic. It's delightful to finally see that what he calls Deep Magic is pretty much a kluge."

"What's Deep Magic?" Alex asks, wide eyed.

"What fools say about programs that are so good it seems they were written by wizards," Mom answers. "Be wary of anyone who says that about his own work."

"I love this," Alex says.

"I'm glad," Mom says, patting his hand. "You're doing a fine job."

"How much more time do you need?" I ask.

"A couple more hours. We'll be fine—out of here by four in the morning."

"Great. I'll be right outside the door if you need anything.'

"Any sodas around here, Donald?" Dad asks. "Can't really call it hacking without sugar and caffeine."

As Donald walks off to the kitchen to fetch some drinks, Mr. Papers and I sit outside the server room. I open up my laptop to check email. It's really early in the morning on the East Coast, so Justine is probably not online, but there might be something in the drafts folder.

Bingo: there's a draft email from Tenzo. In the subject line is "Translation" and there's a Word document attached.

It can only be one thing.

FORTY

I open Tenzo's email. He has written only one sentence:
The world will never be the same.

My throat swells and I take a deep breath before I click on the Word document. I can't believe I'm finally going to see what was written in these books thousands of years ago. These books have ripped my family apart and led me around the world. My beloved Uncle Li died for them. I double-click on the icon and the document opens.

Introduction

The one intelligent and conscious universe has been known for thousands of years. As we move into a period of darkness, that knowledge will be lost and suppressed. These texts will be guarded fiercely. Symbols of old will be carved in stone and in the earth, at all of the most powerful places on this world. Though their meaning may not be apparent, these symbols will still resonate with the truth encoded in them. Those who can see truth will be drawn to these symbols and will work to understand them.

We need not wait forever. The time will come again when all will be revealed. The light will shine on the truth when the winter sun resonates with the full power of our Galaxy's Center. Those who feed on the dark will starve, and those who have been waiting for light will feast as the Pieces of the Sun fall to feed them.

There is enough information in these small books to allow the dark side power beyond measure. This must be guarded against at all costs.

All of the information in this book will be used for power and control unless the true nature of this world is understood.

That true nature is this: The mind is a miniature universe, and the universe is merely an expansion of mind.

There is no difference. There is no separation. There is no thing.

It is Maya, or illusion, that will be the lesson during this next time of darkness. We will feel the pain of believing that self is separate from universe. Our brothers and sisters on the other side of the world, whom we call the Maya, will teach this lesson. With their calendars and their advanced knowledge of the sky, they will show—though it will be long after we are gone—that we are all One.

This knowledge, if it survives, can guide those with light in their hearts to a simple, peaceful, and healthy way of living.

We are all energy beings pulsing with the Supreme Consciousness, which is, at its very base, love.

Wow. Heavy. I'm already intimidated. I scroll down to the table of contents to see what this is all about.

Table of Contents

I try to read the text of the book but it's dense with information and I'm anxious to get it out to the world; this is too important to leave for later.

I peek through the door and ask Alex if he can come help

me for a minute. Sitting next to me on the floor, he leans over and reads my screen.

"Tenzo translated the ancient Sanskrit books," I tell him. "Each one of these nine chapters was assembled and guarded by one man throughout the ages—called the Nine Unknown Men—until they were collected together in two little books and hidden. Now, for the first time, they're translated into English."

"Have you read it?" he asks.

"I've read the intro and looked at the table of contents. There's no way I'd understand it; it's like hard-core science stuff. But we need to get this out. Need to do a mass mailing to all our email subscribers. Do you know how to do that without it getting caught up in spam filters?"

"Aye, no problem. Is it just a Word document?"

"Yep. Here you go," I say, handing over my laptop. "Can you sort by email addresses?"

"Sure, why?"

"Because we need to send this to college kids first. Anyone with an '.edu' address."

"No problem," he replies, typing furiously at the keyboard. "Okay, now I just need you to type up the subject line, anything you want to say in the email, and then attach the document," he says, handing the computer back.

From: info@mayatwentytwelve.com
To: list@mayatwentytwelve.com
Subject: What They Don't Want You to Know

This could be the most important document you
ever open. I know that sounds dramatic, but it's true.

For thousands of years, advanced technology and information has been hidden. Far too dangerous for people who were motivated by power or greed, this information was kept underground. The Shadow Government wants to keep and hide this information, to not let it be free, public information. We have to get it into the hands of the right people. Kids. Smart kids with good intentions who know that truth is more powerful than corruption.

Open this document. Forward it to the best, smartest people you know. Let's change the world.

In lak'ech

I hand the laptop back to Alex.

"You ready to do this?" he asks.

"Absolutely."

He hits send. It's gone. Or maybe it has arrived.

"I'd best get back to helping your father," Alex says, standing up.

"Yeah, sure. Thanks for your help."

I try to think of any other place it would be good to post to, and decide on some of the more credible conspiracy theory websites. This will be like putting a match to kerosene! The kind of people who troll those sites would definitely know what to do with this kind of information.

Finally, I write a draft email for Tenzo to let him know the document has gone out. I also ask him to send it to as many kids at Princeton as he can. Seconds after I hit save, another draft email pops up from him.

Caity! I have been watching this email folder all night, hoping that you would get the translation and contact me. I am so pleased that you sent it off. With your permission, I will forward it to as many student addresses as I have, as well as to all of the science and technology clubs here. After studying what is in the books, I believe we should see a wellspring of potent new technology in just a matter of weeks.

My friend at the Global Consciousness Project is fascinated by your data. The Palenque talk broke a new record for coherence. I should be pleased to see what happens to his readings when this document is opened and studied.

I cannot tell you how sorry I am to hear about Li. I know how much you must be hurting. Be strong, Caity. Know that what you are doing will change the course of history, no matter how dark it may seem.

Justine is well and enjoying her time with her grandfather. All best, Tenzo

My heart nearly explodes when I'm jolted by Dad's voice yelling, "Done!"

"You're done?" I ask, hopping up off the floor.

"Finito," he says, hands in the air, fingers waving. "In the next forty-eight hours all third- and fourth-world debts that were set up for the *Fraternitas* to profit from will be erased. In addition, any public property or social services taken over by the *Fraternitas* have now been deeded back."

"And I've been working on the atmospheric centers in Alaska, Russia, and Norway," Mom adds. "When a solar storm hits and they go to auxiliary power, their signals will be redirected to the coordinates you gave me for Atala's satellite."

"You guys are amazing," I say, knowing at my core that it was no accident that I got them for parents.

"That was incredible," Alex says, looking wired. "I got a lifetime of learning in just a few hours!"

"Aye, but now we've got to get you all out of here," Donald says, looking at his watch.

"I'll just detach the cables and we can use this server cart to roll all these downstairs and out the door," Dad says.

As we're gathering things up to leave, Donald pulls me aside. "One more thing left to do, lass. Come with me."

He leads me to the very back of the floor to what looks like a fuse box. When both the card keys are placed in the slot, the small metal door opens to reveal a computer.

Fascinated by what this could be, I lean over to watch. He asks me to type in the URL for the website where the daily tone is available. I type it in and then he hits enter. "That'll help immensely," he says, closing the panel door.

"What is that?" I ask, wondering what we just did.

"The *Fraternitas* has been using the antennae at the top of the pyramid to put out damaging frequencies. Helps keep people off-balance and in a state of fear. It's in an ultra-low frequency so it can't be heard, but nonetheless it is felt by the hundreds of thousands of people within range of this pyramid."

"And now they'll hear the *Tzolk'in* tone instead?"

"Aye," he says with a wink. "And they won't even know it."

FORTY-ONE

We roll the servers down to the elevator bay on the enormous server cart. I assume we'll all go down together, but Donald says we must go first and exit the building safely before he goes down with the servers to meet the reporter and the film crew.

"None of you can be implicated in any of this, sir," Donald says to Dad. "You're the laird now. You'd best be getting back to Breidablik."

I see a moment of hesitation in Dad's eyes. I don't know if he wants the satisfaction of giving these servers up, or if he doesn't believe that Donald will.

"I'll be sure to have your friend call you to let you know I've delivered them to him," Donald says.

Dad holds out his hand. "Uncle Donald," he says. "What can I say?"

Instead of shaking his hand, Donald pulls him into a hug. "Forgive me," he said. "My path was cloudy."

"No worries, Donald. All that matters now is what happens next."

"I'll do you proud," he says. Then he turns to me and gives me a hug. "Fifty years ago when my father told me of this prophecy, I'm ashamed to say I thought it was rubbish. 'Spose I didn't believe that one person, one wee girl, could change the world."

"I don't think I did much. The world is just ready to change."

"Don't sell yourself short," he says, tapping my nose.

Donald shakes Alex's hand. "Your grandmother used to be a real spitfire," Donald says. "Had quite a crush on her back as a lad."

Alex smiles awkwardly.

The elevator arrives and Donald gives my mom a goodbye hug. "Impressive skills," he says to her. "Impressive daughter."

She smiles and says, "I know."

We make it down to the lobby and discretely get to the parking elevator without being seen by the lobby attendant, who is busy examining Scott Dilazzaro's credentials.

I'm a little surprised to see the car still there. After what we've just done, it seems like the whole world should be upside down.

We're all so tired we can't even talk as Dad takes us back up the winding path though the parking garage. Outside is only slightly lighter than the garage.

"I can't help myself," Dad says as he drives by the front of the building. Scott and the crew are loading the servers into a van. Scott is too busy to notice us, but Donald salutes us as we roll by.

"Where to?" I ask.

"Home," Dad says, getting on the freeway to the airport.

I rest my head on Alex's shoulder and he puts his arm around me. I see Mom look back at us and then give Dad a little look that I'm too tired to attempt to decipher.

We're all bone-weary, yet oddly buzzed. There's no going back. There's no undoing what we've done.

Now we wait and see.

———

Dad is able to get us on a flight to London at noon. We spend the morning in the International Terminal, nodding off and watching the news.

Sometime around midmorning, we hear the news anchor say, "Computer data was surrendered to a *San Francisco Chronicle* reporter today by a man who claims he was part of a powerful organization that has worked outside the limits of government, military, and banking to shape world events. Not much more is known; we'll keep you updated as the story breaks."

While Mom snoozes with her head tipped back, I search her messy bag for her phone. I see a glass phone booth in the corner and walk over. Once inside, I dial Professor Middleford. It's afternoon there, and I'm hoping he's at work so Justine will answer the phone.

"Hello," Justine says, breathless from running for the phone.

"J, it's me! How are you?"

"Oh my God, Caity, it's so good to hear your voice! I can't believe you did it! Or I guess I should say, I can't believe your parents did it … "

"Yeah, they totally pulled off the hacking part. But you are mostly responsible for getting the Sanskrit stuff out—I was so worried about you with those books."

"Tell me about it! The minute I got to town I called Tenzo from the train station. I didn't even go see Gramps first! I had to get those things out of my possession."

"I hope kids can find a way to make that stuff work," I say.

"Where have you been? Have you even checked the website? Comments are in the thousands now, and I was just listing to Princeton student radio and they were even talking about it!"

"No way! Oh, that's amazing!"

"Now that you're releasing the information from the *Fraternitas* headquarters, do you think they'll be out of sight? I mean, are you—you know—still worried about them tracking us down?"

"I don't know, Justine. I would definitely keep a low profile and stay close to Tenzo or your grandpa."

"Have you heard from Clath?"

"Nope. But if she's tried calling, she's getting the kid who took my phone in Chiapas."

"We never really talked about what's next—do you think we'll be expelled?"

"I don't know, J. I'll totally take the fall. I'll tell them I was overcome with homesickness and had to see my parents.

Even if they don't let us back in, maybe they'll at least let us leave with good records."

Justine doesn't respond right away. "I was actually really starting to dig it," she says.

"Yeah, me too."

I hear some mumbling in the background and then Justine says, "Oh, Gramps is heading to campus and I think I'll go with him. I'm not so good with sitting in an empty house … "

"I'll call you from home tomorrow," I say. "By then I should have a plan for what to tell the school."

We say goodbye and I linger in the booth for a moment.

At what point will I crumble? I wonder, thinking of all the people I have, or could, let down.

I look up to see Alex's face outside the glass door.

"There you are, mate. You just missed the piece about the magnetic anomalies being reported 'round the world!"

"Seriously?"

"Aye. Seems *something* has been messing with the electromagnetic field—they haven't made any connection to the Palenque talk or the release of debt, but if you're right about this torus energy, both those things should be factors."

It worked. Our heart waves are now nesting together, not only radiating light and energy, but creating gravity as well. The human connection is getting stronger again. The focus, the tones, the transfer of funds—it's all working toward the transformation.

I shake my head. "I can hardly believe it's all true. I can hardly believe we've started the shift."

"Believe it," Alex says, pulling me up from the seat in the booth. "*Believe it.*"

———

On the train, just minutes from the ferry to Huracan, Dad gets a call from Mrs. Findlay telling him that Monsieur Didier and Professor Clath are at Breidablik. She says they won't tell her what it's in regard to, except that it's a private and personal matter of great importance. It's been making Mrs. Findlay crazy.

Dad tells her to please make them comfortable and to let them know we'll be home shortly.

It feels like forty pounds of lead have been dumped onto my chest. "I hope they'll refund the tuition," I say sheepishly.

"Forget the money—I just hope they don't blackball you from college!" Mom says. "Having you go missing halfway around the world must have scared your Pedagogue to death."

Minutes tick like hours as we get closer to the ferry. I might be more nervous to see Didier and Clath than I was to see my parents.

Thomas meets us at the ferry and I hug him tighter than I ever have before. Good old Thomas, steady and calm. The only person making sure that this prophecy would come to its rightful conclusion.

"Bit of an audience waiting for you back home," he whispers in my ear.

"I'm in deep," I reply.

We all get in the Land Rover and make our way to Breidablik. Wedged between my mom and Alex in the back seat, I ask them to roll down the windows so I can get a good smell of the place. I didn't know that I'd missed the scent of the peat and the lichen and the loch and the sea until just now. Mr. Papers is holding on to the handle above the window, standing in the open window like he's waterskiing. He looks happier than he has in days.

As we pass the island's school—just one building for kindergarten through high school—I nudge Alex. "Looks like we'll be classmates now."

"It's not so bad; you'll see."

My mom looks the other way. Having me back here for school has got to seem like a failure in some way.

Thomas drops us off at the castle steps, explaining that Alex's mom will have his hide if he doesn't get him back right away. I wish I could say a more private goodbye, to thank Alex for all he's done, but it's just too awkward. We wave goodbye and then turn to the big wooden door with the iron straps, unready to face what's inside.

Sometimes it takes being away from a place to make it seem like home. Before, I had only ever considered San Francisco as home. Now, having arrived safely back, I can look at Breidablik Castle as home as well.

Mrs. Findlay runs to the door to greet us. After a bear hug, she holds me out in front of her with both hands and says, "What've you done, girl? They're awfully serious in there … "

FORTY-TWO

I wish I had the confidence to walk in first, but I hide behind my parents so I can see them before they see me. Didier looks calm, but Clath looks like she's going to have a stroke, she's so mad. They're quite a pair: Didier with his beautiful skin and expensive suits and Clath in her Velcro shoes, math sweatshirt, and pull-on denim pants.

They all shake hands, and then I slink out from behind my parents. Clath bites her lip and shakes her head at me.

Once introductions are made, Dad says, "Please, sit down."

"Thank you. Beautiful place you have here. *Trés jolie*," Didier says.

"Thanks. It's a family property," Dad answers stiffly.

"I know," Didier says, settling into an armchair like he's the laird here. "All the way back to Fergus Mac Fireland."

"Did Mrs. Findlay or Thomas give you the history of the place?" Mom asks.

Didier gently removes a piece of lint from his sleeve and says, "No, it was Zhong-Shan Li who told me about it, years ago. Even before Caity was born."

I watch my parents go white. My mouth dries up.

"I don't understand," Mom says.

Didier looks right at me. "Caity, I am a member of The Council of 13:20."

"No!" I say, shaking my head. "No! There's no way. You're totally not Council material."

He laughs. "What proof do you need?" he asks, remaining completely calm while the rest of us look like we're going to crack. "What can I tell you?"

"But you were livid about the Mayan calendar email! You used the words 'cease and desist' and said it was *dangerous*!"

"How else was I going to get those *blasé* kids to look into it? I'll bet my little rant up on that stage drove traffic to the site like you never would have had otherwise."

I'm not sure why I don't want to believe him. He's too slick, too much like Claude D'Aubigne.

"Would it help if I named the other members?" Didier asks. "Bolon, Apari, Tawa, Chasca … "

"What tribe could you possibly represent? Aren't you, like, French?"

"I'm from a very old Pictish tribe, right here in ancient Scotland. You see, the Gauls in France were all descendents from Ireland, Scotland, and Britain."

"Okay, then where are The Council headquarters?" I ask.

"The Muchuchumil Import building in San Francisco, and Atala in—well, I shan't disclose where."

"You just mentioned Atala in front of everyone—even Clath!" I say.

He looks over at her, her eyes wide and mouth half open, and says, "She's too dazed to remember. She thinks I'm here to expel you for leaving her in Palenque with no warning."

"I can still hear you, Didier!" Clath shouts. "I haven't gone deaf. I just have no idea what you two are talking about!"

"Why are you here?" I ask Didier, still not sure if I buy his story. Is he posing as part of The Council to get to us?

"I am here to give you something," he says. "Something quite large and quite valuable."

My parents both look at me. I can only shrug; I'm as confused as they are.

He pulls out what looks like a large jewelry box from his briefcase. When he opens it, I see an oversized golden key with the La Escuela Bohemia spark on the end like a big sunburst.

"*Et voilà!*" he says as he hands the key to me. "La Escuela Bohemia is yours."

All four of us say, "What?" at the same time.

"The school is yours," he repeats. "This has always been part of the plan."

I hold the heavy golden key on my lap. I can't really understand what's going on.

"Can we back up for a minute?" I say. "This makes no sense. If The Council really runs the school, why are the children of the very people who make up the Shadow Government all at La Escuela Bohemia?"

"We think it makes perfect sense. It has been both a way to keep tabs on what the Shadow Government was up to—you would not believe how openly these people talk at school events when they are bragging to each other—and to try to show their children the world. To open them up to a new way of thinking. Of course, the latter rarely worked."

"I don't get how you could draw in the right kids."

"When money and power is all that matters to a person, then they will go looking to flaunt it. All we had to do was create an exclusive school, price it higher than any other in the world, and we knew they would come in droves. And they did."

"And of course it was no coincidence that I wanted to go there."

"You *needed* to go there. It was the only school that would allow you to travel, to be free to do what you needed to do."

"But why are you giving it to *me?*"

"So you can use it to teach the modern applications of the ancient mysteries. Use it to further the information in the Sanskrit books. The Council is at your service, as you need teachers. Bring in the powerful indigenous kids; let them have a place of their own where they can learn the ways of their ancestors who knew the truth. The young must lead the young—*Siga la Chispa!*" Didier says, fist pumping.

I want to be all "Follow the Spark!" but I just don't see how it will work. "Those kids don't have any money; there's no way they could afford La Escuela Bohemia," I say.

"You could teach a thousand students for a hundred more years and still not run out of money. We have been given so much by these families. In addition to endowments of money, we've built archives of jewelry, clothing, art, and furniture that have been donated to the school. It's astounding, really."

"Didier, you really have a lot to explain," Clath says, so mad she's shaking as if she has Parkinson's.

"Professor Clath, you will be Caity's grounding force. Her top counsel and head teacher."

Clath tries not to look pleased, but is no good at it.

Mom holds up her hands. "Let's all just hold on here a moment. You can't just walk in and give my child a school. A school full of money and other people's property—not to mention other people's children!"

"If you feel more comfortable running the school, then so be it," Didier says. "You both have PhDs. Seems perfectly reasonable."

"Oh, come on!" Dad says. "This is nonsense. She has to decline the gift. Really, it's absurd."

For some reason, Dad wanting me to reject it makes me want it even more. "Justine and I did really love the school," I say. "And it would be the perfect place to start research on the Sanskrit information."

Dad looks at Mom. "What's this Sanskrit information you two keep talking about?"

"You haven't told him yet?" Didier asks. I shake my head. He turns to them to explain. "In Palenque, Caity was given two books written by Nine Unknown Men. The Council had been guarding the books for centuries. Full of information on technology that could change the world, these books had been hidden away until the shift happened and the Shadow Government could not corrupt this information."

"And what did you do with the books?" Clath asks, clearly tempted to see them.

"I sent them with Justine to Princeton. Tenzo translated them, and then I … well, I sent the information out to kids all over the world."

"I assure you this was against the better judgment of Bolon and The Council in the beginning," Didier says. "But now we all admit it was a brave and powerful move."

"Wait! Are you saying you're responsible for getting those nine brilliant pieces of technology out?" Clath asks me. "Academic bulletin boards have been abuzz about this—there could be some real merit there!"

Didier and I look at each other and smile. "Yes, Clath, it's quite true," he says. "Caity, you have no idea how the work you have done in just the past few weeks has changed the course of the future for all young people. The shift has begun, in a monumental way—the Shadow Government has been exposed and we are on our way to true freedom."

Clath looks at my parents. "You know, I must tell you that I underestimated your daughter and Justine, but their work has proved to be of exceptional quality. You should see the paper they wrote decoding the Three Hares and how it relates to the Flower of Life."

"Wait until you see what we have to say about the Tomb of Pacal," I whisper to her. "It's gonna blow your mind!"

"We've been quite surprised ourselves," Mom replies.

"You see, this is just the beginning. The tones, the coherence, the unity. The old ways are breaking down." Didier smoothes the thigh of his perfectly pressed pant with his long, elegant hand. "But I'm sure you must be overwhelmed. I think the best thing to do is to get a good night's sleep and talk about all of this in the morning."

Unable to truly process any of what just happened, I absolutely agree.

FORTY-THREE

Taken away to a dreamless place, I sleep for almost fourteen hours. Even after I wake up, I just roll over and burrow deeper into my pillow, enjoying the absolute pleasure of being in bed—not in a plane or a train or a dingy motel or a gold-lined room deep beneath a pyramid. I doze like that for another couple of hours, coming in and out of consciousness, every time reminding myself how lucky I am to still be alive.

Sometime after noon, Mrs. Findlay delivers a tray of food. Mr. Papers follows her, clutching a small package.

"A parcel came for you whilst you were gone," she says as she sets the tray on a corner of the bed. "Papers, be a good boy and hand it over!"

Mr. Papers jumps up on the bed with me and butts his small head against mine. Mrs. Findlay must have bathed him and washed his clothes, because he's looking and smelling nicer than he has in a while.

I reach for the package, but he shakes his head and puts it

behind his back. Then he looks at Mrs. Findlay and motions for her to leave.

"So that's the thanks I get for all I've done for you, you wee scoundrel!" she says, turning on her heel to leave.

I prop myself up in bed and pour a steaming cup of tea. "Okay, let's see it," I say.

He inches over slowly, holding the package out in front of him as if it's the most precious thing he's ever held. Then he hands it to me.

I recognize the handwriting immediately: Uncle Li.

I gasp a little and Mr. Papers comes over and nestles in beside me to comfort me.

The post date on the package is just days ago. He must have had this triggered to send if he didn't report in, just as he had done with his email.

Slowly removing the tape from the brown wrapper, I take a deep breath. The paper opens up to reveal a box about the size of my hand, with a folded note on top of it. I open the note first.

Dear Caity—

If you are receiving this, then I am gone for now. You and I have been connected for hundreds of lifetimes, and will be for many more. We have learned much from each other, and that will never stop.

In this box is a very old symbol, the Ouroboros or Serpent's Coil. This snake eating its tail represents the constant state of creation and destruction and the spin of all things. In creating this symbol, the *ancients were inspired by the Milky Way. In Egypt, where this symbol goes back nearly 4,000 years, it's found encircling the words ALL IS ONE. They knew that we are all just vibrations, spinning in time with one another and connected in a sea of energy.*

You have made me proud. You have held true to your path. And I'm sure you will continue to light the way. The death of Seven Macaw cannot be far off.

You will soon get a call from Monsieur Didier. Please consider his offer very carefully. Though it will be quite a surprise, it may be the way to the greatest good.

Always yours,
Uncle Li

Mr. Papers uses the napkin on the tray to dry my eyes. I take a big sip of tea to unclench my throat and then open the box.

Inside is a gold pendant, an ancient-looking ouroboros. The eye is a faceted pink stone that gleams as it picks up the light. I slip the long, gold chain over my head and around my neck. As I put my hand over the snake, it instantly picks up the heat from my body and feels warm to the touch.

When I hear my parents knocking at the door, I tuck it under my T-shirt. Mom and Dad come in and stand at my bedside like I'm a patient in the hospital. Both of them look older, more worn out.

"Well," Mom starts, "your dad and I have done a lot of thinking about—"

I hold up my hands to stop her. "Please, please. I know you guys don't owe me anything after all the havoc I've caused, but please, I beg you, can we just not talk about this for *one* day? Please?"

Dad jumps in and says, "But we were going to say we're warming—"

I put my hands over my ears like a child and say, "Lalalalalalalal!" until I see them smile. When I put my hands down, Mom says, "You really don't want to—"

I plug them again and say loudly, "I'm not taking my hands down until you promise!"

They both raise their hands as if taking an oath.

"Fine, Caity. Have one day off with your little friend here," Dad says. "Clath and Didier have been talking with Thomas all morning, going over the Sanskrit material. I suppose if this school has been around for decades, one more day won't make much difference."

"Thanks. I just need to pretend life is normal for, like, twelve hours."

"And normal means having tea in a curtained bed with a monkey?" Mom asks.

She has a point.

Dad leans over and kisses my forehead. "Until tomorrow," he says.

Once they leave, I eat every item on my tray, including the garnish, and roll back over, fully intending to sleep for another fourteen hours. I get a pretty good run at it until I wake up to pebbles striking the windowpane.

Opening the window and leaning down, I see Alex standing there in the violet dusk. He motions with his hand for me to come down.

I flash my hands twice to say "Twenty minutes" and then rush to the shower. I can't even remember the last shower I had—was it in Chiapas? That dingy motel by the airport? My hair is a greasy mess.

Quickly undressing in the bathroom, I catch a glimpse of myself in the mirror. The way I had been sleeping pressed the ouroboros onto my chest and made a perfect impression of it right over my heart, which its dazzling gold twin now hangs next to.

I do the best I can with the minutes I have in the shower, then dress quickly and head downstairs. My parents, Didier, and Clath are all in the parlor with a roaring fire.

I'm able to slip out a side door undetected by all but Mr. Papers, who follows me into the moonless night.

Alex leads me to the side of the tower that can't be seen from the castle. We sit on the small stone bench there, close together but not actually touching. Then Alex takes my hand.

"Hi," he says.

"Hi," I reply.

We sit there for a few tense moments.

It's really uncomfortable to have been through so much with someone, yet to have there be this weird intimacy wall up.

Does he feel the same way I do? Is he only holding it back because my parents have been around this whole time? If I can take down the *Fraternitas*, why can't I tell this boy how I feel?

I decide to do it, to tell him.

"Alex, I have to be honest," I begin. It helps that it's dark and I can hardly see his face—it's the perfect format for a confession. "I can't pretend that I'm just a friend, or a friend who gets kisses now and then. I can't sit back and hope it happens, because I've learned that we have to take responsibility for what we want. I'm tall and kind of gangly and not what you'd see in a magazine, but I have heart-stopping, mind-melting, palm-sweating feelings for you. And I can't pretend otherwise."

His hand holds tight to mine. "Good, because I can't either. You have no idea who you are, Caity. No idea how incredible you are. I feel like I've just made some kind of massive discovery, like I've unearthed this treasure and I'm afraid to show anyone because they'll take it away from me. I can't believe that no boy has stolen you away."

I laugh. "I've been waiting to be discovered my whole life."

He puts his hand on my chin, and pulls me in. I can feel the heat coming from his face, that's how close we are. I think he's going to kiss me, but instead he looks right into my eyes and says, "I've got a surprise for you."

It's a cold, clear night and the wind carries just a trace of moist sea air. Alex takes my hand and we duck through the tiny door to the inside staircase and climb the rough stairs, Mr. Papers leading the way. At the top of the tower, we find ourselves under an umbrella of stars. There, in the middle of the floor, is a sleeping bag spread out on the stone floor.

"After you," he says.

I scrunch myself into the bag and then Alex does the

same. In order for us both to fit, he has to put his arm behind my head. I nestle into the crook of his shoulder as he wiggles the zipper shut. Mr. Papers wedges himself between our legs, curling up tightly.

We gaze up at the sky. I don't know where to start looking—it's a mess of stars like I've never seen before. There seems to be no black space whatsoever. It's like being at a buffet and not knowing what to choose first.

"It's too much. It's overwhelming. How do we make sense of this?" I wonder out loud.

"We don't," he says. "Remember—it makes sense of *us*."

"You know what today is?" I ask.

"Aye, of course. It's Six Chuen."

"Aye," I reply. "Chuen, the Monkey, the weaver of time. A good day for new beginnings and discovery."

"And Six, which represents Flow. As in the frequency that helps long-range projects come to pass."

"A good omen, I think." I want to tell him about La Escuela Bohemia, about what Didier has given me, but I just don't have the energy right now. It's too lovely just lying here in the dark with the pulsing sound of crickets and frogs.

For a moment I let myself imagine Alex, Justine, and me running La Escuela Bohemia. Kids from all over the world learning about ancient mysteries and modern science all at once, unearthing the old myths and looking at them in a new light, putting an end to the corruption of power. Most of all, helping make sure that this shift happens, that the Feathered Serpent will rise and spin in all of us.

I inhale deeply and then exhale, trying to feel the universe inside of me, feel me inside of the universe.

"It is all One," Alex says.

"We are all One," I reply.

I believe it, too.

Feeling the warm gold ouroboros around my neck, I tap it with two fingers like a touchstone. There is so much uncertainty right now, so much I don't know about my future. Rolling to my side, I nest my head deeper into Alex's arm. When I put my hand on his chest, I can feel his heart—steady, strong, radiating, contracting, over and over.

We are light and we are gravity, I think, as I feel my own heart swirl, too.

Believe love connects universe.

Acknowledgements

Being new to novel writing, I did not know the proper time to submit my acknowledgements with Book One. When I realized it was too late, I was devastated. This is the first page I turn to when I buy a book and I was aghast at the thought of not being able to thank all the people who helped me achieve the dream of getting published. So please indulge me if I go overboard in this one!

I must start with Julie Inada, lifelong friend and extraordinary writer and editor. It was Julie who encouraged me to take the writing class that connected me with the people who would become most important over the next few years: my critique group. Marcia La Fond, Kelly Hudgins, Erin O'Kelley Muck, Julie, and I met every week for reading and writing. It was with their help that I conceived and wrote *Prophecy of Days*. More recent additions to the group, Jennie Englund Meads and Anjie Seewer Reynolds, have been enormously inspiring, helpful, and supportive. For me, writing would be impossible without your insight and feedback.

Huge thanks to Oregon Literary Arts for awarding me the Holmes Fellowship for Young Readers' Literature. That boost of funds and confidence went a long way! Oregonians are fortunate to live in a state that has such a vibrant and generous literary organization.

Agent Laura Rennert helped get the manuscript into shape—no easy feat. Thank you Laura, for believing my work was worth selling! And what's a seller without a buyer? Thanks must go to Andrew Karre for believing *Prophecy of Days* was a work worth buying. Foreign Rights Agent Taryn

Fagerness sold translation rights to the series, helping my little books reach other lands in other languages. What a thrill!

I am grateful to Flux Acquisitions Editor Brian Farrey and editor Rhiannon Nelson, who along with Sandy Sullivan, Nanette Stearns, and Kathy Schneider challenged my anachronisms and inconsistencies in the kindest way possible. Kevin Brown and Amy Martin blew me away with two gorgeous covers, and Joanna Willis did a spectacular job with the inside. Rhonda Ogren helped me get distribution beyond what I had hoped, and Marissa Pederson, Steven Pomije, and Tricia O'Reilly got the word—and me—out there. And I could not mention publicity efforts without also thanking PR maven Tonya Dressel, my Fixer and dear friend. She never ceases to amaze me with what she can do.

Thanks to Blair and Carol Moody, who indulged my inner hermit with the generous loan of their mountain chalet. The majority of this second book was written in glorious solitude there.

To my extended family of readers—Carole Cameron, Barb Cameron Slaton, Suzanne Slaton, and Janie and Peter Hutchinson—thanks for drudging through early drafts, trying to break me of my comma splice habit, and encouraging me on. Thanks to my sister, artist Cathy Gersich, for the work on first sketches for the book. And thanks to Judy and Keith Countryman, who became my greatest cheerleaders as they traveled the country from Hawaii to New Jersey.

Thanks to Nikki and Steven Davis, who bought the first book I ever signed and became early readers of Book II. Young readers Nora Honeycutt and Hannah Hilden helped tremendously. I'm grateful to Kathryn Hinsch for dreaming big on my behalf, to Acharya for her essential feedback, and to Kim Sellers-Blais for her eagle eyes. Thank you, Teri Hall, for being my go-to person for all things author-y and neurotic-y. Thanks to Peggy Frasse, my intrepid travel partner (and overall book champion) who carries the world in her handbag. Toni Kellerman, Pam Edgington, Julie White, Chris Catton, Debbie Rae, Molly Stephen, Wendy McKay, and Christine Mitchell, thank you for being so supportive of me and the book. You are all proof that friendships made in college can last a lifetime. Thanks to one of my favorite writers, David Sorsoli, for both challenging and inspiring me over nearly four decades, from our humble Ashland homes to Amsterdam, Munich, and Barcelona.

To my parents, Carol Cameron Moody and Jerry Gersich, thank you for raising me with a sense of curiosity (around curiosities). You have both contributed greatly to my love of the mysterious, the hidden, and the bizarre while still managing to appear rather normal to the outside world.

Shantung Hsu, PhD, I am honored to call you teacher and friend (and to be able to base a character on you!). You have taught me so much about the unseen world.

Finally, I am deeply grateful to my handsome husband Scott for his great good humor, steady patience, and boundless love. And to my children, Juliet and Hank, who nip gently at my heels as I run toward my dreams.

I love you all.

Joan Kleen

About the Author

Christy Raedeke's love of mysticism and thirst for ancient knowledge has led her around the world—trekking in the Himalayas, floating down the Ganges, cathedral hopping in Europe, studying feng shui in Kuala Lumpur, cloistering at a hermitage in the Sierra Nevada Mountains, and looking for shaman among the Maya ruins of the Yucatan and Chiapas. She and her husband Scott currently live in Oregon with their young children.